I hope you enjoy it.

A Century of Silence

A Boy Soldier's War on the Western Front

J J FITZPATRICK

Skylarks Animal Management Publishing

First Published in 2018

ISBN: 978-0-9954901-1-6

Cover design: More Visual Ltd, Leicester, UK

Typesetting: David Siddall Multimedia, Monmouth, UK
(10/11.5pt Adobe Garamond Pro)

Contents

Dedication

This book is dedicated to the memory of my Great-Uncle, Private Ben Leeman MM, 15th Battalion, The Notts and Derby Regiment, The Sherwood Foresters – to the 888,245 other men and women of the British and Commonwealth Forces who also fell in the Great War, and to the millions who lived through it, but who forever carried the physical and mental scars of war.

Our Ben 1901-1918

Acknowledgments

There are many people to whom I am grateful for their assistance, and without whom this book might never have been written.

I am in the debt of Maurice Bacon and David Langley, co-authors of The Blast of War, an invaluable resource documenting the 15th Battalion's war, as I am to the Regimental Museum of the Mercian Regiment.

On a visit to Talbot House, Poperinghe, I met Gerry Beevers, a member of the World War 1 Group at the Mechanics' Institute, Bradford, who gave me many invaluable pointers regarding access to regimental and divisional war diaries, which greatly assisted my research.

I would like to thank Mary McCormick and Carol Royle for reading the original manuscripts and for asking so many questions.

And finally, to Julia Kaminski for proof-reading and editing the manuscript – not forgetting Mac the Staffy, for resting at her feet as she worked.

"It is not the critic who counts; not the man who points out how the strong man stumbles, or where the doer of deeds could have done them better. The credit belongs to the man who is actually in the arena, whose face is marred by dust and sweat and blood; who strives valiantly; who errs, who comes short again and again, because there is no effort without error and shortcoming; but who does actually strive to do the deeds; who knows great enthusiasms, the great devotions; who spends himself in a worthy cause; who at the best knows in the end the triumph of high achievement, and who at the worst, if he fails, at least fails while daring greatly so that his place shall never be with those cold and timid souls who neither know victory nor defeat."

President Theodore Roosevelt, Paris, 1910

Introduction

In 2013 Ben Leeman was just a name to me. I knew my Mam had an Uncle Ben, who her Dad, my Granddad, spoke about very rarely as he was invariably overcome with grief whenever he talked about his younger brother and his bitterness about how his own mother never fully recovered from Ben's death.

I knew very little about the Great War. I had never visited the battlefields of Belgium and France. I had heard of Ypres, but did not understand its significance, and whilst the Somme was a place I knew from the History Channel, I had never heard of the villages of Pozieres and Curlu.

All that changed in 2014 and the years that followed, as I walked in his footsteps.

J J Fitzpatrick
25 May 2018

Chapter One

Normandy

Normandy might seem like an unlikely place to begin a story about a soldier in the First World War. Normandy saw no fighting in the Great War, so why start there? Well the reason is that Normandy was the place where the story really began for me, and as I am the one telling the story, I believe it's where I should begin.

When I left the Armed Forces in early 2013 I realised how much time I had spent living away from home and how little I had seen of my Mam and Dad over the previous 35 years. I had visited them regularly and they had always visited me, but sometimes, depending upon distance, this might have only been three or four times a year.

When I retired from the RAF I made a promise that I would try to visit my Mam and Dad each week, without fail. I was self-employed, so I set aside a day each week when I would travel up to Liverpool to see them and stay overnight. Apart from illness and holidays it was a promise I kept whilst my Mam was alive, and it is one I keep; visiting my Dad each week.

It would have been in about February 2014, when during one of my visits I asked my Dad if he would like to take a trip to Normandy for the 70th anniversary of the D-Day landings. I had never been to Normandy, and with the anniversary of the landings I thought I might plan a trip to France in my campervan to see the D-Day beaches and other battle sites.

Twenty years earlier, in 1994, I had been on duty in the Portsmouth and Southsea area. I was on a task at HMS Nelson and around the Royal Navy dockyards and had quite a bit of time off, leaving me free to join in the commemorations for the 50th anniversary of the landings and attend many of the events and speak with some of the members of the Normandy Veterans Association. Fifty years on I had been amazed at how fit and active most of the veterans were at that time, and had enjoyed the commemorative events a great deal. I had never really gone in for people dressing in World War 2 uniforms and stuff like that, but seeing the Normandy Veterans in their smart suits, regimental berets and medals, with their families was a great experience and a memory that had stayed with me.

Now in 2014, 20 years on, the 70th anniversary commemorations were being quite widely reported upon in the press and on the telly and the general opinion of the commentators was that this was likely to be the last such major commemoration at which veterans of the landings would be attending in any numbers; age and infirmity finally succeeding where Rommel and his lads had failed 70 years earlier.

Now to the average reader it should be less than surprising that a person with over 35 years of service in HM Forces should have at least a passing interest in military history and might wish to visit some of the locations where many of the most significant events had taken place, and when better to do so than a landmark anniversary of such an event? My desire to attend shouldn't exactly be a surprise... but doing so along with my Dad would be quite a radical act on my part, especially as the trip would involve me and my Dad sharing a confined space for close on a week.

Not such a big thing to most people, you would think, but bear in mind that for many years me and my Dad couldn't be in close proximity for more than a few hours without it degenerating into an argument over just about anything, no matter how trivial. We were as bad as each other, so planning on spending a week together in the confines of a campervan was about as likely as Churchill and Hitler sharing a berth for a week without a major punch-up ensuing. I'm not sure of the exact dimensions of a boxing ring, but I was sure it was a lot bigger than a T25 VW Camper.

I spoke to my Mam about my idea and she was extremely keen for me to take my Dad with me, probably not because she thought it was a great idea, but because it would provide her with a week of peace. (A few years before, my Mam sent off an application for my Dad to join the British Antarctic Survey on a two-year contract, without telling him!)

Anyway, I took my Mam's positive attitude as a good sign and mentioned that I was planning the trip in a few months. He didn't seem more than mildly interested so I mentioned that if he would like to come, I would be happy to take him along. To my surprise my Dad agreed without a second's hesitation, and so the plan was devised for us to travel to Portsmouth and then catch the ferry for Normandy a couple of days before D-Day on the 4th of June, the last available sailing before the anniversary.

On the 3rd of June my Dad caught the train from Liverpool to

Wolverhampton and stopped overnight with me before we set off on the great adventure. Whilst it didn't quite have the significance of those who had made the same journey all those years before, it did share one similarity... it was just as likely to end in a punch-up.

The great day arrived, and we made our way to Portsmouth. Things went smoothly for the first six miles until we ground to a halt on the southbound M6 just north of Birmingham. Fortunately, we had packed plenty of provisions, so my Dad was able to jump into the back and make a cup of coffee on the stove while we sat on the southbound M6 car park. We had allowed plenty of time to make it to our ferry and having factored in the almost inevitable 90-minute delay, we managed to use up most of this additional time before we had covered the first 10 miles. I remained confident my timings would be spot on.

Having negotiated the M6 and M5 junction we were soon on our way down the M42 and the M40 heading south. The journey was remarkably good and after a couple of hours we arrived at Oxford services and parked up for 15 minutes and a quick piddle-stop. The journey was proving a great success so far, we had made it almost seventy miles without the first major argument and this happy state of affairs was to continue as we made our way to Portsmouth, arriving in plenty of time to make the ferry. I began to wonder if my Mam had slipped a couple of Valium tablets into my Dad's flask, to ensure a peaceful journey... she had previous form for such things.

We arrived at the Brittany Ferries terminal in plenty of time. As we queued for the Portsmouth-Caen ferry I was surprised to see the number of veteran military vehicles making the journey to Normandy for the commemorations. For some reason this wasn't something that I had been expecting and it was a nice surprise and a real point of interest for us as we waited to board the ferry. We spent an hour or so wandering up and down the queue taking photos of some of the fantastic military vehicles that people had preserved immaculately and were crossing to Normandy either to take part in re-enactments, or just to enter into the spirit of the celebrations. I have never been much of a fan of re-enactors, regarding them as a bit "odd" – on a par with train spotters and jam jar collectors, but I had to admit that they certainly contributed greatly to the sense of occasion, and over the course of the following week they attracted a lot of attention from the travelling veterans, no doubt stirring the memories, as if anything other than being back in Normandy was needed.

Whilst I was sure that the seriousness of the commemorations would become apparent during the week as the ship sailed out of Portsmouth

Harbour, past the dock yards and the dwindling presence of today's Royal Navy, everyone on board, Normandy Veterans included, was in high spirits.

I pointed out The Semaphore Tower at the dock yard and regaled my Dad with one of the less glorious moments in my military career when I had run the risk of insulting a high-ranking naval officer.

When my duties took me to Portsmouth I would often end up working in the Semaphore Tower, a historical part of the dockyard and a building where one of the greatest heroes of British and indeed world military history would often work, the Admiral Lord Nelson.

One quiet weekend whilst 'working' in the tower I had received a pre-prepared hot lunch in a polystyrene box. I use the terms 'hot' and 'lunch' loosely, on this occasion, very loosely, to describe the contents. I think they were aspirations rather than actual descriptions.

Anyway, whilst I was sat there looking at the miserable, limp contents, a very cheerful gentleman entered the room and asked me if everything was OK. He must have been in his mid-sixties, with dark, slicked-back hair. He wore a sort of tweed sports jacket and corduroy trousers with brown, slightly scuffed brogues. I immediately noticed the leather patches sewn on the elbows of the jacket, just like my old geography teacher used to wear.

"Hello, Sergeant. And how are you today?" he asked in an ever-so-chipper tone.

"Well the weather's great and the whole day was going really well until the lunch pitched up, fresh from the freezer," I replied.

"If it's cold I could take it and get in heated up for you," he went on, cheerfully.

"Yes, please. That would be great." I replied.

"No problem." And with that he took my soggy box of chips and other unidentified items and shot off, out of the room and along the corridor. About 5 minutes later a Royal Navy officer bearing the rank slides of a Commander entered the room. I stood when he entered.

Looking around the room as if to locate something he had mislaid, he enquired, "Hello Sergeant, I'm looking for the Admiral, you haven't seen him, have you?"

Considering at one point he had looked under a table, I thought the missing Admiral must've been either very small, or half-cut and so likely to be located under a table.

"No Sir, I haven't. The only other person who has been in is the chap with the tweed jacket," I replied.

"Yes, that's him!" He replied, his mood brightening, just as I began to get a horrible sinking feeling in my stomach.

"In that case I have seen him. He's just nipped off down the corridor to microwave my chips for me," I replied, whilst pointing towards the corridor down which the Admiral had disappeared with my box of limp chips.

And with that the Commander spun around and shot off down the corridor in hot – well hotter than my chips – pursuit of the missing Admiral.

A few minutes later the Commander entered the room, followed by the Admiral who was carrying a tray, with some nice plated-up hot chips, fish and peas. A mug of coffee and a can of coke, which he deposited on the bar room table in front of me. I leapt to my feet and stood to attention. (I was about to say 'snapped' to attention, but any former soldiers will know that most RAF personnel are incapable of doing so.)

"Enjoy your lunch Sergeant, I think we will need your expertise in about half an hour, so you've got plenty of time to enjoy it," he said, before leaving the room in his customary jolly fashion.

I thought my Dad would be impressed with this hilarious and true tale, but he was more interested in surveying the historical buildings in the dock yard.

"Did you hear what I said, Dad?" I asked.

"Yes, of course I did, I'm not that deaf you know. Anyway, were your chips OK?" he replied.

And we continued to sail out past the assembled ships, out from Portsmouth Harbour, past the Spinnaker Tower and out into the Solent, heading for the English Channel.

As we made our way through Portsmouth Harbour we were treated to a bit of a flypast from the Coast Guard and the Royal Navy and a few of the Royal Navy ships fired their water cannons towards the ferry. The ferry was full of Normandy veterans, they were a great sight to see: standing proudly in their best suits, blazers, regimental ties, berets, and almost without exception a chest full of hard-earned medals. The veterans weren't just men, there being a great many women who had served with equal valour during one of the most dangerous times in the nation's history. The veterans were accompanied on this emotional journey by many war widows, sons, daughters, and grandchildren, proudly wearing the medals earned by a loved one on their right breast.

It was an honour and a privilege to be on this journey with them, particularly those sporting the Normandy Veterans Association badge, who were going back to a place where they had helped shape the history of Europe, and indeed the world, 70 years earlier.

A few days before we set sail there had been many television programmes featuring stories of the Normandy landings, and interviews were conducted with many of the veterans who fought. I remembered one interview with a former tank commander who had gone ashore at Normandy in one of the tanks that were fitted with skirts all around them in order to make them amphibious.

When he was asked whether he had been afraid to be facing the Germans and what they would throw at him when he got ashore, he explained that he was more worried about what would happen once they left the safety of the landing craft and made their way through the choppy seas as they made their way towards the beaches. I can't remember the exact numbers he gave during the interview, but I think he said that of the twenty-odd tanks in his squadron that set off from the landing craft towards the beaches, only six made it ashore; the remaining tanks were swamped by the waves, filled with water and were lost, with their crews trapped inside.

He said he couldn't wait to get on the sand as at least he was confident of his ability to fight against a well organised and disciplined enemy, whereas the sea and the weather conditions were something that you could do absolutely nothing about. He and his mates had been entirely in God's hands at that point and sadly, God didn't appear to be on his best game that day.

As the journey progressed the veterans moved about the ship, most of them quite slowly, some of them in wheelchairs. Almost all were accompanied by carers or family members, determined to make sure that this visit, if it was to be the last, was a memorable one.

There were many television crews on board ship, conducting interviews. Whilst we were sat at the table with a couple of elderly gentlemen I realised that one of them was the same former tank commander who had given the TV interview about the amphibious tanks. A small TV crew arrived and asked if they could interview him and he kindly agreed. My Dad and I offered to move to allow the television crew better access to carry out the interview, when a young researcher just tapped my Dad on the hand and whispered, "Stay there. You really want to hear what these two men have to say."

We stayed and listened to the interviews, and it was hard not to be moved to tears as both men spoke about the friends they had lost that day seventy years earlier. You could see that as they were telling their stories, they were almost seeing it all again in their minds, almost living it once more. Both once again reiterated that during the landings the German Army and their response to the invasion held no fear for them, just the weather conditions and their less than seaworthy amphibious tanks.

When asked, "Where you scared when you hit the beaches?" he replied, "Of course we were all fearful, but we were never going to fail... we knew we could overcome that fear and press on. That's exactly what we did, we overcame our fear and pressed on."

There was nothing but modesty in the words of both men as they went on to explain their actions that day, and how fear was never going to stop them and their mates. They were going to achieve their objectives or die in the attempt as they knew exactly what was at stake. The young interviewer was dead right. What I heard at that table was something I will never forget.

The other thing that struck me about the interview was the genuine interest of the young interviewer, his researcher, and camera crew. As I sat and listened to the gentlemen at my side I looked at the faces of the TV crew and I could see how much they were taking in and how much the words meant to them. For them this wasn't some glib interview that was going to be forgotten five minutes after recording it. I reckon we were all aware that what we were hearing was a first-hand account of one of the most significant moments in history, and we all knew how fortunate we were to be present. In a few years these men would no longer be here to tell their stories and the only record of it would be in the history books or on film. We were privileged to be in the company of many who had created that history, on a ship taking the same route to Normandy that they had travelled so many years before.

When we were in mid-channel there was a ceremony at the stern of the ship. A wreath-laying ceremony held by many of the veterans and their associations to commemorate lost comrades. It was an extremely moving ceremony, accompanied by a piper and a bugler, who played The Last Post as the wreaths floated on the calm sea, remaining in mid-channel as we left them far behind and continued our journey towards Normandy. It was surprising how that channel wind can cause your eyes to water. It had the same effect on everyone present – veterans, relatives and just those who wished to pay their respects.

As we approached the Normandy coast looking towards the west, all the D-Day beaches were set out before us, and disappearing into the distance, with small clusters of lights just coming on in the towns and villages along the coast. As daylight became dusk, we slowly sailed into the port of Ouistreham, a few miles from Caen.

The hundreds of vehicles slowly disembarked, and we wound our way from the port into the town, before taking the coast road to the west. On the night of the 4th of June 2014, we parked up about five miles from Ouistreham on a hard-standing twenty yards from the sands of Sword Beach. We got out of the van and had a brew, before finishing the night with a beer and then off to sleep, listening to the waves crash on to the beach. It didn't take me long to nod off and as I drifted off to sleep I thought, "I hope I've put the handbrake on!"

My Dad and I spent a fantastic week visiting the many museums and the beaches in Normandy. At midnight, as the 5th June turned into the 6th, I stood with hundreds of locals on the beach at Lion-Sur-Mer as a fireworks display lit up the whole Normandy coast from Sword Beach in the east to Utah Beach in the west. It was a fantastic sight to see. It seemed as if the whole of the town had turned out and stood on the beach just watching the fireworks; those few locals who were old enough remembering, and everyone else having to imagine the events of 1944.

On the 6th of June 2014, the sun shone, and my Dad and I spent the day at what was once Sword Beach, at Lion-Sur-Mer. We sat in a beachfront bar drinking beer and watched a family with their children running up and down the beautiful sandy beach, in the warm sunshine, throwing a tennis ball for their boxer dog, who charged in and out of the sea to retrieve the ball. This is what it had all been for. So that French families could behave like families should in their own country, free to enjoy a family day out in peace. The Normandy landings were the start of almost another year of struggle and sacrifice that would eventually bring long-awaited freedom to families all over Europe.

It was a great week. We lived on coffee, beer, Warburton's crumpets, with a few Jaffa cakes thrown in for good measure. The weather was kind to us and the locals hospitable. A couple of days before we were due to return home, we had yet to book the return crossing. My Dad phoned my Mam and had a good conversation with her before passing the phone to me. Although I didn't know it, the conversation that followed was to make a large impact on my life and it would lead me into the story I'm about to tell.

"Hiya, sunshine boy. How are you getting on with your Father? At least it looks like neither of you have strangled the other one yet!" She jested.

"No, Mam, actually the week's gone really well, I can't believe how well we've been getting on," I replied.

"What? You haven't even had an argument yet?" exclaimed my poor little astounded Mother.

"Not yet!" I replied. The line went very quiet, apart from a small thump which I took to be my Mam keeling over and falling to the floor in a state of shock.

"Really? You're not just saying that? One of you hasn't got an arm or leg in a sling?" Mother asked.

"How do you get your leg in a sling?" I replied.

"Well, you know what I mean. I can't think properly. I'm in a state of shock!" She said.

"Yes, Mam, I'm sure, we've got on really well this week; it's been great." I responded, as surprised as she was.

"Well that's great. I don't really want to push my luck and ask you this but I'm going to anyway. Don't think you have to say 'yes', just because it would mean the world to me and would break my heart if you refused," said my devious, manipulative little Mother.

"Go on then Mam, what you want?" I asked.

"Do you remember my Uncle Ben?" Mam enquired.

"Yes, I do. Why do you ask?" I replied.

"Well your sister has been online and she has found the cemetery in France where he is listed on a memorial wall. I don't suppose you fancy taking a trip up to the north of France and seeing if you can find it for me, do you?" she asked, slightly casually.

"Bloody hell, Mam! Do you know how far it is from Normandy to northern France?"

"Well it can't be that far, and I mean they have motorways and everything in France these days, don't they?" said my mother.

"Well the roads might be great, but I don't really fancy dawdling along the motorways in an ancient camper for a few hundred miles to try and find somewhere that we've never been, when I'm not really sure where we're going. I don't reckon Father is going to be the best navigator in the world. He couldn't find his own backside with both hands!" I responded. Job done I thought.

"Oh well, I just thought I'd ask. I mean it's just that no one from the family has ever managed to track down where Ben's memorial is, and I just thought that as you are in France it might be the only opportunity any of us would ever get to pay a visit. Still if it's too far I'll see you when you get back," replied my deflated little Mother.

"How do you know where the memorial is? I don't really want to go on a wild goose chase and spend a couple of days running around trying find something that might not be there," I said, trying to excuse my reluctance.

"It's at the Pozieres Memorial Cemetery and as you go into the cemetery his name is on the second column on the right-hand side of the altar. It is panel number 52, and his name is about halfway down on the right-hand side of the panel," she replied without pausing for breath.

"I don't suppose you have a GPS location for that memorial slab, do you Mum?" I replied, sarcastically, my resolve weakening all the time.

"What a GPS?" she asked.

"Never mind, I'm sure we'll find it," I replied; my resolve broken.

"So, you're going to travel up and find it for me?" she enquired, just doing a double-check that she had won.

"Of course I am. You didn't think I'd say 'no' did you?" I responded.

At this point I heard my mum shouting to my sister, "They're going to find Ben. I told you they'd go."

"OK, Mam. Check up on the internet and get the exact location. We'll probably set off tomorrow. Can you please tell Carol that I'll get in touch with her in a day or so to arrange for us to come back by the Eurotunnel rather than the ferry?" Would you like to speak with Father before we set off?" I asked.

"Yes please, sunshine boy. Thanks." Replied my jubilant Mam.

"That's fine Mam, it'll be great." I turned to me oblivious Father; "Dad, Mam wants to have a word with you. She says we've got to stop off and buy you some new underpants... we're heading for northern France."

"What do you mean, northern France?" asked my confused father. "Where the bloody hell is that?"

As I handed the phone over to my dad, I asked, "Well, remember when you looked at the French map book?"

"Yes," he replied, as he took the phone from me.

"Well northern France is the top bit and southern France is the bottom bit. We are somewhere between the top bit and the bottom bit, so we'll head more towards the top bit than the bottom bit. Stop me if I'm getting a bit technical, or I'm going too fast."

He ignored me and spoke into the phone, "What the bloody hell is he rabbiting about, Alice?" He asked.

Everything went quiet for a couple of minutes as Mam explained the situation to my increasingly worried-looking Father. After ending the conversation my Dad stared blankly at the phone handset, expecting it to switch itself off. When nothing happened, he passed it to me saying, "You'd better switch it off. I don't know what the bloody hell I'm doing."

"That makes two of us, Father. I know you're a bit shit with phones, but I hope you're a lot better at map reading, because you're going to be getting plenty of practice tomorrow."

*****

The following day my Dad and I set off from Normandy to the Somme. According to the satnav the journey should have taken about 4½ hours, although travelling in a 30-year-old camper meant it would take considerably longer. I calculated it would take about 8 hours, and due to the slow running speed of the camper – on average about 50 MPH – I thought it was best not to travel on the motorway system, but to stick with the A roads. The plan was set, and the pair of us went out for a few beers before getting an early night.

The following day we woke at about 8 o'clock, a bit later than usual, and enjoyed a breakfast of coffee and crumpets. By this point I was getting a little bit tired of crumpets; however, we still had another couple of hundred stored in the back of the camper that needed to be eaten or disposed of before we got back, and I had to face the wrath of my Mam for wasting food.

The journey started well as we headed towards Le Havre and it was at this point matters started to go a bit pear-shaped. As we approached the metropolis that is Le Havre, we began to see warning signs above the carriageway, which in my rudimentary schoolboy French I translated to mean that there was a bridge closed up ahead.

A swift U-turn took us into a trading estate. I retrieved the map book from under Father's seat. It was studied, by me, not 'Bear Grylls', who was staring out of the window, having developed a sudden interest in French cement factories, whilst 'bricking it' in case I passed him the map.

I worked out a detour, realising it would need to be quite a short one, otherwise Father would not have been able to follow it on the map. (As it happened, regardless of how short the detour was, 'Mr Magoo' wasn't going to be able to follow it because the print on the map was far too small.) The only alternative was to bin the map after selecting a location well away from the 'Pont Ferme' and setting the satnav to get us there, then, having arrived at the new destination, resetting the satnav to get us to Pozieres.

The detour added about an hour and a half to the journey time, but I wasn't in a great rush and once back on the road to Pozieres it was quite pleasant travelling through the French villages. Whilst travelling around Normandy, every village we visited was a hive of activity, but these were almost deserted.

I'm not sure whether it was like this all the time – obviously with the 70th anniversary commemorations in full swing the Normandy villages were bustling with locals and visitors. As we travelled towards the Somme we noticed that many of the villages we passed through were almost deserted. It was as if the locals had been beamed up by visiting aliens. In many places we didn't see a single person, a shop open for business, or a moving vehicle. We started to play a little game of spot the human and we became quite jubilant when one of us saw somebody. If that person was under the age of 70, we almost did a lap of honour.

We came across a fishing lake and stopped for coffee and crumpets. It was at this point I discovered a packet of Jaffa cakes that had slipped down behind the crumpets, so we had a pudding to follow our main course. We felt quite posh as we enjoyed our coffee and crumpets, finished off with a couple of Jaffa cakes apiece. Who said fine dining was dead?

As we approached the area of the Somme we noticed a change to the landscape: we began to travel through wide expanses of flat farmland, enabling us to see as far as the horizon. Soon, indications that we were approaching the battlefields of the First World War began to emerge.

The frequency at which military cemeteries began to be signposted increased; at first a single sign pointing down a small lane, then as we got closer, the single signposts became far more frequent, until they were replaced with three individual signs attached to a single post, each pointing in different directions to more military cemeteries.

Most of the signposts belonged to the Commonwealth War Graves Commission with their distinctive green and white livery indicating a British, Australian, New Zealand, Canadian, or South African cemetery. The sign itself was quite small and plain, but the significance was unmistakable. Each sign directed you towards history; a history that was paid for with the blood of millions of young men from the British Commonwealth, from France, from Belgium, and from Germany. Whilst the shape and the colour of the signs changed, depending upon whether the cemetery in question was maintained by the CWGC, or the French, Belgian or German authorities, all pointed to the final resting place where thousands of young men silently lay, and had done so for a hundred years.

The first sign we saw almost created excitement, as we knew we were getting closer to our goal. We pointed out the first sign, then a few miles later, a second. Within thirty minutes we started to see more and more signs, and the enormity of what we were both witnessing began to sink in, as we drove along the quiet country road that was leading us back into history. Slowly, each sign began to take on a completely different meaning as we took turns to read the name of each cemetery, becoming ever quieter, more reflective and respectful. The ever-growing number of signs now became unwelcome.

About ten miles away from Pozieres we stopped to check the email my Mam had sent to us. It detailed the exact location of the cemetery and where Ben was commemorated. The description was detailed, and we were confident that we could follow it straight to where the name was engraved. We brewed up, but there was no appetite for a Warburtons before we continued towards the cemetery.

The map and the satnav told us that the cemetery was on the main road between La Boiselle and Pozieres. During the last part of the journey the road was straight and wide, with trees planted sparsely along the edges of the road and open farmland on either side. We travelled the last few miles in warm sunshine and saw the cemetery, standing white, remarkably white, almost glowing in the sunshine. I reduced speed for the last few hundred yards, and then indicated left and pulled into the layby outside the gates of the Pozieres British Military Cemetery.

Surprisingly, despite travelling for about 10 hours, neither of us was in any hurry to get out. We sat in the camper for some time, just gathering our thoughts. A final check of the email giving directions, and together we stepped out of the camper into the bright sunshine, just outside the open gates.

The gates were of black wrought iron, or rather wrought iron painted black. As we looked through them, the graves were divided in half by a broad grass path that led 50 or 60 yards to the altar and the cross, both of which were illuminated in the afternoon sunshine. We stood for a minute in complete silence until my Dad spoke.

"Do you know where we are going? he asked.

"Yes, Dad," I replied, little knowing where the short grass path in front of us would eventually lead me.

As I looked around the peaceful, sun-bathed cemetery, the lightest of breezes moved some of the flowers growing on and around the headstones. Over to our right were 3 local workers tending the graves. One was using a small hoe to break up the dried soil just beneath each headstone and around the small shrubs planted there. Another had a set of long-handled shears and was trimming the edging on another grave, ensuring all lines were perfectly straight and the grass was an even length. It was comforting to see how well cared for this place was, each grave carefully maintained, each stone clean, and the soil freshly tilled to allow the plants to flourish.

Some of the graves had a little shrub planted on them, others had an ornamental rose. Not every grave had a plant, but that didn't detract from the care that had been given to each soldier's resting place. Some graves had a tiny poppy stuck into the ground, others had a national flag stuck into the soil. There were one or two union flags placed on the graves of British soldiers, a few tricolours to mark the grave of an Irishman and more frequently, Australian flags marked the resting places of some of the thousands of 'Diggers' who lay here; every single one of whom was a volunteer.

As we walked slowly along the path I took in the inscriptions on the gravestones, noting the different countries and long-disbanded regiments of the soldiers who now lay in France, although that's not strictly accurate because as I understand it each of these cemeteries have been gifted in perpetuity to the countries concerned by France and Belgium, in gratitude for the part that British and Commonwealth soldiers played in the defence and eventual liberation of their countries.

50 yards in, we arrived at the altar and slowly climbed the steps following the instructions on the sheet of paper I held in my hand. I took my Dad's right arm and helped him climb the steps towards the altar and then round to the right and towards the walls that enclosed the cemetery, and on which were inscribed, from top to bottom, the names of soldiers who had no known grave. We arrived at panel number 51, and then stepped to the right to panel 52. We slowly lifted our eyes, and there, about three-quarters of the way up the right-hand column of names, was inscribed LEEMAN. B

That was all it said; LEEMAN. B. Nothing more, nothing less – just that simple inscription. A simple inscription that brought a lump to my throat and tears to my eyes for a man, or should he be described as a boy, who had lived and fought close to this spot 97 years earlier, before giving his life for something, now so difficult to understand, but which in those times probably made perfect sense. My Dad and I just stood in silent sadness and stared at the inscription. It was engraved a little too high for me to touch, even when I reached up with my right hand.

LEEMAN.B – each letter precisely 2 inches high, carefully spaced, exactly the same as the dozens of other names inscribed on panel number 52 and the thousands carved on the dozens of other panels. Just seven letters, with a space and a full stop, was all that acknowledged the life and death of my Mam's Uncle Ben, my Great Uncle.

My Dad took a couple steps back and sat on the little wall. I joined him, and there we sat looking up in silence, until the clank of the gate made me turn to see the gardeners leaving the cemetery and gently closing the gates behind them. It suddenly struck me that all the time they had been working they hadn't spoken to each other, but had worked in silence. I wondered if they didn't speak because we were there, or if they always worked in silence, either out of respect or maybe because each of them knew the job so well there was no need to speak. They just knew what had to be done and did it, quietly and without fuss or ceremony.

Then my Dad said, "I wish your Mum could have seen this. She would have loved it. I just wish she could have been here to see it."

"She can see it," I replied.

I left my Dad sitting on the wall in front of Ben's name and walked back to the campervan. I collected my phone and switched the ringtone off. I would have been horrified if I'd received a call in the cemetery. I stood outside the cemetery gates and switched the camera to video, then retraced my steps, slowly and deliberately recording everything that I'd seen as I walked down the path, climbing the steps towards the altar, around the cross and over to panel 52 where Ben's name was inscribed so that my Mam could follow our exact route. When I finished recording I re-joined my Dad and just sat with him, in silence, for another 30 minutes.

Without speaking we got to our feet and walked around the panels that surround the cemetery on three out of the four sides, taking time to read the names and the different regiments from which the soldiers came. There were so many names I'd never heard before, long-disbanded regiments, from tiny geographical locations. Others that had been absorbed into larger, more anonymous regiments.

After looking at many of the inscriptions we walked quietly among the headstones. It was comforting to see several graves of Ben's fellow Sherwood Foresters. There were several headstones bearing the badge of the South Staffordshire Regiment, the area in which I now live, and from where these young men travelled almost a century ago and to where they would never return. I remember thinking that one of my neighbours could well be the great-nephew of one of these soldiers and

I would never know it. But I was grateful for the opportunity to read their names and let them know that on this day at least, they had been remembered and had a little prayer said in their memory.

Before we left the cemetery, we went to the register that was kept in a small, brass box, built into the wall just inside the gate. There were half a dozen books in each of the two safes, and in each book were listed in alphabetical order the name of each soldier buried or commemorated within.

I found the directory listing the soldiers whose surnames began with the letter L and began to thumb through the pages. I wasn't in a hurry to get to Ben's name, so I took a little bit of time to read some of the other names in the book. I was going to read Ben's name in a few moments, but it struck me that most of the soldiers recorded in this book had never had a family member hold the book and read their name, so for a few minutes, instead of just looking at the names, I decided to read them aloud. After all this time it was the very least that they deserved – just once to have someone read their names out loud and think about them. For each name I read aloud, I wondered what the initial meant: Lewis. C. I wondered what the letter C stood for. Christopher? Charles? I'd never know, but it didn't matter. I'd taken a few seconds to read their names aloud and remember them as men, not just an inscription. To pay them just a little of the respect they had earned.

Eventually I got to Ben's name and I noted that after his name the initials MM had been inscribed in the ledger. This was the first time I learned that Ben, at the age of 16 or 17, had been decorated for his courage. As if just being here wasn't enough, he had gone beyond what was expected of him, of any British soldier, to earn such an award. I read and re-read the entry – LEEMAN. B MM – in silence and respect.

My Dad took another book out with a different set of initials on the cover and slowly read through some of the names contained in it. I don't know if he had the same thoughts in his head as I did when I read the names. It didn't seem the right moment to ask him. It was a time for silence and reflection for Ben and all the others.

We left the cemetery and returned to the campervan and again sat quietly. I don't think there has ever been a time before or since when either my Dad or I had been so quiet; no jokes, no arguing. After a few minutes I drove us towards Pozieres, a few hundred yards away, and headed for a small restaurant at the side of the road called 'The British Tommy'.

I pulled in, yanked on the hand brake and switched the engine off.

I spoke first. "Do you fancy going in here for some scoff and a beer?"

"Yes. Come on. Let's just hope they don't serve bloody crumpets!" he replied. We both sat and laughed for the first time in a few hours, before getting out and entering the cafe for a beer and a crumpet-free lunch.

*****

A year later in June 2015 I returned to the British Military Cemetery at Pozieres, with my Mam. The camera footage of my previous visit was greatly appreciated, but I knew my Mam had to visit and see it herself.

We approached through Pozieres and a quarter of a mile beyond the village I stopped the car in the layby outside the gates and helped her out. As she took in the exterior of the cemetery, I took her 'wheels' out of the boot and set them up, quickly picking up the three pots of yoghurt and two bananas that had fallen out of the seat on to the ground and which were to sustain my Mam throughout the day, courtesy of the breakfast buffet at the Hotel Regina, Ypres.

I gave Mam her wheels and then I just left her to it. This was her time. Her time and Ben's time. She had waited seventy-four years for this moment and I knew she would call me when she was ready for me to join her. As she moved down the centre path towards the altar, she stopped at a headstone, the second stone in from the path, and bent down to it. There were a couple of small weeds on the earth, which she removed. She scraped a little hole in the ground and taking a small set of rosary beads from her pocket, placed them in the hole and covered them over. She stood up and leaned on her wheels for a minute or two, before heading to the steps up to the altar.

A world-class mountain biker couldn't have got up the steps on those wheels, so I joined her, first helping her up to the level bit, then returning to get her wheels. Once she was equipped with her transport, I made myself scarce and allowed her to visit panel fifty-two, alone with her thoughts. She spent the next thirty minutes just sitting quietly and then she gave me a wave and I joined her.

"Can you help me climb up there to touch his name, sunshine?" she asked.

"Bloody hell Mam, are you mental?" I replied.

"Of course I am. Now stop whingeing and give me a leg up," she insisted.

Well, with a bit of heaving and pushing, up she went. Once on the ledge she looked to the name about a foot above her head and slowly reached up with her right hand and traced the letters with her fingers. Once again it was just her and Ben. There was nothing to be said.

After a few minutes she turned around and I helped her down. She was a fair old weight for a little 'un. No wonder she packed so much power into those clips around the ear, which I frequently experienced, well into my early fifties.

Once again, as on my previous visit, the sun shone on the headstones and panels and the place was pretty and peaceful, just as it should be. As we turned to leave she said: "I promised you I'd visit your Ben one day, Dad."

Then she turned to me and said, "Let's go to that café we passed on the way in. I'm dying for a cup of tea."

We slowly walked from the cemetery and as we passed the grave where she had buried the rosary, she stopped and put her hand on the top of it. The inscription read: "Known unto God".

"This might be him, mightn't it?" she said.

"Yes, Mam. It just might be," I replied as we walked back to the car.

As we left the cemetery through the high, black-painted, iron gates she turned for one last look and took hold of my hand before saying, "Thanks for bringing me. I've kept a promise I made to my Dad, to come and find Ben. Now it's done. I'll never come back here again, but make sure you do, sunshine boy."

"I will, Mam. I promise." And I put my arm around the shoulders of my little Mam and gave her a kiss on the side of her face. My Mam never visited again, but I did... many times.

Chapter 2

Introductions

The journey back to the Somme had been straightforward. I'd made it many times since my first visit and here I was again, having returned for Ben's centenary, which would happen in the next day or two, depending upon which of the official records you went by.

It was about eleven o'clock at night, when, unable to sleep, I slipped silently out of bed, gathered up my clothes, slipped on my trainers and gently slid open the camper door, before stepping out onto the grass. In silence I dressed. Standing on my right foot, I kicked off my left trainer, put on my left sock, slipped my left leg into the left trouser before placing my left foot back into my left trainer, then repeated the process with the other leg. I pulled my trousers up and then laced up my footwear. I pulled a fleece over my head on top of my t-shirt, then fastened my belt. So far so good.

Now I had to close the door. The wheels and runners of the camper's sliding side door were slightly rusted so they made a sort of screeching noise. If I tried closing the doors too slowly the noise would have been bound to wake my missus, Carol, who was enjoying a rare peaceful night's sleep without the customary weight of Molly cat on top of her. Usually, to ensure that the doors do not make this screeching noise I closed them quickly, as running the door along the rail fast and with some force cuts out the squealing noise, but culminates in a loud bang as the door is slammed shut.

I considered my options carefully; closing the door slowly would make it screech. Carol would wake up and would certainly want to know what I was up to – and to be honest I didn't really know myself. She might even insist on coming with me. Closing the door quickly was almost certain to wake her as it slammed, but by the time she'd woken properly I'd be away on my toes legging it down the drive, out of earshot and away from a thousand and one questions as quickly as possible. I opted for the second choice. I slammed the door and I was off like a whippet down the drive, about twenty yards away from the camper.

I stopped and turned my ear towards the camper to listen and heard... nothing. Ninja!!

All I had to do now was to quietly negotiate my way past the barking Chihuahuas who patrolled in the extension to the farmhouse and I would be away. I opted to walk gently on the grass rather than the gravel path. Thirty-odd years of military service taught me that gravel is generally noisier to walk on than grass. Whilst this piece of knowledge doesn't exactly qualify me as a potential Special Air Service Trooper, it is one of the three most valuable lessons I learned, the other two being; 1). when making a brew in an arctic environment don't use the yellow snow, and 2). never go on a date with a woman who has a thicker neck than you.

A few minutes later, having escaped from Carol and evaded marauding Chihuahuas I felt that the only thing I was missing was my Indiana Jones hat and bull whip. Still, I was content with having the satnav from the camper.

I had a rough idea where I was going and finding my way would be much easier with an illuminated satnav. I set the picture smaller, so I could get a good idea of the layout of the countryside around the campsite. When we drove in I noticed that the most likely place to gain access to where I was going meant I had to turn right out of the campsite and up a small incline to the centre of the village, passing the village war memorial. A little further up the road was an old barn and grass track leading up an incline to the right and away from the road. According to the satnav it was less than 200 hundred yards to the memorial and another 40 to the right turn.

I walked slowly along the quiet street. I was surprised at how old some of the buildings in the street appeared, bearing in mind a hundred years earlier there was probably nothing left of this area. The village was silent as I walked along the pavement on the right-hand side of the road with an old ivy-covered wall against my right shoulder.

It was very different from the village where I lived back home – almost eerily quiet. This was something I'd noticed during my regular visits to France, places often appear to be completely deserted, not seeing so much as a single pedestrian as you drive through. When you are in the cities and towns, they appear busy, but in the villages, there always appears to be something of a voluntary curfew, most unlike any village I had ever visited in the UK.

I soon reached the war memorial. In the UK many of the memorials are quite similar, which makes the war memorial in my home village a bit special. Whilst I'm not exactly an authority on them, ours is like no other war memorial I've ever seen in the UK. It is simply a full-size crucifix in a sort of grotto. Quiet, peaceful, and thought-provoking. This French memorial was like many others I'd seen in France, except that although this one featured the obligatory soldier, he was accompanied by a child – a young girl.

Memorials back home have inscribed the names of the soldiers, sailors, and airmen from the town or village who lost their lives in both world wars. In later years, the names of service personnel lost in Northern Ireland, Korea, the Falkland Islands, Bosnia, Kosovo, Iraq and Afghanistan have often been added. When you read that list of conflicts, the 70-odd years of peace since the Second World War doesn't appear quite so peaceful.

I suppose French and Belgian memorials differ from those at home because so many of the names inscribed on them are civilians. Most of the names on this memorial were not soldiers, they were farmers, butchers, shopkeepers, men, women and children, illustrating the differences in the war experience of the British and French people. We've had so much to be grateful for. The courage and strength of the Royal Navy, the Army, the Royal Flying Corps, (which became the Royal Air Force), but perhaps the greatest debt of all needs to be paid to the English Channel, an insurmountable barrier for almost a thousand years.

I must have spent about fifteen minutes at the memorial, walking around it, looking at it from all directions. Things look different when you look at them from a different angle. The detail on both figures was remarkable. Cast in dark metal, the soldier in his uniform with his trademark Adrienne helmet with the crest on top. The small girl grasping him, with both her arms wrapped around his legs and her head resting against his left hip. The soldier held her close, his left hand resting gently on her left shoulder. In his right hand, he held his rifle, with the butt resting on the ground. The rifle had both sling and bayonet fitted. He doesn't look down at the girl, but stares into the distance. Why does he do that? Why does he not look down at the girl? I thought of a similar memorial in Alfreton in Derbyshire, depicting a soldier and young lad and I had seen a similar one in a Belgian town. Do any of them look at the child?

The girl doesn't look up at the soldier, but looks down towards the ground. Why doesn't she look up at the soldier? Maybe it means that this doesn't represent a father and daughter, but an anonymous soldier comforting an unknown child.

I wondered what their names were. Were they named on the memorial? Or were they just generic figures? Were their names important? Should they be identified as real people? Is it better they are anonymous representatives of a country's suffering and loss?

Perhaps we should view the figures as real people, because unless we do so, maybe they don't properly represent individuals who had feelings, emotions, families and life.

I remembered watching the film Saving Private Ryan and recalled the resentment which the Rangers, who had been sent to rescue Ryan, felt about losing their friends on their mission to save Ryan. Having found Ryan, one of the Rangers was angry with him, because they had lost three of their friends to save his life. The anger and resentment felt by the Rangers dissipated when Ryan asked one important question; 'You lost three of your friends? What were their names?' In asking that simple question he acknowledged that those men weren't just soldiers who had given their lives for him, but were people, they were individuals and they mattered.

I walked around the memorial and looked at the soldier and the girl from the front and then circled around it in an anticlockwise direction. The girl's right arm was wrapped around the back of the soldier's thighs. The soldier wore the usual puttees, wound around his lower legs, covering the top of his boots, keeping out water and winding upwards from his boots to a point just below his knees where the top of each puttee was tucked into itself, to prevent it unravelling.

Looking at the soldier's back, he wore a leather belt and the webbing straps that crossed in the middle of his back went through his shoulder tabs. The detail of the soldier's webbing and equipment might have been aged by a hundred years of time and weather, but it was still clear in every detail. The lower front hem of his greatcoat was folded upwards towards his waist and buttoned in place to reveal his bayonet scabbard, which was empty, as the bayonet it usually housed was fitted to his rifle.

I wondered if this statue was based on a photograph, or just the imagination of the artist. But if it was imagination it must have been based on a thorough knowledge of a soldier's personal equipment. Did the artist ever witness a similar scene played out for real? Or had he just imagined a frightened, lost child holding tight onto something, someone, who might keep her safe? Nothing in the soldier's facial expression gave a clue to his thoughts. His gaze went off into the distance, not towards the girl. What was he looking at? What he was thinking? I began to feel a bit of an affinity with the soldier and the little girl. They stopped being a soldier and little girl and started to become my soldier and little girl.

I had now moved three-quarters of the way around and I was at my soldier's right side, looking at the detail on his rifle with the bayonet attached. How long had he carried that rifle? Was it a new one straight out of the box, never having seen action? Or was it a tried and trusted friend to my soldier, keeping him safe during many battles when his life depended on it? I wondered how many times the rifle had been fired. And how many times the shot fired had found its target, taking the life of a German soldier. When the enemy soldier was struck down, did it hurt? Was his life snuffed out in a split-second, so he wasn't even aware it was gone?

When you switch a light bulb off it goes from light to dark in a split second, but the light bulb doesn't know it's no longer illuminated. It doesn't understand that a second ago it was light, but now it's dark; that once it was working, but now it's not. Of course, lightbulbs and human beings aren't the same at all. If you switch a lightbulb off you can just as easily and quickly switch it back on, so that the darkness once again becomes light. Sadly, it doesn't work like that with people, once that light has gone out, it's gone for eternity, never to be lit again, or to shine on the face of a loved one, for the rest of time.

If my soldier took the German soldier's life with his rifle, what was the reaction of the man's family when they were informed of his death in action? How did they feel? Did they believe he had died in a noble cause serving his country? Or were they struck down by a grief so deep that they never recovered from it? Perhaps he was never spoken of again, or perhaps at this very moment his great-nephew or great-grandchild was seeking out a grave in northern France and thinking about the great-uncle or great-grandfather that they had never known.

The bayonet was about a foot long. 'That's a serious piece of kit, that bayonet,' I thought. I wondered if it was ever used in anger, and how many lives it had taken in the battles to defend France.

I completed the circuit and was back in front of my soldier and little girl having viewed them from all sides. The backdrop when viewed from the front was an old barn with a tiled roof and big green double doors. It was a typically French scene. I moved slightly to the left, then to the right. Whichever way I moved it seemed the backdrop to the statue made it was clear that you were in France. The houses were typically French, the inscription on the statue was in French. I couldn't be anywhere else but France.

I moved in much closer and looked upwards to the soldier's moustachioed face beneath his helmet. Behind his head was a clear, dark sky. There were few streetlights in the village, so there was little light pollution, which so often obscures the stars in the sky. The sky wasn't quite black, but an inky, dark blue, with the stars clearly set against it. If it was on an ink bottle it would have been called blue/black. Every now and then one of the bigger, clearer stars would appear to twinkle, whilst others appeared to change colour slightly and shimmer with a hint of red, or green rather than white. Why did they do that? Where's that Brian Cox bloke when you need an answer?

Looking up, my soldier and child were set against the infinity of space. It was no longer apparent that we were in France. From this angle there were no clues to our location, other than the soldier's uniform. Without a uniform he could have been any nationality and the three of us; soldier, child and me, could have been anywhere in the world. It made me realise that whenever we look up, we all look at the same sky regardless of what country we live in, what values we hold, or what God we believe in, if we believe in any God at all. It made me think, not in any earth-shattering moment of wisdom and insight, just how small we were and perhaps how futile it had been to fight and die over the tiny bits of soil, grass, sea and stone that we call countries.

I thought how futile it appeared from 100 years distance, without appreciating the irony of thinking this way, as just 5 years earlier my own boots were kicking up the dust of Afghanistan whilst fighting against Afghans in their own country, a few thousand miles from home, just because my government disagreed, rightly or wrongly, with the way some of them wished their country to be run. At least this memorial was closer to home.

Although war might be about a piece of land, or a noble cause – to defend, or promote a way of life that we value and hold dear – or for ideals with labels like democracy, freedom, and stuff like that, when you are on the ground and the battle is going on all around you, you don't fight for Queen, or country, or democracy. You fight for those you love and when the shit hits the fan, the person you love most is your mate, an arm's length away from you; you fight for him and he fights for you.

I realised that I was crouched down on my haunches looking up, so quickly stood up, checking to make sure no one was watching, thinking, 'What's that bloody nutter doing over there?'

I reached up and touched the head of my young girl, who still hadn't let go of her soldier. But then, she'd been holding on for nearly 100 years, so she wasn't about to let him go now – nor was he about to let her go. I put my right hand on top of my soldier's left hand, which was on the little girl's shoulder. I let it sit for a minute or so. His hand was cold, but after a few seconds it felt warm to the touch. I gave my soldier's hand a little squeeze and the little girl's head a gentle stroke before stepping back a couple of paces. If I had been an American I would have thrown up a smart salute, but being British, I wasn't going to be a dick. In any case I am sure the touch of a hand would have meant more to them both than any salute.

I turned to my right and slowly walked away to cross the road towards the grass track leading out of the village. As I reached the path I looked back towards them for a second, but neither of them looked back at me. They remained still, as they had done for most of the past century and as they would continue to do for the next century and beyond. I stepped on to the path and walked into the darkness.

*****

The grass path was wet and slippery. The warmth of the evening had dried the pavements on the main street, so they showed no evidence of the rain that had recently fallen. The grass path told a different story; it was wet, and the beads of rain sparkled like little fairy lights on the tips of the grass. In other books I have read these beads of light are often described as little diamonds, but I don't have a great deal of experience with diamonds so can best describe them as fairy lights.

Without warning the battery in the satnav died, but I knew where I was heading. I walked carefully and slowly, climbing slightly as the barely visible path rose above the village. Some distance away I could see the lights of a nearby town, maybe five miles away. I couldn't see the town, just the glow that lit the sky above it.

I continued slowly up the gentle incline to the crest of the hill, if you could call it a hill, as it was more of a slight bump or undulation in the field where I stopped to survey the landscape. If my understanding of the tourist pamphlet I had read earlier was correct there would be a small regimental memorial about 400 yards ahead of me close to the path, and, 100 yards off to the right of the memorial, a small British cemetery.

I reached the crest of the bump and looked down the slope on the other side towards the memorial and cemetery. Both were just about visible as vague shapes in the darkness – the moonlight providing just enough illumination to make out the outlines. I started down the slope, which was a bit steeper than the climb. It was bloody slippery, and I took it slowly, going down sideways, right foot first, left foot remaining still to help me balance and sort of shuffling down sideways, so as not to fall.

Unfortunately, the footwear chosen for my night-time walk probably wasn't the most effective and I began to slide sideways, slowly at first, but gradually picking up speed like a middle-aged snow-boarder, before hitting a bump and falling backwards. Landing on my arse, I continued the downward journey feet first, on my back, looking up at an inky-blue, starlit sky. As I picked up speed I put down my right hand to stop my slide, but only succeeded in spinning myself around a hundred and eighty degrees, so that instead of sliding down the slope feet first on my back, I continued the downward journey headfirst, on my back.

After about another 10 seconds I ground to a halt, mainly due to the amount of grass and mud that was packing down the top of my jeans, filling the backside of my pants. The last time my pants were this full of brown squidgy stuff was about 53 years earlier, if you exclude a night out in Nairobi circa 2007 that involved copious amounts of the local beer and a dodgy zebra steak in a Brazilian restaurant called 'Carnivores', but that's another story.

Having ground safely to a halt my serious mood evaporated as I burst into laughter. I lay back on the damp grass and looked up at the sky. My fleece had ridden up and my back was soaking wet. I climbed to my feet and began shoving my left hand down my belt at the back of my jeans to begin fishing lumps of grass and mud out of the arse of my pants. After removing a couple of handfuls and chucking them on the path I had a horrible feeling I was having a stroke.

Someone once told me that one of the first symptoms of having a stroke is that you detect the smell of burning and I could definitely smell something burning. I stopped laughing and started to feel my face with both hands. My hands and face both appeared to be functioning normally. I opened and closed my mouth without any problems; hands face and mouth all appeared to be working normally. What a bloody relief! I wasn't having a stroke... what a knobhead!

The fall and slide had left me facing back up the slope in the direction I had just come from. Pulling my jeans up and my fleece down, I turned back towards the memorial and cemetery. As I did so the source of the burning smell became apparent. Just ahead of me and to the right of the path it looked as if there was a small fire with a thin plume of wispy, grey smoke drifting up into the dark night air. I walked towards it and I then realised that it wasn't a fire I could smell, but the pong of a cigarette. It was strong, thick, heavy smoke. It wasn't like the cigarettes I used to smoke when I was a 40-a-day lad and it wasn't like any French cigarette.

I'm not claiming to be a world-renowned authority on the smell of fags around the world, but from my time in Afghanistan I do remember the distinctive smell of the cigarettes the French soldiers smoked... a bit like someone barbecuing a pair of manky socks! I became quite familiar with the smell as the French Army appeared to regard smoking as some sort of national sport.

No, this smell was vaguely familiar from my childhood when people would smoke unfiltered cigarettes like Senior Service and some of the old fellers that went to the pub with my Dad would smoke Capstan Full Strength, or Woodbines. This smoke was just like those. I didn't even know if you could still buy Woodbines or Senior Service these days. I moved closer until I was about 10 or 15 paces away and I could see the outline of the smoker.

He was sitting on the grass with the back of his left shoulder facing in my direction. He sat cross-legged on the floor – like we used to sit in school assembly when I was a kid – the way that only schoolchildren, or people in dodgy, lycra leggings practising yoga sit these days. His clothing was dark, something like a heavy woollen fleece in a sort of brown colour, although in the darkness it could have been any dark colour.

I couldn't see the length of it because the smoker was sitting, so I assumed it was a bog-standard fleece. As I approached I could see it was a long coat made of a coarser material, with a big collar. I continued down the path until I was almost level with where the smoker sat, a few feet off to the side of the path.

I suppose I assumed he was a camper, but I didn't think to look for a tent or anything like that. All I was thinking about was the unusual smell of the burning ciggy. It was completely out of context, a right blast from the past, but it wasn't any more unusual than the sight of a person sat in a field in the middle of nowhere at almost midnight. The presence of a late night rough-camper didn't strike me as odd, because I could think of nothing but the weird fag smoke I was breathing in.

As I drew level with him I thought to try out my advanced French courtesy of a two quid phrase book obtained from Bargain Books.

"Bonsoir!" I let rip in my best schoolboy French.

"Bloody hell! There's nothing sounds dafter than an English bloke trying to speak like a Frenchie," he replied.

No guardsman at the trooping of the colour could have come to a more abrupt halt. Despite many years in the Royal Air Force and quite a few parades, it was the best halt I'd ever managed, although that won't come as much of a surprise to any soldier who ever witnessed the Royal Air Force attempting to march.

Funnily enough, although the words brought me to a complete halt, for some reason I didn't think to turn around and look at the smoker sitting cross-legged on the ground. I just stood, dead still, with my back to him. 'Why the hell don't you turn around', I thought to myself. But I couldn't. I was frozen, everything sort of just stopped. It wasn't like my brain wasn't telling me to turn and my body was disobeying. My brain wasn't doing anything at all. I just stood like a statue in the darkness facing towards the small regimental memorial.

Then the silence was broken, not by a voice, but by the sound of my fag-smoking companion slowly climbing to his feet. I still had no desire to turn around. I thought 'What the hell's going on here! You're in the middle of nowhere, in the middle of the night with a frigging weirdo stood a few feet behind you and you don't turn around to see what he's up to!' The reason I didn't turn was simple; I was shitting myself.

Then he spoke again and introduced himself: "I'm Private Ben Leeman, Z Company, 15th Battalion, The Notts and Derby Regiment, The Sherwood Foresters."

I turned and looked at him. There he stood; bare-headed, in a long greatcoat, unbuttoned, under which I could see the familiar British battledress tunic. His trousers were barely visible due to the length of the greatcoat, his puttees were missing and his trousers covered most of his boots.

"I'm your great-nephew," I replied.

"Yes, I can see that. We've both got the same squashed, Leeman nose. Shall we sit down and talk for a while?" asked Ben. "It's been long a long time since I spoke with anyone." And with that he beckoned me to approach. As I took the few, slow steps towards him, he took off his greatcoat, and with a bit of a flourish, a sort of bullfighter movement, he spread it on the ground, with the inside facing upwards. He squatted down on the collar end of the coat and pointed to the bottom of the coat with his right hand, indicating where I should sit... on his coat.

I walked towards him and slowly and a bit stiffly lowered myself to the ground and sat with him. As I lowered myself down, Ben crossed his legs and again took up his "lotus" position, like I did in PE when at primary school, but not at any time since.

"How is this going to work? Do you just talk, or do I ask you questions and you answer them?" I asked.

"How should I know? I've not done this before. I'm sure we'll work it out before morning," said Ben, before adding, "Would you like to tell me your name, or do you want me to guess?"

"My name's John," I replied. I looked at his 17-year-old smooth and slightly dirty face and his short-cropped hair. "Do you mind if I just call you Ben, rather than Uncle Ben?" I asked.

"Why? Are you ashamed to be my great-nephew?" he responded, in a serious tone.

'Shit!' I thought. He's waited a hundred years to speak and the first time I open my trap I've offended him.

Then his face burst into a wide grin. And I immediately recognised him as a typical, mickey-taking Leeman.

"I'm not being funny," I said. "It's just that I'm 57-years-old and you are 17. Calling you uncle, or even great-uncle, to give you your proper title, seems a bit weird."

"How do you think I feel? I've just met my great-nephew for the first time and he's the same age as my bloody grandfather," Ben replied.

"There is another reason," I said.

"What's that then? It's not the boots is it? I can see you keep glancing at them." Ben said, and he poked a finger into a hole in the sole of his left boot, adding, "If I'd known you were coming, I would have worn my Sunday best."

"No, it's not the boots, it's just that you can buy boil-in-the-bag rice and it's called "Uncle Ben's."

"What's boil-in-the-bag rice?" Ben asked.

"I'll tell you later. I think we've got more important stuff than rations to talk about," I replied.

We sat quietly for a few minutes. Ben took out a packet of cigarettes and offered me one. I shook my head. I was surprised to see they weren't Woodbines, as I thought that was the only type of cigarettes the troops had. But these were a packet of Black Cats, which I had never heard of.

He took a fag from the pack, and, striking a match, with his hands cupped around the flame to prevent the non-existent breeze blowing it out, lit his smoke. He blew out a cloud of smoke and then he spoke.

He turned his head and looked all around him, "It's so quiet around here now. Is the war over?" he asked.

"Yes. It's over." I replied.

"When did it end?" Ben asked.

"In 1918. It officially ended on the eleventh of November at eleven o'clock in the morning. The eleventh hour of the eleventh day of the eleventh month. I suppose they were trying to make it symbolic in some way," I said.

Ben responded, "Symbolic? Yes, they would do that wouldn't they?

Symbolic! It would have been better had they settled for 'sooner' instead of symbolic. November 1918? I was always afraid that it would never end. It seemed like the war would never end, that it was just going to go on forever."

"Well it did end," I assured him.

"Good," he replied and then sat in silence.

"Well, don't you want to know who won?" I asked.

"I suppose so. It's just more important to know that it's over. I thought it might be still going on. That it had just moved on past this place, that maybe we had finally pushed them back and were now fighting in Germany, or even worse that they had pushed us back, maybe even over to England."

"Anyway, I can see you're dying to tell me, so go on, tell me; who won?" Ben asked, somewhat reluctantly.

"We did," I replied.

"What did we win?" asked Ben.

"Well, that's a bit trickier, and to be honest I'm not exactly sure. The war ended with an armistice rather than a surrender by the Germans, even though they were on their arses. We claimed to have won, the Germans were forced to accept extremely harsh terms in order to secure peace and not be ground into the dirt but be allowed to return to Germany, with at least some scrap of pride intact."

"Britain was never invaded, the Americans came in late in the day (no change there, I thought) and so got to play a part on the world stage for the first time, and the French got Alsace back, well at least until 1940," I explained.

"What happened in 1940?" Ben asked.

I stayed silent for a while, ignoring that uncomfortable question. I sat and watched him taking a drag on his smoke and looking around him.

"So where should we begin? The war, or before all that stuff?" Ben asked.

"Before all that Ben, tell me about your family... I mean our family," I replied.

Chapter 3

Family

"Where would you like me to start?" asked Ben.

"I'm not really sure. Where do you think your story begins? I replied.

Ben gathered his thoughts and went on: "Well, I could talk to you about being a kid, growing up, about my brothers and sisters, I suppose that is as good a place as any to start.

"I was born in Lincolnshire, and before volunteering I lived all my life in the town of Grimsby. I have two brothers and three sisters. I'm the youngest of the boys and I suppose I was always a bit competitive with Charlie and George, they're my two brothers by the way, not my sisters. Charlie and George are a few years older than me. Our Charlie is the eldest, four years older, and our George is about two years older than me.

"My sister Florence is the second eldest, coming between Charlie and George. Our Edie is almost a year older little than me. Nora is the baby, a couple of years younger than me. Nora is named after our Mam and she looks just like her. George is named after our Dad.

"I would have liked to be the oldest or the youngest. That always seemed to be the best place to be. Our Charlie was always treated as our Dad's right-hand man and our Nora was the baby. No, maybe I wouldn't have wanted to be the youngest.

"I wasn't as clever as Charlie and George. They both did really well at school. Well, maybe they weren't any cleverer than I was, maybe just that they were a few years older, so had learned a lot more than I had learned. I was a bit jealous of them when they were both working, and I was still at school. I couldn't wait to leave school, but our Dad insisted I stay at school for as long as possible. I was almost 13 when I finally left school.

"Charlie worked in an engineering workshop. He was always good with his hands. He always smelled of oil when he came home from work. Even when he came home he was always taking stuff to bits and putting it back together. Our Mam would go mad every time she caught him dismantling something, but everything always worked as good as new when he put it back together. Better sometimes, because he was always mending broken stuff and getting it working again," he said.

"Our George worked in a shipping office down by Grimsby docks. I'm not sure what his job was, but he used to come home and talk about the far-off places where all the ships were heading. Some of the places that he talked about I can still remember, although I never found out exactly where they were. I suppose George was always a bit envious of those who crewed the ships. He spent his time sending those ships to far-away places, but they were places that he would probably never see himself and might never know about except through reading books.

"Talking to George must have had a big effect on our Charlie. Charlie loved working in the engineering workshops, but I think the stories that George told him about the destinations where he was sending those ships must have got him thinking, because a couple years into his apprenticeship he came home one day all excited and announced that he'd joined the Merchant Navy as an engineering officer cadet.

"Bloody hell! Our Mam went mad and Dad said nothing. I think they were both in a state of shock. I think our Mam thought us kids would always be within arm's reach, just as she and our Dad had stayed within arm's reach of their Mams and Dads. Although our Dad was shocked, it was the timing of the news, not the news itself, that surprised him.

"Do you know, on the day I left home to go for my army training I travelled further from home in a single day than our Mam and Dad had ever travelled from home in their whole lives? If only I'd known where that road would eventually lead me, I might have stayed at home listening to stories from our George and reading letters from our Charlie."

Ben continued: "Growing up in Grimsby as a young lad was great. I wasn't bad at school. I worked quite hard because our Dad was always going on about the importance of getting a good education. We weren't at all well-off as a family, but we weren't poor either. Our Dad always worked hard. He was a foreman in a wood mill that made the sleepers for the railways. Our Dad must have earned a decent wage, or at least I think it must have been OK because we always had good food for our meals and a dry, warm house, which was more than a lot of my school friends ever had.

"Our clothes were always clean and well looked after, but not expensive, and there was plenty of stuff handed down from Charlie to George to me, and just the same with the girls' dresses. Our Mam always made sure we took care of everything we had – clothes, toys, books – so it could go from brother to brother or sister to sister. I always remember that our Nora always wanted a pair of trousers from me, but our Mam was having none of that!

"Our Mam always reminded us of the importance of keeping things nice and everything I ever had always just appeared to be on loan. I always felt I was keeping it for someone younger, so it could be passed down to them. I suppose that was just something that our Mam and Dad always instilled into us. We were a family and what we owned belonged to all of us. If it belonged to the family it had to be respected, cared for and passed on. When I grew out of my stuff there wasn't a younger brother, and Nora wasn't allowed trousers, so our Mam took all the stuff I had grown out of down to the local church for them to pass on.

"And I'm not just talking about a pair of shoes, or a Sunday coat, I'm talking about other things as well, like reading, or anything one of us learned, we were expected to pass it on to our brothers and sisters.

"Our Dad had learned to read as a kid, even before he went to school. He was a great reader and he kept our house stocked with interesting, exciting books. He looked after all those books carefully, but they were family books, not just his. He shared his books with us, but not just the actual books. He shared his love of reading and he spent so much time with all of us kids, boys and girls, instilling in us the same love of reading and providing us all with the same opportunities to learn and to better ourselves.

"I remember our Dad sitting at the table in the corner of the living room with a small lamp over a book and reading it to one of us kids. He would explain the meaning of words and sayings in the book, so it wasn't just a story, but a story with the meanings explained. He did this with Charlie, Florence, George and Edie. And when they were old enough they all invested that same amount of time in me and Nora. Our Dad made sure that all of us kids could read and write as well as any adult. He encouraged us to read his books on all sorts of stuff, history, geography, science, so we all learned of things that were far beyond the end of our street, town and even our country.

"We lived quite close to the middle of the town, but the town wasn't that big really. The best part about living in Fildes Street was the river that crossed the end of the street leading to Cartergate. You could spend ages playing down there. I remember trying to catch fish and our Mam came out and gave us a right telling off, because she said the river was dirty, and she didn't want any of us catching anything horrible from anything we might hook. It seemed a bit odd to have those concerns considering the river was called the Freshney. She needn't have worried, in all the times I went down there to fish, I never caught a thing, just got wet shoes and socks.

"As a kid I loved our little dog; Nan, a golden cocker spaniel, and I loved football; playing it, watching it and even reading about it in the newspaper. I would take any opportunity to kick a ball. I was always getting told off by our Mam for coming home from school with scuffed shoes. Always just the right foot, because that was the foot that I kicked with most of the time.

"Our Mam would tell us off and remind us how much shoes cost and how I should look after them. Our Dad would lift his head from the book or the newspaper that he was reading and when our Mam left the room would say quietly; 'Ben... you need to use your left foot more. It'll make you a better footballer and even if it doesn't, it'll be less obvious to your Mam that you've been kicking a ball.'

'But won't I just get into more trouble for scuffing two shoes, instead of just one?' I replied.

'You might have a point there! Forget what I just said,' he'd say with a grin, or a wink, before going back to his reading."

"While I was still at school I always had a little job to earn pocket money and I would usually spend it going to see Grimsby Town play. It was really exciting having a big team like that. I never really understood why the team was called Grimsby Town though, because their football ground was in Cleethorpes. I suppose it was because when the team was first formed it was a Grimsby team, called Grimsby Pelham after the family of one of the local bigwigs. I only ever remember them playing at Blundell Park, in Meggies though."

"What do you mean, Meggies?" I interrupted.

"Cleethorpes. 'Meggies' is what we call Cleethorpes," Ben replied, before continuing, "We weren't a bad team. We won the Lincolnshire Senior Cup most years when I was a kid. We usually ended up playing Gainsborough Trinity or Lincoln City in the final. We won it in 1913. I don't remember there being a cup final in 1914, maybe it was cancelled because of the war.

"I think as much as watching the game I was impressed that teams came to play here from such a long distance away. Some of the places sounded a bit exotic and very distant. Back then I'd hardly ever been outside the town, other than to go to the coast for days out, or to watch the ships arriving or departing, and that was only on the other side of the town, close to the football ground in Cleethorpes.

"Our mam and Dad hadn't moved more than thirty miles from home in all their lives and until I went to Lincoln, when I first tried to enlist, I had never gone further than I could comfortably manage on a bike."

"The team lost a lot of players to the army in the early part of the war. Many of the players joined up and left the team... I wonder how many ever got back home to play for the team again?" Ben thought aloud.

"Did you have a team shirt?" I asked.

"What, off one of the players, you mean?" Ben replied.

"Sorry Ben, it was a daft question. Kids today nearly always have a copy of their team's football shirts to wear to the games, so they look the same as the players, well except a bit smaller! Did you have a football scarf? You know, in Grimsby Town colours?" I asked.

"Yes, I did, how would you know that?" Ben replied.

"We still have them today," I answered.

Ben continued, "Yes, our Mam knitted me a black and white one when the team changed its colours when I was about ten or eleven years old. She knitted it for me and gave it to me for a Christmas present. I remember wearing it to a game on Christmas Day."

"Don't you mean Boxing day? I didn't think they played football on Christmas Day," I said.

"They didn't, except in Grimsby and Hull. Our teams had special permission to play on Christmas Day because of the trawler fleets from both towns. They didn't play at Christmas very often, but I am sure it happened.

"I always thought it a bit odd that Grimsby Town didn't actually play in Grimsby. When I started working at Bennett's Sleeper Mill with our Dad I would often go to the football after working on a Saturday morning. The mill and creosoting plant was near to the Alexandra Dock, but it was only a short walk back to Corporation Street and over the Corporation Bridge. Blundell Park was only a mile or so further along after crossing the bridge. You had to keep an eye on what was moving on the river, because it was a swing bridge, and it took quite a while to open and close. If there were a few boats on the river, it could be quite a long wait before you could cross. When we were leaving work, heading for the match, it would look like a stampede sometimes with everyone running to make the crossing before it swung open. There were a few times when someone made a jump for it and ended up in the river.

"I know I called them boats, but they might have been ships, I was never sure what made a boat into a ship. Our Charlie and George would definitely know," Ben stated confidently.

I cut in, helpfully; "It used to be having three or more square-rigged masts, but once they did away with sails, I wouldn't know now."

"Oh, right." Ben went on: "A short way past the football ground was the promenade at Meggies. If it was a family trip, rather than me going to see the football, we would usually walk, but occasionally we would jump on the train from the town to the station right on the promenade."

"You would be amazed at how much football has changed, Ben. Do you know that most footballers now get paid far more money than the Prime Minister? Some get more in one week than the Prime Minister earns in a year," I said.

"How's that possible?" Ben asked.

"Don't ask me, mate. I don't understand it any more than you," I replied.

We sat in silence thinking about the madness of that revelation, Ben once again looking down at his crossed legs, me, staring at him, trying to take in every detail.

Ben looked up and spoke, "Well, maybe they get paid more than politicians because they deserve it more. I mean, I bet no footballer has ever signed a piece of paper sending millions of soldiers and men, women and children to their deaths, have they?"

"No, Ben. I'm pretty sure they haven't," I replied.

"And if they all get paid so much, I bet their Mams don't worry much about scuffed shoes," said Ben.

"At least one thing hasn't changed; Grimsby still play at Blundell Park," I said.

Ben smiled and nodded, before going on; "I loved going down to the docks when I wasn't in school. I loved watching the ships arrive and the sailors coming off the ships from different countries. Sailors from all over the world and of every colour too. Some of them were black, or at least very dark brown. I'd never seen a black man before, except in our Dad's books, but even then, they were only ink drawings, not even photographs, so it wasn't the same as when you really saw them in front of you.

"I can remember as clear as day, when I was about eleven years old, I saw a tall black man coming off a ship. At first, I thought he must've been a miner, well obviously not a miner, because even then I knew there weren't mines on ships, but I knew from our George and Charlie that they used to burn a lot of coal to fire the ships, so maybe he was one of those sailors who worked at shovelling coal. But as he came down the gangplank I saw that he wasn't dirty, that the black was the colour of his skin.

"Then a second man started down the gang plank and he was black as well. Yes, a black face and black hands and I remember walking next to him for a long time watching as he walked down the street away from the docks and into the town. I walked close to him and I was going to reach out and touch his hand, but I was only a kid and he looked like a giant, so I was too scared to reach out.

"I suppose that we were lucky, living in a town that was a seaport, a sort of opening to the rest of the world because we saw things that people who lived away from the coast just didn't see.

"I loved going to Meggies on family trips or just on my own, with our Nan. She was the deepest golden-coloured spaniel you ever saw. Nan was a great little dog, all excitable and wriggly. Sometimes she would wag her tail so hard she would hit herself in the face with it.

"If it was a nice day and the family took the train, I would sometimes walk with our Nan and meet them at the station. She would run and run on the beach and loved swimming in the sea to fetch sticks. We had to be careful because of the deep mud in some places on the beach, but she never slowed down one little bit. Sometimes our Dad would help me to sneak her on to the train at the end of the day, but I think that was because I was exhausted, not our Nan."

After a short pause Ben went on, "I never imagined anything would separate us as a family. I just thought we would be together forever and that is how it was until the beginning of 1913, when our Charlie came home and told our Mam and Dad he had signed up with the Merchant Navy, and how our Mam cried at the thought of losing him. I always thought our Charlie was my Mam's favourite. Even though our Dad was probably sad as well, I'm sure our Dad knew full well when he was educating us kids, he was preparing us for life way beyond Grimsby and way beyond the world that he and our Mam had lived in all their lives.

"Even though our Mam was sad to be losing Charlie, I won't ever forget the look on her face when he first came home in his Officer Cadet uniform. If pride could have made a heart burst from a chest that would have been our Mam's last second on earth. The pride that shone from her face is something I will never forget. The whole family was there, outside the house, our Mam and Dad, Florence, George, Edie, Nora and me. All looking at our Charlie in his uniform. I suppose it wasn't just our Mam and Dad who were proud of him; we all were."

"That image must have been very important to you, Ben." I said. "Most people would settle for a memory that lasts a lifetime, but that one has lasted for another hundred years. It must have been very special to stay with you, even now?"

"Yeah, I suppose you're right. It wasn't like that when I came home in my uniform to give our Mam the good news. She smacked me across the head, knocked my bloody cap off and called me all the stupid buggers under the sun. See, I told you Charlie was her favourite!" And we both laughed.

"She was quite proud of me when I left school and got a job at Bennett's. I'm sure our Dad helped me get in, but I didn't mind. I was ever so proud going to work alongside him. That walk to work alongside him, carrying my snap. For a short time each morning it was just us two, walking to work, side by side. I didn't have to share him with the family. I felt like a man, not a boy I was so proud of our Dad. He was well respected and liked by the other chaps. Yes, he was a good man and I was so proud to be his son and his workmate. After about 5 minutes or so we would begin meeting up with all the other fellows going to work, at the mill and at other places down near the docks, but that time alone with him was great."

As Ben talked about his Dad, my Great Grandfather, his eyes lit up and it was as though he was re-living every step of that walk they made together, his pride and his love for his Dad was clear. As his words tailed off he dropped his head and looked down again at his crossed legs. That was to become a pattern in our conversation. As he recalled happy or exciting times, he would sit upright and lift his chin. I could see the sparkle in his eyes. When recalling a sad event his eyes would drop, and he would hunch over as if talking to the earth, his voice tailing away to not much more than a whisper.

Again, his voice became quieter and his posture changed as he added, "I suppose the memory of our Charlie in his uniform is so strong because it was the last time the whole of our family was all together to celebrate something. A day or two later Charlie left to begin his cadetship. I think he went to Liverpool. I well remember the next time I saw our Charlie, but for a different reason.

"It was the middle of summer in 1913. I had been working down at Bennett's with our Dad, for a good while. As I said we always walked to and from work together every day, unless I was going to the football. It would have been about the beginning of July when our Dad began to fall sick. At first, he just missed a day, then a week or so later, he'd miss another day. By the beginning of August he was having a day or more off each week.

"Sometimes, he would come downstairs in the morning, dressed for work, but our Mam would send him back to bed. He looked terrible. He would try to argue with her, but she was having none of it. By the time I came home in the evening he would rally a bit and look a bit better. He would ask me about work and what everyone was up to. I was worried though, because he wasn't eating much at meal times. The next day he would seem better and it would be work as usual, but he walked slowly, he would tell me to walk on ahead, so I wouldn't be late, but I didn't want to leave him, so we began to set off for work ten minutes earlier, so we could walk together, just a bit more slowly.

"In mid-August he stopped coming down in the morning on the days he was unwell. I went to his room to say goodbye and he was in his bed, lying flat. I walked to the side of his bed and looked at him. He was so small and frail, almost like he had shrunk overnight. His skin looked too big for him. I leaned over him and kissed him on the forehead. 'I'll see you tonight, Dad.' I said.

"He took my hand and said 'Bye son, be a good lad. Now give me a kiss and get off to work.' I leaned over and kissed him on the forehead. He squeezed my hand, but there was nothing in it. No trace of the man who could move a railway sleeper by hand across the mill, without any help.

"I set off for work on my own, but it didn't seem right. A couple of times I almost turned around and went back home, but I kept going. When I got to the mill I went to the office to let them know that Dad was ill again, 'That's OK, Ben. Make sure you give him our best wishes,' the manager said – he didn't seem surprised.

"The day dragged and all I could think of was getting home. When we finished for the day I set off from work as usual, but for some reason instead of walking I started to trot along, then got quicker and quicker until by the time I reached the end of our road I was running full pelt. Crying my bloody eyes out, I crossed the bridge at the end of our street and as I did so I could see our Charlie and our George on the front step.

"George was down on his haunches smoking and Charlie was standing with his arms folded, but not folded like a schoolkid, sort of wrapping his own arms around himself, hugging himself, if you know what I mean? I knew something was wrong. Dad and I always got home from work before George and what the hell was our Charlie doing at home?

"As I ran towards them, our Charlie saw me and turned towards me. I could see he was crying. I tried to sidestep him and get to the door, but he blocked me, sort of tackled me, wrapping both arms around me and lifting me off my feet. Before I knew it, our George was on his feet and around behind me. He put his chest to my back and his arms around me and right around our Charlie. The three of us stood there in the street. Me, sandwiched between my two older brothers, and I knew that our Dad had gone. That's why he had said "Bye, son," when I had left for work. He knew it was goodbye. I wish I'd known.

"I have no idea how long the three of us stayed like that, but I felt safe between my brothers. Eventually we went inside our house and I heard sobbing. I walked to the living room door and there was our Mam. Sitting on the couch with Florence, Edie and Nora kneeling in front of her, with their faces buried in her skirt; sobbing into her lap.

"The next week was just a blur of tears and hunger. All of us kids just cried and cried. I am surprised the house didn't flood. I never thought we would stop. All except our Mam, who never cried. She just comforted all of us. Sometimes there would be three or four of us in her lap at once, all sobbing, and she would stroke our heads, or cup our faces in her tiny little hands and kiss the tears away, but it was a hopeless task. There were just too many of us and too many tears, but she never stopped trying.

"I never saw our Mam cry for our Dad. But I heard her cry. Every night in her room, she cried like her heart would break into pieces. She cried every night until I left home...I'm glad I wasn't there to hear her cry for me.

"I felt like losing our Dad was the end of being a kid. Even going to work alongside our Dad, all dressed up like an adult, I don't think I really felt like one – not really. Losing our Dad changed everything, for all of us. Charlie had gone, and our George really stepped up as head of the family alongside our Mam. Charlie came home on leave once or twice in the next year, and he wrote regularly and sent an allotment home to our Mam, but it was our George and Florence that really helped get our Mam back on her feet. Then just as there seemed to be a little light at the end of the tunnel, we were at war."

*****

Ben continued: "I had been reading about the build-up in the newspapers. I suppose I followed the example set by our Dad, reading every day and trying to understand what was going on in the world. It seemed that just about half of the countries in Europe were spoiling for a fight, so it was no surprise when it all went off." Ben shook his head.

"How old would you have been when the war started?" I asked.

"I suppose I would have been about 13 or 14. I'm not exactly sure. When I tried to enlist I didn't take a birth certificate. I couldn't exactly ask our Mam for it could I? I never saw my birth certificate; I don't even know if she had one for all of us.

"We all sort of worked out how old we were from where we fitted into the family between our brothers and sisters. I know that our Mam and Dad didn't know the exact year they were born. They knew where they were born; they could name the parish, but not their exact birth dates.

"I always thought I was born in either 1900 or 1901, because I remember being told I was the first Leeman baby to be born in the new century. Our Edith was born just before me and we always thought we were almost the same age. But if I was the first in the new century then she must have been the last in the old century.

"The war started in August 1914, but I can't really remember the exact date. Charlie had been in the Merchant Navy for well over a year before the war started. He wasn't one of those that volunteered after the war began, he was already serving when it started. I don't think Charlie being at sea gave me the push to try and enlist.

"The first change the war made to our family was the reduction in letters sent by our Charlie and those he did send were brief and lacking in any sort of detail. Later, after enlisting, I found out it was due to censorship.

"The other noticeable thing was the decrease in the number of ships docking in Grimsby. I would still go down to the docks regularly with our Nan, and noticed there were fewer and fewer ships docking at Grimsby. I didn't know why, and I still don't. Perhaps it was that the west coast was safer for shipping than the east coast, due to the German Navy.

"Our George had some long conversations with our Florence about whether he should join up. He told her he wanted to enlist in the Army, which surprised me, as considering his job in a shipping office and his interest in seeing far-flung places I would have thought the Navy would have been his choice, but no, he appeared to be more inclined towards enlisting in the Army.

"Florence wasn't keen on him enlisting at all. She pointed out that he was the head of the family and how much our Mam relied on him. George was almost torn in half. I know how much he wanted to enlist. Of course, I wasn't part of those conversations, I was just listening in to the whispers.

"The more I read, the more I listened to whispered conversations and the more I saw the fellows from the mill leaving their jobs and going off, the more I became convinced that I had to enlist. I only ever really considered the army. My main problem was that I was a bit on the short side. It was one thing to look young, if you are young and tall you could get away with claiming to be 19. But if you looked young and were a bit of a tiddler there was no chance of fooling anyone in an enlistment office. It didn't stop me trying though." Ben chuckled quietly and smiled, shaking his head.

"What happened?" I asked.

"It was January 1915. I got up early one Saturday morning and caught an early train to Lincoln where I knew there was a big recruiting drive on. Many of the families who lived in our area of Grimsby had seen family members go off to join the Grimsby Chums. Men who worked on the docks, or in the factories, all working together would also be able to serve together in a single unit. I thought this was a great idea until the entire Chums Battalion was decimated in 1916 on the first day of the Somme. Imagine the devastation that caused to the whole community. In one swoop all the men, young men and older men with families, just gone.

"When I heard what had happened I remember thinking it would be bad enough for me to be killed and my family suffer my loss, but how does a town cope when all the men who lived in your street and the street next to yours and the street next to that one, and who all worked together, are all killed together?"

"Why do you call them the Grimsby Chums? I thought those battalions were called Pals Battalions?" I asked.

Ben replied: "That's typical of Grimsby folk... always have to be different. You're right though, I think just about everywhere else they were known as Pals Battalions, but in my town, they were Chums, so I think of all those battalions as Chums, not Pals. Officially, the Grimsby Chums were the 10th Battalion, the Lincolnshire Regiment. They were formed by the former headmaster of Winteringham Secondary School. I'm sure he meant well, but as things turned out, he has a lot to answer for.

"Anyway, for a few months before Christmas 1914, after paying our Mam, each week I put a little money aside to get some clothes that fitted and looked like they were mine. I spent my savings on a suit. It was the most I had ever spent in one go. Come to think of it, I never spent anything more on anything in my whole life."

"I don't think I would have fooled anybody at the enlistment centre had I turned up in our Charlie's old stuff, which was miles too big for me. Even the most desperate recruiter would have had no choice but to turn me away. Borrowing a pair off our George wasn't an option either, as he was three inches taller than Charlie. I would have looked like a circus clown wearing a pair of his trousers. There was nothing else for it, I would have to invest in a suit of clothes and a shirt to make me look the part.

"Once I'd saved enough money, the next decision was where to buy it. Obviously, I couldn't go to any of the local shops. Where I lived, everybody knew everybody else and I couldn't risk our Mam passing by and the shopkeeper telling her 'Oh, your Ben was in here the other day. He looked very grown-up in his new clothes.' There would be little point turning up in the recruiting office in my new clothes with a cauliflower ear after our Mam had boxed it. Although looking back now, it might have made me appear a little less childlike and a little bit tougher." Ben laughed.

"I would have to travel to the other side of town. When our Charlie left home he left his old bike, which was leaning up against the privy in our yard. It had seen better days, the tyres were deflated, the frame was rusted, and the brakes didn't work. I asked our Mam if I could have the bike if I fixed it up. Our Mam said I should write a letter to our Charlie asking if I could borrow the bike whilst he was away, but she also said she didn't think Charlie would object to me doing it up while I was waiting for a reply, with the post taking so long now, due to the war. Our Mam said she couldn't see a reason why Charlie would say no and would probably be happy that I was taking an interest in fixing things.

"I wrote the letter to Charlie asking his permission to fix up his bike and use it until he came home. I never asked to keep it, just to use it and look after it until he came home and wanted it back. I posted the letter addressed to Charlie's ship and set to work on the bike with our Mam's permission.

"The first task was to remove the tyres and check the tubes inside. When I checked the tubes by putting air in them, dipping them in a bucket of water to check for leaks, I found that there was no air escaping from the inner tubes. At this point I thought that I should have tried inflating the tyres while they were still fitted to the bike before pulling them apart. I knew our Charlie wouldn't have made that mistake. Can you imagine him pulling the engine apart on a ship before checking to see if it worked? I don't think he would have been quite that daft. Maybe that's why he was an engineer and I wanted to be a soldier.

"At least taking the tyres off gave me the chance to check the wheels and they looked fine. When I spun them on the spindle and checked to see if there were straight everything looked good. The bearings ran quietly and smoothly, and the wheel ran true. I checked the brakes, which were a bit stiff, but with a bit of oil they were as good as new.

"I asked one of our Charlie's mates from his old engineering works if he could get me a small bottle of oil to help bring Charlie's bike back to life. Charlie's mate nipped inside and came back a few minutes later with a small bottle of golden oil. He asked me to send Charlie his best wishes and the best wishes of all the lads in the factory who remembered him. I said I would, and then made my way home, with the small bottle of engineering oil safely tucked in my pocket. By the time I got home it was too dark to work outside, so I covered the bike with an old tarpaulin and on the next Saturday afternoon when there was no football, I set to work stripping the brakes and all connecting rods, cleaning and oiling them then reassembling them before checking that they worked. I checked the brakes on the wheel rims before refitting the tyres.

"I turned the bike upside down, so it was sat on its handlebars and its seat, and I spun the front wheel by hand before bending down and applying the brake, which brought the wheel to a stop. Then I turned the pedals, by hand, and the back wheel spun fast and true. I applied the rear brake gently and once again the brake bit into the wheel rim and brought it to a halt.

"I removed the wheels again, refitted the tyres with the tubes inside and then replaced each wheel into its forks before inflating the tyres, which I did with a small hand pump. I took a small spanner and ensured the nuts holding each wheel were tightened properly and then I turned the bike upright, so it sat on its wheels.

"Our Mam came out into the yard to see what I was up to and I remember her saying to me; 'Our Charlie would be so proud to see what you've done with his bike, son.' I tried to smile, but it was more of a sickly, guilty grin. I felt like a criminal. She had no idea why I'd been repairing the bike. It was one of the few occasions when I deceived our Mam and it's something I wasn't proud of. I regretted my slyness at the time and I still do.

"I opened the back door and pushed Charlie's bike out into the ginnell and wheeled it slowly past the back doors of our neighbours' houses and onto Somersby Street. I squeezed the brakes whilst I was pushing the bike. First, I checked the front brake, which was very sharp and resulted in the back wheel lifting off the ground. I then pushed the bike a little further and applied the rear brake, which resulted in the rear wheel locking up and the tyre scraping on the stones. Now it was time to ride the bike. I was right pleased with my handiwork and I knew our Charlie would have been pleased that everything was working perfectly, even though he would have disagreed with my motives for fixing it up. Perhaps I should have considered an engineering career in the Navy after all.

"I stood on the pavement and parked the bike in the gutter and threw my leg over the seat, put my right foot on the raised pedal and pushed off. The bike moved forward smoothly and before I knew it was whizzing over the cobbled stones down towards the end of Somersby Road, where it joins Alexandra Road.

"I applied the brakes and came to a perfect stop on my highly engineered bike. Unfortunately, I'd forgotten that Charlie was a good few inches taller than me and that when I got on the bike, it was in the gutter and my standing foot was on the pavement which was much higher than the road surface on which the bike was resting. As I came to a halt at the junction and tried to put my foot on the ground I realised my foot was about four inches short of reaching the ground. The bike tipped on its side, dumping me onto the road with the right pedal dug into my shin, leaving a decent sized hole. It would have been quite painful, but I was distracted by my right elbow smashing into the cobbles, taking the skin off right down to the bone.

"I did my best to ignore the pain as I was more concerned that no one had seen me fall, so I jumped up quickly and looked around to see if anyone had been watching. Nobody had, and I picked up the bike and rode home. Despite the blood running from the hole in my leg and the warm stream of blood running down my sleeve, I was proud of my efforts and, being an optimistic sort of fellow, I was grateful that it had happened while I was wearing a pair of old trousers rather than a good pair, or even worse, my soon-to-be-new suit. I mean it's one thing to have a hole in your leg that could soon be cleaned up, but trousers cost money, of which I had very little.

"The following Saturday, with my savings in my pocket, I rode to a small clothing shop on the other side of town. I looked at the suits in the window before going inside. I stepped inside and was greeted by a smart-looking gentleman standing behind the counter, with a tape measure draped around his neck. 'Good morning, Sir. How may I be of assistance?' he said. I had never been called 'Sir' before, I'm sure I must have checked over my shoulder to see if someone else had followed me in.

"I told him my requirements and in minutes I was being pulled, pushed and measured. Jacket on – too long, trousers on – too baggy, try this one, try that one, take it off, pass it through the curtain to the back room and in about thirty minutes, with freshly shortened sleeves and trousers, I stood before the mirror, not recognising my reflection.

"I paid for my suit and it was carefully folded and wrapped in brown paper, secured with waxed string. I cycled home with my package tucked inside my coat, a lot poorer but happy. I was skint but a lot closer to my goal.

"The suit had cost a little bit more than I had planned, so my trip to the recruiting office in Lincoln had to be delayed until after my next pay day. In the meantime, I received a letter from our Charlie giving me permission to fix up his bike and use it until he returned home. I wrote back straight away, thanking him and passing on the best wishes from all the lads at his old engineering works, just as I had promised.

"The great day came, a few days into the new year, which would be 1915. I woke early, dressed downstairs and set off to walk into town, where I caught a train to Lincoln, about thirty miles away. The journey seemed to take an eternity and by the time I got there I was starving. In fact, by the time I was halfway there I was starving. By the time I got there I was ready to eat one of my fellow passengers. As the train travelled further I noticed that it was slowly filling, stop after stop, with men; young men and older men, but no ladies. It appeared that most of the men in the area had the same idea as me and were heading off to enlist. By the time we reached the middle of Lincoln it was standing room only. Seats had twice as many passengers as they were designed for, on them, and every spare inch of floor space was packed.

"I'd never seen anything so crowded... that was until we arrived in Lincoln and I saw the queue for the enlistment office. 'Flipping heck,' I thought, it wasn't a couple of sandwiches I should have brought, it was a pillow and a blanket. Looking at the length of the queue, I doubted I was going to get to the front of it in a single day. As things turned out, I needn't have worried.

"We lined up in the street about three abreast and slowly, like snails, we shuffled along towards the enlistment office. Everyone around me looked much older than me, which is probably because they were much older. I don't really know why I thought I could get away with it – blind optimism, once again."

"As the queue crawled onwards I saw many soldiers from different regiments handing out leaflets to people in the queue. I think they were trying to steer the potential recruits towards their own regimental enlisting officers. I had heard that the recruiting sergeants were paid for every person they signed up. Looking at the queue that stretched out in front of me and behind me, as far as I could see, I thought that if this was true, they would be rich men by the end of the day.

"I inched forward, eyes down, staying close to the wall so that I couldn't be seen by the soldiers who walked up and down the shuffling line. As I got close to the front I caught the eye of one of the sergeants who was passing out the leaflets. He beckoned me with his finger to leave the queue. I looked away and pretended I hadn't seen him, which considering his size was difficult. Then he called, 'You boy! Come out here. We need to have a chat.' Once again, I carried on looking straight ahead at the back of the man in front of me. I heard the crunching of his boots on the pavement as he approached, but I still didn't move my eyes from the back of the man in front of me, until a small cane tapped me on the shoulder and the same voice rang out again, 'You boy... come with me.' There was no chance of escape, so reluctantly I turned towards him and then followed him away from the safety of the queue and over towards a small monument or fountain."

"The sergeant appeared to be a giant who blocked my view of everything around me. As I stood in front of him I remember thinking how small I must've looked to his eyes. It was just like being back at school with the school master towering over you to give you a telling off for something you had done wrong. This was even worse, this was something much worse."

"He asked; 'What's your name, son?'

'Who me, Sir?' I replied.

"He leaned forward and made an exaggerated show of trying to peer round me, first to the left of me, then the right as if checking that there was nobody hiding behind me."

'I can't see anybody else standing in front of me sonny, so who do you think I'm talking to?' he asked.

'Me, Sir.' I replied.

'That's a good answer, son. So now that we've established who I'm talking to, would you like to answer my question?'

'What question is that, Sir?' I asked.

'Well son, you won't be much use to the army, with you having such a poor memory. I mean, I only asked that question about two seconds ago and you've already forgotten it. How do you think you would ever learn to be a soldier with such a poor memory? Would you like me to give you a second chance and ask you the question again?'

'Yes, Sir. I would like you to ask me the question again, please.' I said.

'What... is... your... name?' he said, very slowly.

'Ben, Sir.' I quickly replied.

'Is that your surname, or your Christian name, young man?' he asked.

'It's my first name, Sir,' I replied.

'Well would you like to tell me your surname, or would you like me to try and guess it?' He said, through gritted teeth.

'No, Sir. I'll tell you what is.' I replied, although I made the mistake of not actually saying my name.

"At this point the sergeant appeared to lose all patience with me. He leaned forward to put his nose against mine. But either he was too tall, or I was too small, so all I could feel was the peak of his service cap resting on the top of my head.

"Then he bellowed, 'Well go on then... you bloody idiot!'

"The force of his voice almost knocked me off my feet. I almost turned tail and ran for it, but I don't think I could have moved even if I'd wanted to.

"Taking a deep breath, I stood my ground and replied, 'I'm Ben Leeman, Sir. I'm here to join the army.'

'Come with me, son,' he said, turning quickly on his heels and marching away.

"Bloody hell, he couldn't half move. I had to run to keep up with him. Not only was he about seven feet tall, but his legs must've been five feet long. I never again saw a man with such a long stride. After about fifty yards I realised he had taken me away from the enlistment office and I thought I was in for a battering. He turned to face me once we were well away from the prying eyes of those others in the enlistment queue.

"There we stood for a couple of seconds in front of a wooden bench. Without speaking he sat on the bench and removed his peaked cap, placing it on his lap. I saw that he had a large scar running right across his brow parallel to his eyebrows. It was a red, angry, raised scar, but it appeared to be well healed.

'Take a seat, son. And he patted the bench for me to sit on his right-hand side. I sat.

'Well, Ben Leeman, what are you doing here today?'

'I've come to join the army, Sir.'

'And how old are you, Mr Leeman?'

'I'm 19, Sir.'

'And what was your year of birth?' He asked.

'1896,' I replied.

'What is your date of birth?'

'The second of January, Sir,' I replied, thinking on my feet.

"I had been rehearsing this conversation in my head for such a long time and I had always been worried that when under pressure I would get the year wrong and give the game away. But even under this intense pressure from a terrifying sergeant I'd held my nerve. I was sure I'd proven myself worthy of a place in the army, being calm under pressure. I was so proud of myself at this point I seriously considered asking if I would be eligible for a commission.

'Very good, Mr Leeman. Despite your short stature and your youthful looks you are clearly a young man the like of which we are keen to have serve in the British Army,' he said, and smiled, for the first time since he had begun speaking with me – probably for the first time in a long while, truth be told. I was relieved to have passed this test.

"Then he spoke again. 'I'm surprised you're here today though, it being your birthday.'

"I suddenly realised why this date had come to mind so easily... it was written on my bloody train ticket.

'So, tell me again Mr Leeman, how old are you? And please tell me the truth this time.' There was no anger in his voice. Although I had been caught telling lies, there was just a hint of sympathy.

'I'm 15, Sir. But I'm ready to serve. It's what I want to do,' I blurted out.

'I understand, Mr Leeman and I want you to serve... but not just yet. I'm afraid that there will be plenty of time for you to serve when you reach the age of 19. Do your parents know that you're here?'

'There is only our Mam, Sir. She doesn't know,' I replied.

'Well if she's anything like my Mother, and judging by the calibre of young man she has raised, it appears she is, I don't think she'd be very happy with me if I signed you up. And the last thing I would like to do is get on the wrong side of an irate mother. I'd rather face a charging Jerry. Where have you travelled from?'

'From Grimsby, Sir,' I replied.

'What time does your train return to Grimsby?'

'4 o'clock, Sir.'

"The sergeant stood up, put his cap back on his head and straightened it. He put his right hand into his tunic pocket and pulled out a shilling piece."

'Have you ever heard of accepting the King's shilling?' he asked.

Yes, I have, Sir,' I replied.

'Well this isn't the King's shilling, it's Sergeant Johnson's shilling. And now it's yours Mr Leeman.' And with that he handed the shilling to me.

'You're a brave young man Mr Leeman, and this country is going to need young men like you, but not just yet. There will be time enough for you to do your duty, but that time isn't now. Now get yourself back to your Mother. Come back in a few years when you are old enough and I will happily take you with me to the war. Who knows? By then you may have grown into that jacket,' he said, and smiled for a split second... then he stopped smiling.

"Sergeant Johnson checked the straightness of his cap, picked up his stick and marched smartly back towards the line of men that continued to snake towards the enlistment office. I made my way slowly back to the station."

"Did you ever see Sergeant Johnson again?" I asked.

"No, I didn't. He was in the Lincolnshire Regiment, not the Sherwood Foresters, but I often thought about him and his kindness. I'd like to think he survived the war to return to his family. But I never knew."

"I'm beginning to feel a bit like Sergeant Johnson myself, Ben," I said.

"How do you mean?" Ben replied.

"Well he never got a straight answer from you and neither have I. I wanted you to tell me how you came to join the army and you've given me a brilliant account of how you didn't. Still evading the questions, eh? Sergeant Johnson would be proud of you," I said.

Ben laughed, "I'd like to think so," he replied.

As he spoke Ben undid the right breast pocket of his tunic and put his hand inside, fumbling in search of something, and as he did so he asked me, "Do you know what I did with the shilling that Sergeant Johnson gave me that day?"

"You kept it with you, didn't you?" I replied.

"Did I buggery? I bought two cups of tea and the biggest piece of cake I could afford before catching the train," Ben replied, before bursting into laughter, as did I.

We laughed and laughed, before falling backwards onto the old greatcoat, in the middle of a damp, dark, French field; me aged 57 and my Great Uncle, aged 17, pissing ourselves laughing; nothing unusual about that.

When we stopped laughing, we lay there trying to catch our breath for a few minutes, until we sat up again.

*****

Ben eventually continued with his tale: "I returned home from my trip to Lincoln a bit downhearted and on the way home I sat and gave some serious thought to what I would do next. I decided that I would wait at least another year before trying again. Give myself time to grow up, as all my efforts to encourage growth had failed so far.

"I had to make sure that I didn't stand out from the crowd and my height, or lack of it, was just too obvious. It was one thing to look young, it was another thing to be under the 5'3" minimum height for the army.

"Now, they didn't measure you to the half inch, but I was at least a couple of inches under and I already had experience of being picked out due to looking too young. I was sure that my lack of height was the first thing that attracted attention to me that day. I had to think of a way to get up the line and in front of the recruiters to stand a chance.

"I planned to grow a bit in the coming year before my next attempt. I had some great plans which I wasted no time putting into practice. If I could speed things up, I would.

"Every chance I got I'd hang from the wall in our yard. I'd go out to do some work on our Charlie's bike and as soon as nobody was watching I would open the back door leading into the ginnel, jump up and grab onto the top of the brick lintel over the opening. I would hang there for ages trying to stretch myself. Sometimes I even put stones in my pockets to make myself heavier, but then I realised the stones were making holes in my pockets and our Mam would have gotten suspicious.

"One day when I had taken our Nan down to Meggies beach, I found a large smooth stone which had a hole worn through the middle of it. It was the perfect shape to tie a piece of rope through it, then loop it around my waist. Using it would stop my pockets getting holes. I don't know if doing all this would have made me grow at all, or if I would just get really long arms, like a monkey in one of our Dad's books. I did have a really strong grip though, I could hold on for ages." Ben laughed and shook his head.

He went on; "I know that you must think all of this sounds daft, it even sounds daft to me while I'm telling you, but I was desperate not to be caught out a second time and the best way to improve my chances was by not standing out too much. I even considered trying to grow a moustache, but looking at my top lip there was little chance of that.

There was so little growth on it, and what fluff there was would likely be blown away in a stiff breeze."

I thought back to my own first attempt to grow a moustache and my Dad telling me 'Don't bother shaving, son. Just dab a bit of milk on your top lip and let the cat lick it off.'

"So, when did you try again and had you grown at all? I asked.

"Well, all my plans went out of the window a month or so later. I was at work. During my break I was eating my snap and reading a newspaper. It told the story of a Bantams Battalion being raised by the Notts and Derby Regiment in Nottingham. It was a battalion specifically for soldiers who were under the minimum height for the regular army.

"I couldn't believe it. A few miles away they were actively recruiting under-height soldiers. That was a place where I could blend in with the rest of the recruits. I made up my mind to try again with the Bantams.

"As soon as the opportunity arose I skipped work and travelled to Nottingham, still no taller and still not filling my jacket. I felt sick all the way there and arrived just before midday. I walked from the station to the recruiting office at the Mechanics Institute. It took about fifteen minutes. My heart was beating so fast and I could hear the blood pulsing in my ears. It sounded like when you put your ear to a sea shell.

"As I arrived at the office there was no queuing in the street. I walked in and there were about half a dozen men ahead of me, standing before a desk. I joined the queue. I was behind a man who was no taller than me, although he was as broad as he was tall. I just stared at the back of his neck. I heard someone walk in and stand behind me. I didn't lift my eyes. I couldn't even describe the room. I just looked forward. The man ahead of me spoke with the recruiting soldier at the desk and then turned to his right, removing his jacket as he walked through a door a few feet to our right.

"I stepped up to the desk. The seated soldier did not raise his head, but looked at a ledger he had on the desk in front of him.

'Name?' he said, presumably to me.

'Ben Leeman.'

'Age?'

'19'

"Date of birth?'

'The second of January 1897.'

'You do realise that makes you 18 years old? I'll ask you again, date of birth?'

'The second of January 1896, Sir.'

'Good answer, Mr Leeman.'

"Then without looking up, he handed me a sheet of paper on which he had recorded my details."

'Remove your jacket and take this form into the next room for your medical.' He nodded towards the door to my right, through which the stocky man had disappeared."

"I did as I was instructed, and the next 5 minutes were a blur as I was pulled, poked, weighed, measured, told to bend this way and that. Mouth opened, light shone in my eyes and down my ears, before being declared "Fit!" and handed a stamped piece of paper before being ushered into another adjoining room where I was inducted into the 15th Battalion Notts and Derby Regiment, The Sherwood Foresters. Five minutes later I walked out onto the street, carrying a handful of papers to get me home and back again, instructions of where and when to report, and my second shilling.

"I returned home, but instead of telling our Mam, I said nothing. I didn't let on. I couldn't. I said nothing to anyone, just carried on as normal. I went to work, I came home from work, I played on the beach with our Nan and I went to the match. The day before I left to begin training, I told my manager at Bennett's. He was shocked. He went to a cabinet in the corner of his office and returned with a decanter and two glasses. He poured out two measures of what turned out to be whisky and gave me one. We both drank. It nearly bloody choked me.

"He said he would have my wages drawn up first thing in the morning for me to collect, but I told him I was leaving early and asked that they be delivered to our Mam.

'Have you told your Mam, Ben?' he asked.

'No Sir, I haven't,' I replied.

'You should tell her, son. She needs to know. Have you told your Dad?' he asked.

'What do you mean?' I replied.

'Go sit with your Dad and tell him. He'll let you know what you should do,' he advised.

'I will, Sir,' I said, taking in his advice.

'Good luck, Ben. Come back and see us. Your job will be waiting.' And he smiled.

'Thank you, Sir,' I replied, and with a handshake I left my old job behind. I walked from the sleeper mill to the cemetery and sat for an hour with our Dad."

"What did you say to him?" I asked.

"I'm sorry, that conversation was just between me and him," Ben replied.

I didn't press the point.

Ben continued; "The next day I got up early and dressed. I left an envelope for our Mam, which contained some money I had saved and a letter containing a long explanation of what I had done. I begged her not to try and find me. I didn't tell her which regiment I had joined, in the hope it might deter her from trying to find me. I stepped out of 41 Fildes Street and made my way to the railway station.

"I arrived in Nottingham early afternoon and reported to the HQ at St Mary's gate. Within hours I was on an omnibus with about 30 other men heading for the camp on the outskirts of the city. The next few days were spent being kitted out and organised into some sort of order. I was disappointed to find that I was earmarked as part of the Battalion Reserve and would be staying to train in Nottingham, whilst those that had joined earlier were to move to Yorkshire to start their training for overseas service.

"About a week later the HQ and the four companies moved to Yorkshire. I watched them form up and leave. It was a terrible feeling to be left behind. A bloody reserve. I felt as though I should have stayed at home, but within days I was on my way to Masham, where I was instructed to report to Z company. Apparently, in the first week there had been a weeding out of those unfit for service and those who were under age. I probably replaced an underage soldier who was older than me!"

"So, the reason you joined the Sherwood Foresters was just because of the height limit being reduced?" I asked.

"It was at first. That was what caught my attention. Like I said, my original plan was to wait until I had grown a few inches. But the reports in the newspapers were more concerned with the toughness of the Bantam recruits. The papers kept going on about how these men were drawn from the ironworks, the dockyards and the coalmines. That they were hard men – tough, fit little buggers who would take the fight to Jerry. That was exciting to me.

"When I joined I was as proud as you could imagine to be joining this group of tough men. I knew it was something I would have to live up to and I was determined not to let them down.

"During my first year in the battalion I was worried about growing too quickly. 19-year-olds don't tend to grow very much, and I was worried that if I started to grow, it would be noticed, and they would realise that I was a lot younger than I was claiming to be. One minute I was trying to stretch myself, now I was desperate not to grow.

"I even used to round my shoulders and developed a bit of a hunch when I was trying to look shorter, which was easy when trying to keep the rain from running down the neck of my tunic or trying to keep the cold out. One of the company officers once asked me If I'd ever had quicksilver poisoning.

'No, Sir!' I replied, 'Why do you ask?'

'It's just that you always seem to grow by three inches whenever the sun comes out!' He laughed. "I was sure he knew I was under age, but he was equally certain that I was up to the job. I was certain too."

"In late 1916 after a year in France, the 35th Division was unable to get enough under-height replacements of the right toughness and had to recruit regular-height soldiers. I joined as a Bantam and a Bantam I wanted to stay. Some of the original lads didn't really rate the new taller replacements. They didn't feel they were good enough for the battalion. I don't know about that. I thought they fought just as well as the rest of us, but even so, I went from wanting to grow taller in order to get past the recruiters, to not wanting to grow, so no one would doubt I was a Bantam; a real Bantam, who had been accepted into the Battalion as one of a special group."

Chapter 4

Bantam

"I was relieved to be joining the battalion at Masham. Although I had been kitted out at Nottingham, remaining in reserve meant that while I had my uniform, and had started training, not being part of a company in the battalion meant I didn't really belong. Joining my company let me feel like I was becoming a soldier, not just dressing up and training, just for the sake of it. Joining my company meant I was training with the fellows I would be fighting alongside. I was part of it. Although I had always been proud to wear my uniform, until then I didn't believe that I had earned the right to wear it," Ben said.

"Was your uniform comfortable... was it up to the job? I asked.

"The tunic and trousers were made of wool and when they were new they were very scratchy and itchy. But this could be helped by using a razor or the blade of a sharp knife to shave the inside of the collar of the tunic and the inside of the trouser legs. When I was first issued with mine the tunic and trousers were too long, but by the time we arrived in France a few months later both fitted well and were soon getting a bit on the short side as I grew.

"Once I was familiar with my uniform I realised it was quite well designed, with pockets for personal items and pay book. As well as the large breast pockets on the outside there was an internal pocket where you carried two first field dressings – one for the bullet going in and the other for it coming out. Above the breast pockets there were thicker patches called rifle patches and these were to prevent wear when firing the rifle, but they also reduced the rubbing of your webbing when it was new and needed to be broken in. They didn't stop you being rubbed sore, only wear and good adjustment did that, but they helped a bit.

"Our shoulder tabs were sewn to the tunic, and it was on these that we wore our brass regimental titles, in our case Notts and Derby. Our peaked caps were made of the same material as the tunic and had a metal and brass cap badge. I was so proud of that badge. I'm sure every regiment is proud of its cap badge, but I always felt ours was special because in addition to the Notts and Derby title it bore the words 'Sherwood Foresters'. I always felt that this was a special title that set us apart, you know, due to the Sherwood Forest and Robin Hood links. I suppose it made me feel like we were fighting for a just cause.

"I quickly crumpled my cap, to give the appearance of a seasoned soldier, but I don't think I fooled many people. I'm sure I looked like a boy who had just crumpled up his cap. When I had my photograph taken and sent it home to our Mam, the first letter I got back from our Florence said, 'Mam thinks you look very smart in your uniform, but what happened to your hat? Did you accidentally sit down on it?' That's exactly what I had done!

"When I was first issued with my uniform at Nottingham I was issued with leather 08 pattern webbing. The army had been issuing this pattern, but made from thick woven cotton, instead of leather. The cotton webbing was better; more comfortable and requiring less care to keep in good condition. Due to the sudden and massive increase in the size of the army this was in short supply and most units were issued with the leather type and only exchanged it when they moved to France. Our battalion must have been fortunate, as most were issued with the cotton webbing variety, but being held back as a reserve, I didn't get it.

"When I joined my company at Masham, one of the corporals told me to get over to the Quartermaster and ask to exchange my webbing with one of those who was being removed from the battalion. 'They won't need the good stuff when they are peeling spuds,' he said."

"I made my way over there and was told by one of the staff to go and swap with someone who was close to my size. I picked out a lad who was about my size and about my age and asked him to swap. As he took off his webbing and handed it to me his eyes welled up with tears and I felt sorry for him. I even told him I was sorry as we swapped. He just nodded and said nothing.

"Our webbing could carry just about everything you needed to carry with you. It could be stripped down when you needed to move quickly or be added to when moving long distances.

"I eventually added bits or made alterations to my webbing as I gained experience – we all did – but everyone's kit was pretty much the same. The belt and braces with left and right ammunition pouches at the front, good for carrying 75 rounds of ammunition in each, and most of the lads, me included, scrounged some additional pouches. We also carried a bayonet in its scabbard and an entrenching tool with the blade in a webbing holder. We usually carried a small haversack with personal stuff and food inside, and a large pack was carried at times that contained your greatcoat and blankets. We could put our waterproof sheet in it, but I always attached mine, folded on the top of my pack, to keep the rain out. There was a space in the large pack for your mess tins, but I always carried them in my haversack. I never wanted to be more than arm's-length away from my eating kit!

"One or two of the lads acquired some additional bandoliers, but they weren't generally issued to us infantry. Most of the cavalry units had them, probably because they couldn't wear pouches comfortably when they were on a horse.

"Our boots could be described as the best piece of equipment we had and the worst. Once broken in they were strong and comfortable, but when they were new, you didn't know if you were going to break them in, or they were going to break you. Under normal circumstances they were good at keeping your feet dry, and when wet they dried out quickly. The puttees were awkward, but effective in the same way. Unfortunately, France and particularly Flanders were far from normal conditions and our boots gave little or no protection from the elements and the ailments that came with the constant wetness.

"I was proud when I first put on my uniform and that feeling never left me throughout the war. I believed it stood for something and I think others did as well. I saw it on the faces of people we met in France and Belgium. I think it meant something to them; that they had someone there who would stand by them, not abandon them. Someone who would do their best to help them, not harm them. Course, it didn't always work out like that, but that was the intention.

"Does that sound stupid? Perhaps it was, but I suppose I was always a bit of an idealist. I think we all were in our family. I know our Charlie and George were. I think we must have gotten that from our Dad. Our Dad would never shirk his duty. It didn't matter whether he was at home or if he was at work, he always did his best. I think he instilled that into all of us, both boys and girls.

"I remember something he read to me once. Do you remember when I said that our Dad would read to us? And not just the words of a story, but he would take time to explain the meaning behind the words, the real meaning of the story... the moral of the tale, if you like?" Ben asked.

"Yes, I remember," I replied.

"Our Dad would always do that, but there was one time when I clearly remember him not doing it; one time when he didn't explain the meaning of what he was reading to me from a newspaper. He just read it to me, slowly and carefully. After he read it to me, he passed me the paper, so I could read it myself. Our Dad would never have done something like that unless he wanted me to look for my own meaning.

"I was only a youngster, maybe 10 or 11 years old, and I read it over and over, trying to understand the meaning. It didn't take me long to memorise it, word for word, but it took me many years to fully understand it. It was made by the American President, Mr Roosevelt, in Paris in 1910."

Ben closed his eyes and recounted the words of the speech, slowly and deliberately, just as I imagined his Dad read the words to him from the newspaper;

"It is not the critic who counts; not the man who points out how the strong man stumbles, or where the doer of deeds could have done them better.

The credit belongs to the man who is actually in the arena, whose face is marred by dust and sweat and blood;

who strives valiantly; who errs, who comes short again and again, because there is no effort without error and shortcoming;

but who does actually strive to do the deeds; who knows great enthusiasms, the great devotions; who spends himself in a worthy cause;

who at the best knows in the end the triumph of high achievement, and who at the worst, if he fails, at least fails while daring greatly, so that his place shall never be with those cold and timid souls who neither know victory nor defeat."

When Ben finished speaking he kept his eyes closed for a few seconds more before opening them, going on; "That's a good speech, don't you think? It took me a long time until I truly understood the meaning, probably at Houthulst, towards the end of 1917."

"I suppose the words are even more effective when you try to live by them, to live up to them. I think that's what our Dad wanted me to understand, what he wanted us all to do. Not just to understand the words, but to try in our own way to live up to them.

"I don't know if I managed to do that. But when things were hard, and I wanted to give in, those words and the memory of our Dad reading them always made me give a bit more, for my mates and for our Dad." When Ben finished speaking we sat in silence. He took out his fags and offered me one, which I declined, sparked up and took a deep drag, holding his breath for about five seconds before exhaling through his nose. His nose twitched, and he rubbed the apparent itch with his left cuff.

*****

Ben continued: "As I said, I was so relieved to be moving to Masham to join the rest of the Battalion, along with about a hundred others, to replace those who had been accepted at the recruitment centres but who had quickly proven to be sickly, unfit or under age.

"Moving from Nottingham to Yorkshire and joining my company was exciting, but a bit daunting. I think being younger than most of the others, maybe I was a bit more optimistic and enthusiastic. I'm sure I was a bit homesick, at least for a time, but it was an adventure for me – then again, I didn't have to leave a wife and children behind.

"I later felt guilty because I never considered the effect it would have on our Mam if anything was to happen to me. But after losing our Dad, I suppose I felt that at least she didn't have to provide for me, and I could play my part in providing for her and my sisters, even though she didn't have to depend on what I sent back... not like the families of the married men, who had to depend solely on the soldier's allotment that was sent home.

"I found the first month or two of training to be interesting and exciting, as I was learning lots of new stuff, but it soon became routine and a bit boring. It was quite hard physically and some of the lads struggled at first. I was quite fit, so I managed reasonably well. I hurt in places where I wasn't used to being exercised, but I quickly got used to it and I knew that we still had recruits waiting in Nottingham wanting to join from the reserve, and I wasn't about to be earmarked as a weakling and sifted out and replaced.

"The worst part of it as far as I was concerned was breaking in my new boots. We were issued with two pairs of boots, which were as stiff as iron. So much of the training was route marching carrying our equipment. That first week those boots tore my feet to pieces. I'd never seen blisters like that before. You knew when they'd burst inside your boot because the pain stopped, but not for long. You could feel that the inside of your boot was wet, a mixture of pus and blood. The relief from pain was only temporary. The blister soon started to form again – any relief was short-lived.

"After a couple of weeks or so, your feet toughened up and the boots softened up. It was like the hardness left the leather and entered your feet. Suddenly marching became easier, which was a good thing, because the routes became longer and longer as training progressed.

"Then I had to decide what to do about the second pair of boots. I thought it best to start breaking them in as soon as the first pair were done. I didn't want to get too comfortable in the first pair and have to start all over again months later. I didn't look forward to it, but I reasoned that it was best to do so as soon as possible while my feet were still hard from breaking in the first pair. I didn't want to have to break in the second lot in France, when I was worrying about a visit from Jerry or charging towards him in a pair of boots that were crippling me.

"I broke them in as soon as possible, using a few new tricks I learned from the first pair. I don't think I went for a piddle for months without doing it in the pair of boots I wasn't wearing at the time, to soften them up," Ben joked.

"Did it work?" I asked.

"I think so. And even if it didn't, at least it stopped any other bugger pinching them whilst they were half full," Ben laughed, before going on: "I can't believe I ever thought a pair of stiff boots would be painful enough to hinder my running after going over the bags. On those occasions the state of my boots was the last thing I was worried about.

"Our physical training was constantly being made tougher, building up to route marches of about 15 miles in full kit. We would usually have a five-minute halt to rest and drink water every hour. Towards the end of a day's march I hated taking a rest as getting moving again was so hard. Some of the chaps would lie on their backs and gulp down their water. Whenever possible I'd remain standing, just so I wouldn't have to struggle back to my feet again.

"Our packs, ammunition and rifle weighed in at over seventy pounds. It was heavy to begin with, especially before you got used to carrying it. But on top of our own kit we shared the burden of carrying additional ammunition and spares for the machine gunners, bombers and mortars, which really added to the load.

"When it rained, our kit seemed to double in weight because our uniforms were like a massive sponge. If you threw your waterproof sheet over you and your pack to keep the rain out, it made you sweat so much that you were even wetter on the inside than the outside. Everyone complained about marching in the sun. Not me. It didn't bother me at all; but the rain – I hated marching in the rain.

"Musketry practice was a break from the hard, physical grind. I had never fired a rifle or a shotgun before I started training, but I really enjoyed it. By the end of training I was an excellent marksman, so much so that a training sergeant said I should consider requesting a sniper training course. I had no idea what a sniper was, so I said I would consider it. When I found out, I didn't apply. It wasn't the job for me.

"I enjoyed training on the Lewis gun. When I was training they were still new in service and our battalion was only just receiving a few of them because the Flying Corps had priority.

"They were a decent bit of kit. Heavy; easily a couple of stone, but nowhere near as heavy as the Vickers, and they could be operated by just one soldier, rather than a crew. The pans were fiddly to charge up and quite heavy to lug around. You could empty the pan in a flash, you had to go easy on the trigger as it could be emptied in about 5 seconds if your finger was a bit too heavy."

*****

"The next move was to Tidworth barracks at Bulford on Salisbury Plain. It was the furthest south I had ever been. I remember seeing Stonehenge for the first time and being amazed at the size of it. Not just the height, but the massiveness of the stones. It was an incredible sight and the first thing I mentioned the next time I wrote home. I had seen drawings of it and photographic plates in our Dad's books and a few newspapers, but they didn't prepare you for seeing it in real life... the first of many things I would see which photographs, drawings or even training didn't prepare me for – just about every part of the war that I saw in France and Flanders.

"Throughout training we kept hearing rumours that we would soon be ordered overseas. I don't know if they were just rumours and so just fizzled out, or if we were being prepared only for plans to change. Experience would teach us that orders were changed more often than a Tommy changed his socks."

I chipped in; "There hasn't been much change in the past hundred years, Ben. It's much the same today, 'Troops get on the bus... troops get off the bus.' The story's pretty much the same and so is the frustration. Even though you know you are going somewhere dangerous, once you have trained for it and prepared yourself in your own head, all you want to do is get on with it."

Ben nodded and replied, "That's progress for you!" and we both smiled at how little had changed.

He went on; "Following the excitement and interest of Stonehenge the rest of the time on Salisbury Plain was pretty mundane, and as we approached Christmas 1915, it had become bloody tedious and depressing. We were still there at Christmas.

"We spent so much time slogging our way in columns, for mile after mile across the plain – setting up camp – digging trenches – manning them in the freezing weather for a couple of days – filling them in, some of the time – packing up all the kit – marching to another location –

doing the same again – marching back to barracks.

"December was a bloody miserable time and apart from Wipers it was my lowest point in the war. Nothing ever compared to the misery of Wipers, but at least there we were doing it for real. Here we were just killing time and the boredom was killing us. Even the time on the musketry ranges became tedious. There were only so many thousands of rounds you could fire at wooden targets, before you started wishing they would fire back," Ben reflected.

*****

"How well do you think your training prepared you for what was to come?" I asked.

Ben considered his response, before answering: "Our training prepared us for almost everything... except the shock of seeing death close up and without warning. And the other thing it couldn't prepare us for was the feeling of fear. Those two things – death and fear, are things that training can't fully prepare you for, and even after you have experienced both on the battlefield they still have a powerful effect on you.

"Fear was the worst... it could eat right through you if you let it and there's no point denying I was afraid many times. To be able to go through all that without fear would make you less than human. Don't get me wrong, I was always able to do my job, to soldier on, even though at times I was almost on my knees. Apart from Wipers, the fear came and went – there, fear was with you almost all the time. Sometimes it was obvious, sometimes less so, but it was always there.

"During training in Blighty there was no fear, just a feeling of anticipation, the same when we sailed for France. Even knowing what we were heading into didn't frighten me. Looking back, that lack of fear was just down to ignorance. Even experienced soldiers who had served in other campaigns were completely unprepared for what they were going into. It was like nothing before.

"During our first month in France, whenever we were training the sound of artillery was always within earshot and you became comfortable with it. The first time on the line we were shelled regularly, and you learned to fear it, when you saw the damage it did, but you lived with it. But the sound of the barrage that our lads fired at Jerry before the advance on the Somme in 1916 was terrifying and that was our guns firing. Nothing could prepare a soldier for that, because nothing like it had ever happened before. Can you imagine how it was for Jerry, who was on the receiving end?

"I suppose it was during the Somme offensive that I first struggled with the sight of death and trying to overcome my fear. We were moving forward and passed through the remains of a Royal Artillery unit that had been hit by a Jerry barrage – it was carnage. A complete slaughter of men and horses, with the remnants of their guns scattered far and wide.

"I don't know which part of that scene hit me so hard. I suppose it was the sight of the dismembered horses mixed in with the shattered bodies of the gunners. The men looked small and puny next to their magnificent horses. But despite their strength and power, the horses were just as dead. I remember thinking that none of those poor animals had volunteered, none collected a shilling for enlisting, none swore an oath to serve King and Country – but they paid the price with their lives all the same.

"I can still see and feel what it was like even now as I'm telling you about it. It was like walking through a painting, one of those creepy ones depicting hell and the devil. The funny thing is that as far as I can remember there was no colour in the picture except for the red of the blood. I can't remember the colours of the horses, or the colour of the guns and the uniforms, they are just like a photograph, just shades of grey, but the blood was red and fresh, not black like old blood.

"And the smell! It was the smell of fresh meat, not decaying meat, which we all became familiar with, as the war went on. It was the smell of freshly slaughtered men and horses. The day was warm, and the air rose up to meet you. As you breathed in, the scent of the flesh and blood was sweet and sort of sticky. You could taste it on your tongue, not just smell it... and there we were carefully picking our path through all that death.

"Yes, that was the first time I struggled with the feeling of true fear. Not just thinking about it, you know, in my head – but real and physical, inside my chest, like someone had put a hand inside me and squeezed, causing my chest and guts to sort of cramp up. It was physically painful." Ben finished speaking and looked down at his boots. He pulled the sleeve of his greatcoat down over his right hand and leaned forward and wiped some imaginary dust from his boot.

After a minute or so he continued: "There is quite a list of things that frightened me, but for the most part I managed to deal with them. First, snipers! Theirs not ours... unless you beat one in cards and he owed you money. Jerry snipers were to be feared, but if you moved about properly and kept below the rim of the trench, then you were safe from a sniper. When moving over open ground, moving fast, low and zigzagging gave you a chance.

"Second, going over the bags. The first time I saw another battalion going over the bags I couldn't believe how slowly they moved... like they were already dead – carefully lifting their feet over the barbed wire as if afraid to snag their trousers. I remember thinking 'Sod that!' When I moved I went like a bloody hare with a hound on my tail.

"Third, whizz-bangs. You know, the ones that burst over your head. You learned to react fast and live with it, or if you didn't learn, you died. The single shells right out of the blue were the worst. You had to react in a split second – if you didn't, you'd cop your iron rations. I once saw someone with his head split completely down the middle because one caught him in the trench wearing just his field cap – that would have been in 1916 before we were all issued with our own tin hat, until then they were passed from one man to the next as you went on post.

"Fourth, trench raids. Theirs, not ours.

"I don't think I was ever afraid on one of ours. I suppose I had confidence in my own soldiering. As a Bantam I was small, fast and fit, faster and fitter than most of the other Bantams, and they were faster and fitter than most of the Jerries we faced. I used every bit of cover and being a tiddler, I could get by on the bare minimum – keeping low and moving fast or crawling at a snail's pace depending on the circumstances.

"I didn't see fighting close up like during trench raids as something to be feared. I wouldn't say I enjoyed it, but I didn't hate it either. Maybe it was because I was young and felt invincible. It must have been different for those fellows who were married with children and responsibilities at home. My responsibility was to my mates.

"After my first face to face with Jerry, I was never again afraid of him, especially when close-up, but when I was running fast towards him through a trench I often saw his fear. Moving with a bomber; fast, low, no straight lines. Even though I was just a kid I was pretty tough – and a good little soldier." Ben finished speaking and a hint of a smile appeared on his face.

There was an intensity in his eyes. For the first time I saw the fighter inside the lad a few feet in front of me and I began to appreciate why he was well able to scare the shit out of a "soon to be dead" German.

Ben went on: "I think our training was a good as it could have been. Without it I'd have been lost, and while it couldn't prepare me for the death and the fear, it gave me a fighting chance, which was just as well, as we were soon on our way."

*****

"It was at the beginning of February 1916 when we moved to France. It was good to be leaving the training camp at Tidworth and it was even better to be moving to France, rather than Ireland as had been rumoured. I mean, who would want to spend the duration of the war in Ireland? Not me, that's for certain. I couldn't wait to get over there to France after the months of training.

"We moved by train to Folkestone, to be shipped across the Channel. We were expecting to land at Calais, which was the shortest crossing, and as the Channel wasn't the safest place to be at that time, we expected to be on the ship for the shortest time possible. Instead we were shipped to Boulogne, which added a couple of hours to the journey and a lot more sickness during the crossing. I must admit that although I was excited to be going to France, the crossing itself wasn't something I was looking forward to.

"Embarking on the troop ship felt like the start of some great adventure. I wasn't stupid enough to think that fighting a war was going to be fun, or a happy experience; I knew it would be hard and frightening, but I was ready, and I knew that my mates were ready too.

"Our company commander, Captain Barnett-Smith, was respected and well liked. He was an experienced soldier, having fought in the South Africa campaign. We had confidence in him and I think he had confidence in us. He stood at the foot of the gangway as we were embarking and had a bit of a laugh and joke with us as we made our way aboard.

"The crossing was quite smooth. There was very little wind and the sea was calm, but it still resulted in quite a bit of seasickness. Some of the fellows were sick before we got under way and continued until we had our feet down in France. I wasn't sick. I mean I didn't throw up, but I felt quite ill for about an hour. The feeling of sickness came over me and I felt terrible, but as quickly as it started, it disappeared. By the time we disembarked I felt fine. We made our way to a field kitchen close to the quayside, brewed up, and had a decent breakfast. Within the hour we were on the move, heading east... towards the war."

Chapter 5

Stand To

"Moving inland from Boulogne, our first stop was a place called Renescure, where we remained for over a month, drilling, musketry training and going through the final preparations for the front line. We even managed to find time for Kitchener, no less, to inspect the Brigade. Imagine how happy we all were! Well, we were told it was Kitchener, but from the distance I saw him it could have been a scarecrow with a big moustache.

"In early March we were attached to the 10th South Wales Borderers at Le Touret, so we could sharpen up our trench routine with an experienced battalion. We had our first casualties within days, but the three wounded soldiers recovered. That was a real shaker for a few of us. We were all expecting casualties, but it is different when it happens to one of the fellows that you have lived with and trained alongside. The biggest shock was just how indiscriminate it was. It wasn't as if they were doing anything they hadn't been trained to do, yet they were still hit. I suppose up to that point I was sure that so long as I did what I had been trained to do, I would be safe. How gullible was I?

"On the 26th of March almost 700 of us took post on the front line at Laventie, where we relieved a battalion of the Scottish Rifles. Before marching forward, we were paraded on the Commanding Officer's orders. Before the march we were all instructed to apply whale oil to our feet so as to prevent foot ailments. We each carried all our personal equipment, including a greatcoat, waterproof sheet and cape. We all carried two sandbags per man, which were to be filled and placed on the fire step, so us Bantams could stand post without reducing the height of the parapet because most of the Jocks who we were relieving were a good bit taller than us.

"All our webbing was checked for uniformity. The CO was determined that we would make a good impression and once he was satisfied we moved forward according to our orders crossing the Estairs – Sailly road just after 6.15pm.

"The weather was bad... cold, rainy and bloody snow flurries. It was freezing cold and we were glad we had been ordered to wear our greatcoats. In the darkness we made our way in columns to the level crossing at Laventie Station, where we were met by guides from the Jocks. W Company led off to the level crossing with X, Y and us in Z Company following at 10-minute intervals.

"We continued towards the trenches led by our guides, with 200 yards spacing between each platoon. As we moved forward in the dark and the snow, I remember thinking that the column looked like a train in the dark with the breath of the Tommies rising like the steam from an engine. The moon kept breaking through the clouds and lighting up the clouds of breath and snowflakes. It looked like some illustration in a book of Grimm's fairy tales, except this wasn't going to be a fairy tale, we all knew that.

"We moved into our positions; W Company took the right at Erith Street, with X and Y Companies in the middle and us in Z Company on the left. At 9.30pm we very quietly 'Stood To' for the first time as a battalion, at full strength, most of us previously rejected as being too short for service. But one thing was for certain, Jerry was going to have his hands full. We all felt we had something to prove and we were determined to give a good account. I'd come a long way from Fildes Street. I remember hoping our Dad was looking down, feeling proud."

"Three days later 2nd Lieutenant Bridgwater copped it. Our first death in action."

*****

"The whole of April was spent rotating in and out of the trenches in the Laventie area. I think we were all a bit worried about the state of our equipment and if we had enough stuff to go around. I don't know whether ammunition was in short supply, but even though we had room in our webbing for a hundred and fifty rounds of rifle ammunition, we were only issued with one hundred. We still didn't have enough tin hats to be issued with one each, so the lads who were on the step had them and they were passed from relief to relief. The periscopes we were issued were a welcome piece of kit, meaning you could steer clear of Jerry snipers, especially as our own snipers had just been issued with special scopes for their rifles... so we all reckoned that Jerry would have them as well.

"I can't tell you how disappointing France was during those first months. I always imagined that France would be a lot warmer than home. I always pictured it as being a bit exotic, but those thoughts turned out to be wishful thinking and France turned out to be a bit of a let-down, and that was even without some bugger trying to kill you all the time!

"The weather was bloody freezing for the time of year, like a winter day on the beach at Meggies. The cold hit us hard and we lost a fair few men to frostbite... in April! Most of the cases were treated locally, but some were serious enough to be shipped back to Blighty for treatment.

"There were a few bright times though and things did warm up a bit, but only when a barn we were sheltering in was hit by a Jerry shell and went up in flames before you could blink. Fortunately, even though the barn was packed tight with Tommies – mostly from Z Company, but Engineers and Pioneers as well – everyone escaped unscathed, which was more than could be said for our Company Commander's famous white trousers, which he never missed an opportunity to tell us he had worn in South Africa. Sadly, a proud military career was coming to an end and those breeches met their fate on that cold night. They were reduced to a few burned scraps of cloth. Captain Barnett-Smith was so distressed, we fully expected him to bury them, or what was left of them, with full military honours.

"The lads thought it bloody hilarious, but we made sure Captain Barnett-Smith never caught us. Pleasant chap that he was, he took the loss of those breeches hard. Who would have thought that being shelled and almost burned to death could be so entertaining?

"Shortly after the fire we captured our first Jerry prisoner. Perhaps 'captured' is a bit of an exaggeration as it gives the impression that we had set out to catch one; 'bumped into' our first Jerry prisoner might be a more accurate description. For whatever reason he had become separated from his unit and, getting lost, he just wandered into our barbed wire, got himself well and truly tangled and woke everyone up by shouting for help. After about ten minutes of struggling he freed himself and was called forward and slipped into the bag.

"At the end of April we moved off the line into the Divisional Reserve for a short time. I'm sure it was during this time that the Division began getting replacements that weren't Bantams, but regular-height soldiers; replacements from other regiments, who were returning from wounds, or because their original battalions were being wound up. Cyclists and dismounted cavalrymen. I reckon most were good fellows, but we weren't too happy.

"We were rotating in and out of the line with the 14th Gloucesters. They were good lads and we got to know many of them quite well during our time in reserve and whenever we rotated. One lad was about my age and was also named Ben. He was also a bit of a boxer and footballer and we used to lark about a bit, sparring and discussing what we were going to do to each other at the divisional sports. He joked about retiring me from boxing with a 'cauliflower arse' from all the times he would knock me down. He always wore a scarf sent to him by his Mam, so I would tell him he could wear his scarf in the ring, so "Little Mammy's Boy" wouldn't get cold whilst he was asleep.

"At the end of May we were in the Neuve Chapelle sector and we were handing over to the Gloucesters. Our Lewis gunners, snipers and signallers had already changed over and moved back, when we began to take a right pounding from the Jerry guns.

"The very first shell that came over exploded right above our heads and a piece of shrapnel came down and killed Ben outright. One moment we were standing joking together and the next he was down... gone. One of the Gloucesters got down to him to try and find where he had been hit. But it was clear he had gone, so he just dragged him under cover as all hell broke loose.

"The shelling was so intense that it destroyed the barbed wire and the communication wires that linked the companies together. It meant that each company was fighting alone, with no idea what was going on further along the line. Runners were sent to try and pass messages and keep contact with the companies either side, but most of the runners never returned.

"The sound was deafening, especially when our own artillery fired back at the Jerry guns and tried to put them out. W Company was on the right of the line next to the Lancashires, who took such a hammering that they were almost reduced to nothing.

"A gap opened up in the middle of the wire and it wasn't long before Jerry rushed through it and dropped into our fire trenches. It took over an hour for the companies either side of the breach to close in and drive them out. But as they pulled back they took quite a few of our walking wounded with them as prisoners.

"Once we had driven them out, we set about repairing the fire trench. It was a desperate, hard slog and we were fully expecting further raids, so we were split into those on the step, who were constantly firing at anything that moved, and others who were trying to repair the damage to the trenches. By first light we had repaired and secured the line.

"Our lads and those from the Gloucesters gave an excellent account that night, but none more than the Medical Officer and the stretcher bearers who grafted like demons all through the night, completely ignoring the hell that was breaking loose all around them.

"It's one thing to appear brave when hammering at Jerry with everything you have, it's quite a different thing to shut out everything around you and do your job; moving the wounded from harm's way, giving treatment and, when no treatment would be of use, just comforting a dying man. Those fellows did that all night long, with no regard for their own safety; putting their trust in us to keep them safe, which we tried our best to do. That takes a special kind of courage.

"When it was all over, before moving off the line we helped to remove the dead. A couple of the lads pulled my mate, Ben, from where they had put him. He was still wearing his scarf. It had his blood on it and one of them took it from around his neck and handed to me. The whole night had left me dazed, but uninjured. When the scarf was handed to me I sort of stumbled backwards and ended up sitting on an ammunition box. I sat there and just held his scarf in both hands, looking at it, while the lads lifted him onto a stretcher.

"I remember looking at a patch of his blood, which looked dark, almost black, as it had soaked into the dark green wool. Jim came over and stood over me. I looked up at him and he said, 'Give it to me.' It was more of an order than a request.

"Before I had the chance to hand it over he took the scarf from me, walked a few steps to a shallow pool of water and crouched down to wash the bloody patch out of the wool. He stood up, then rubbed the wet patch of the scarf on the wooden planks of the trench wall and then against the front of his greatcoat. He put the cleaned piece of the scarf against his cheek. It was obviously still wet, because he rubbed it against the front of his coat again for about a minute before checking it against his cheek again.

"He walked back to me and offered me the scarf, saying, 'Put it on and try to stay warm. You need it now, he doesn't.' I looked at the scarf in his hand, but I just couldn't take it from him. 'Take it, or someone else will. He liked you, even though he was planning on kicking your arse in the boxing ring. He'd gladly let any of us have it, but if he could speak he'd want it to be yours.' I reached out and took the scarf, but I didn't put it on.

"I just sat with it in my lap and stared at it. I sat there as Ben was lifted and carried away along the trench. I sat quietly, alone, staring at the scarf and trying to clear my head. I felt responsible and wanted to cry and shout out that I was sorry, but I didn't cry, and I didn't shout out. I just squeezed the scarf in my fists until I got cramp in my hands.

"That night was our first big test, and apart from the terror of the first couple of seconds, everything I had trained so hard to do just clicked into place. I think that was the night I became a soldier. It was also the first time, but not the last time, I lost a friend." As Ben finished speaking, we both sat in silence.

Ben took out a fag and lit it. He had half-finished it before he spoke again: "It would have been late June, about the 24th, when the guns began their bombardment before the advance on the Somme. We all knew something was coming, we'd all been hearing constant rumours that the French were pressing for a major attack to relieve the pressure on their army at Verdun.

"Once the guns started firing they just carried on without any let up until the 1st of July, when our infantry went over the bags. I heard that over a million and a half shells were fired in order to destroy the Jerry barbed wire and defences, but apparently it didn't work.

"We were a long way from the guns, but even from many miles away the sound was enough to drive you mad. It kept on and on, day and night. Even though we were probably 20 miles away, we could always hear it. On or off the line, you could always hear them, thumping away in the distance.

"A gunner told me that we used over 800 of our 18-pounders, as well as hundreds of other types of gun. The 18-pounder could fire 3 or 4 rounds a minute and they worked in teams, so they really banged the shells out.

"When I say they could fire 3 or 4 rounds a minute, they didn't do that very often. It was exhausting for a gun crew to keep it going for any length of time. It also damaged the barrel of the gun if you kept it up for too long. The crew would fire a couple of rounds a minute for long periods and then up the rate to 3 or 4 in the last few minutes before the infantry went over.

"This increased rate kept Jerry well pinned down, but it also warned him that an attack was about to begin. Someone once told me that artillery was responsible for more casualties than the machine gun, but I never felt it did us much good before going over. There was just too much barbed wire for enough of it to be breached creating a decent-sized gap, and this meant you had to choose between trying to get through the wire, or being funnelled towards the small gaps, and making a better target for the Jerry machine gunners. The 'Grimsby Chums' learned this lesson the hard way and were simply slaughtered on that first day of the Somme offensive.

"I don't think anyone realised how well Jerry had prepared. We were in trenches, but our trenches were nothing like the Jerry trenches, which were like warrens, almost underground villages. So far down underground that even the biggest of shells couldn't dent them and as soon as our artillery fell silent Jerry was out of his bunkers and back up on the fire step waiting for us.

"We found out later that we had spent months tunnelling under the Jerry lines to blow up the trenches and bunkers from underneath as going in from above was useless – although we didn't know about the tunnelling at the time – not until the explosion at La Boiselle. That was as much of a surprise to most of us as it was to Jerry.

"We learned some of the lessons from this mess and in later advances against their multiple lines of defence, we used a 'creeping barrage' with the shells landing just ahead of the following infantry. This kept Jerry's head down for much longer, but anything dropping short landed amongst the advancing Tommies. It also depended on different companies advancing at the same pace, which was impossible given the differences in ground conditions, and this hampered us during the fighting at Houthulst Forest in 1917.

"But in the main the creeping barrage worked, keeping Jerry's head down, sometimes until we were right on top of them and in some cases in their fire trenches, and once in amongst them we could take control with our Lewis gunners, bombers and bayonets moving quickly through the interconnecting trenches."

"What do you mean bombers?" I asked.

"The lads who were loaded up with the Mills bombs, you know? 'bombers'. That's what we called them. We all trained with the Mills bomb, but those lads were given extra training courses. They could drop one down a rat's lug hole from 30 paces.

"As I said, there were lots of expensive lessons learned, the main thing I learned was that despite what we had been told, there is no safe way to advance towards a thousand Jerries firing bloody machine guns; it's always likely to end badly," Ben joked.

*****

"During June we had spent only a short time on the line and our casualties were light, with just a few wounded and only one drawing his full ration. We moved into reserve and then a couple of days after the initial advance on the Somme we took the train to support the offensive.

"We were held back in reserve during the initial offensive, which didn't please us at first. Later, when we all heard the number of dead I think most of us were quietly grateful and understood just how lucky we had been. None of us would ever say it, but I bet I wasn't the only one thinking it.

"It was the middle of July when we entered the line near Maltz Horn Farm, south of Trones Wood and linked up with the left edge of the French frontline. We lost quite a few wounded to heavy Jerry shelling even as we made our way forward. The rain and the shelling were incessant, and we were exhausted even before we reached our positions.

"We were entering the line where a short time earlier The Buffs had taken a right hammering and it was awful to see the bodies of so many of their lads strewn everywhere. In the darkness, it was all we could do to avoid standing on what was left of some of those poor lads. Often it was only the smell that told you there was a body close or when your foot slipped because you were standing in the remains of some poor bugger. Nobody had yet had the opportunity to recover the unfortunate souls, because of the constant shelling and the regular Jerry attacks.

"On the 19th we were ordered to advance and seize the Jerry trenches opposite our positions. We were all ready for it after sitting for a couple of days taking everything they could chuck at us. There were regular gas attacks and we had spent long periods in our gas hoods. X and Y Companies had taken the worst of it so far and had been worn down by the constant shelling and gas attacks, so it was decided that rather than the whole battalion attacking, W and Z Companies would go in, supported by 2 companies of Manchesters.

"Our Company formed up in the dead ground behind our fire trench at about half past three in the morning for a final briefing. Just over an hour later we attacked, trying to make best use of the remains of long-abandoned trenches, and the natural dead ground. We still had to cover a lot of open ground before we made it through some large gaps in the wire, but before Jerry knew it, we were on top of him.

"The Jerry regiment in this area had built quite a reputation with their aggressive raids, but while we had only been on the line for a few days, with all we had taken during that time we were all in the mood to see just how tough they really were. Most of us were hoping Jerry would fight, not run or surrender, and we were in so fast and hard that they didn't have the chance to throw their hands up. They either ran, or we bombed and shot them down on the spot as we made our way north along their trenches – and that suited us just fine.

"As we rounded the end of a Jerry fire bay, we came upon a heavy machine gun crew, which was hammering away with their 08, down the length of their trench at the W Company lads who were working their way towards us. A couple of our bombers almost dropped their Mills' down their tunic collars and we were in before what was left of the machine gunners had fallen back to earth, to finish off everyone in front of us, before dealing with the occupants of a large dugout positioned just behind them.

"The whole thing was over in less than thirty minutes and once the 08 crew and their mates had been packed off to Valhalla, we linked up with W Company. We were ordered to hold our positions and await a counter-attack. As we made our way back along the trench to set up defensive positions we had to jump over the bodies of Jerries who hadn't been aggressive or quick enough and now littered the floor of the trench, and I thought about the lads from The Buffs who we had stepped over on our way in, a few days earlier. I stupidly thought that at least we had taken some revenge for those lads, but really, we hadn't.

"For once, we were quickly reinforced and supported by a barrage from our guns pasting Jerry's second line and support trenches. We were ready and waiting for the counter-attack, but it never came." Ben paused.

After a few moments of reflection, he went on: "We took a lot of casualties over that time on the line, over fifty dead and about the same missing, with well over a hundred more wounded. They were fellows you had lived with for such a long time and now they were gone, some forever. Me, I was unhurt; just lucky I suppose.

"The following hours were a bad time, they always were after a big scrap. Once you have calmed down, the relief that you had come through in one piece was enough to make you want to cry, but of course you don't. Didn't someone once say that the only thing as sad as a battle lost, is a battle won?" Ben asked.

"The Duke of Wellington: 'Nothing except a battle lost can be half so melancholy as a battle won.' He said it after Waterloo," I answered.

"Well, he was bloody well right. Who would have thought a lowly Tommy would ever agree with anything said by a General? Especially after this lot," Ben said.

He went on: "A day or so later I learned that before our attack went in there had been an incident in Y Company when a corporal just cracked under the strain and tried to lead his section off the line. He was challenged by an officer and the whole lot of them were quickly arrested, before panic spread through the rest of the company. I don't know what punishments were given to the lads, but the corporal was court martialed a short time later and I am sure that he was put in front of a firing squad in August. The CO was making sure it never happened again."

*****

"At the beginning of August, the whole division was moved off the line for a period of rest in the 10 Corps area. We were all exhausted and being moved by train was a welcome luxury. When we arrived at the destination railhead to continue the journey on foot, our stretcher bearers, most of who were bandsmen, exchanged their stretchers for their instruments.

"We marched to the camp behind our band. Under normal circumstances that might have been a bit of a chore, but it raised our spirits. Our time in camp was split into resting and training hard to bring a large intake of replacements up to standard. It wasn't an easy task; as the Cheshires had found a few months earlier, many were just not up to the job, being just weedy and sickly – definitely not Bantams.

"By the late August we were back on the line at our old stomping ground in the Matz Horn Trench and after a short, quiet period, we prepared for a raid. It went badly wrong. As we were assembling before moving off, we were shelled, heavily and accurately by Jerry; it killed a dozen of the fellows. It was no coincidence, and the raid was cancelled. Although it was a blow to lose that many of the lads, I reckon that, fortunately for the rest of us, Jerry had jumped the gun. Had he waited for the raid, which he obviously knew was coming, he could have sprung the trap and taken a lot more of us – grateful for small mercies I suppose.

"In September we moved to the trenches around Arras. This was a quiet time. I think both sides were exhausted after the previous couple of months and had lost the appetite for a scrap. I reckon we all needed the time to lick our wounds and recover," Ben reflected.

*****

"How the hell did you manage to keep your spirits up in the middle of all of that madness?" I asked.

"It didn't take much, to pick us up. During September the weather had turned warm and our time off the line was spent playing sport, visiting local towns well to the rear, and musketry training. Our time on the line was mundane, but reasonably comfortable. Morale, which had started to wear down, picked up again," Ben replied, taking out his packet of Black Cats and offering me one.

"No thanks, Ben. I've still given them up," I said.

Ben lit his fag, but this time, instead of putting out the match, he slowly let it burn down, almost to his fingers, before dropping it on the ground. "I suppose you just had to try and keep your chin up. I mean, what was the alternative? Every one of us knew how important it was; from the Tommy in the trenches, up to our CO and right up to the generals.

"Good and bad morale is easy to see. It's possibly the most important thing to an army – more important than any single piece of equipment. Without good morale the other stuff doesn't work as well; sometimes it doesn't work at all.

"In our platoon and the whole of Z Company, the NCOs and officers did as much as they could to keep spirits up. Maybe I was lucky. Speaking with some of the other lads in different battalions in the 35th Division, they had NCOs who were nothing but bad for morale – harsh bullies who kept their lads in line by fear. Don't get me wrong, you wouldn't want to cross some of our sergeants and corporals, but none of them were bullies. They were good fellows; hard but fair. The same for our officers. There wasn't a single one who I wouldn't have liked, in different circumstances – even if they were a bit posh.

"Standing up to your knees in mud and ice-cold water is a bit of a leveller. We had an older lieutenant who would spend hours on the fire step alongside the lads, talking to them and keeping them company. He would talk about all sorts of things, not just the war. I think some of the other officers thought he was a bit of an odd-bod, but I remember having many a conversation with him about four in the morning, and I think I got to understand a bit about his motives for spending so much time with the lads.

"I reckon the first reason was to prevent him going out of his mind thinking about home and what he was missing, but I think he wanted to be a good officer and he wanted to experience what the lads under his command were going through. I mean, unless you have been in someone else's shoes, well, waterlogged boots, you won't understand how they feel. By sharing their discomfort and what they endure, you are in a much better position to know their limitations, because you are feeling the same pain.

"I think this helped him to judge the morale of the lads. If you ask a man how things are on a sunny day, he'll probably tell you he's fine – which is nice to hear. Ask the same man in the freezing-cold rain, in the dark, when you are both unable to feel your hands and feet, and he'll tell you exactly what's on his mind. It helped make him a better officer and earned the respect of the lads. He was a good example to the younger and less experienced officers who tended to follow his lead. He was sadly missed and mourned as much as any mate when he was killed.

"But it wasn't just the officers and NCOs who realised the importance of keeping spirits up. We all took responsibility for it and did our best to look after it... and each other. We kept an eye on each other.

"Letters from home were as valuable as fags. If a lad had a good letter from home it would give him a spring in his step, at least for a time, but sometimes it would be short-lived when he realised what he was missing. Getting regular letters from home was important and I really felt for the lads who didn't get much, or in a few cases didn't get any mail.

"I was lucky and got a fair bit. Our Mam wasn't much of a writer, she would usually tag a few lines on to the bottom of a letter from one of my sisters. George would often do the same – just a line or two at the bottom of the page, but each of my sisters wrote regularly, and I wrote back as soon as I got a letter... whenever possible. The best letters were the ones which sent me news of our Charlie. He couldn't write to me, nor me to him, but the girls kept each of us informed about the other whenever they could. Yes, they were the best letters. I bet most Tommies wrote more letters in those few years than they did in the rest of their lives.

"Sometimes, even the most cheerful of us needed a reminder. I remember the CSM telling me. 'Leeman, this is one big, horrible bloody war. None of us wants to be here. Not even the professional soldiers. The only ones who want to be here are the lunatics and psychopaths and there aren't many of those. But here we are and that's a fact. Now you can be here and be happy – or you can be here and be miserable; but make no mistake, happy or sad, here you will stay; at least until Jerry relieves you of your cares.' He was dead right.

"None of us could change the fact that we were here, but you could try and change the way you felt about it, and keeping your own spirits up had a knock-on effect. It rubbed off on your mates and made the bond between you stronger. Who the hell wants to be around some miserable bugger?

"We were moved off the front line as regularly as possible and that was always good for morale. Even when you were heading back on to the line, at least you usually knew how long it was for and you could tick off the days. There was an end in sight.

"In early 1917 we heard about mutinies amongst the French, and not just a few isolated cases, but up to half of their army. That worried us. We were worried that they would collapse and leave us on our own to hold the whole of the line. Things improved after they sacked the head of their army and replaced him with another general, who visited the front line, spoke with the 'Poilus' and made sure that those at the front were rotated regularly, rested and given leave. I suppose he just treated them like soldiers, not cattle, and it worked.

"For me, being moved to a rear trench a few hundred yards behind the fire trench was almost as good as being in camp. Being used on work details like track laying and road repairs kept us busy and our minds off other things... most of the time.

"Moving back to the training camps was best. I enjoyed the training, especially the physical training. I always felt unfit after a few days in the trenches. It was good to get to the camps and stretch your legs, play some sport, or just fill your lungs with fresh air.

"As I've told you I loved boxing and playing football. We would compete against other units in the brigade. We'd compete against the Cheshires, the Gloucesters and the Trench Mortar Battery. We also played against the 105th Machine Gunners. I wasn't that keen on them.

"The boxing was great, and I would fight as a lightweight – I did well. I only lost one of my fights and had a draw as well. I won about fourteen or fifteen fights, even fighting against some of their heavier lads. My only loss was against a lad more than a stone heavier, and if I'd had more time I would have worn the bugger down with my body punches.

"I only wished I'd got to fight my mate from the Gloucesters. I bet it would have been a cracking match and I'd have been proud to shake his hand... after he'd been revived and helped back to his feet." Ben smiled at the thought; just a weak smile, but it was better than nothing.

He continued; "The football was very competitive, and we had some great games, particularly against the teams from the Cheshires. They had some really good players. I always played right full-back. The 16th Cheshire's had a great outside left and I enjoyed playing against him. He would turn you inside out if you let him, but I always held my own against him. To be honest I couldn't tell you the result in some of those games, but I could tell you how many times he beat me, or I stopped him in his tracks. It was like our own game inside a game.

"He was badly wounded in 1917 during the fighting at Houthulst. I heard that he survived but was in a bad way and was shipped back to Blighty due to his wounds. I hope he got through it. He was a smashing lad."

I cut in, "So, were you a good player then?"

Ben responded without hesitation; "Uncompromising! I like to think that I was uncompromising. Sometimes the ball would get past me – sometimes the man would get past me – but very rarely both together! I remember being warned by the referee following one of my more enthusiastic tackles that I shouldn't be doing Jerry's job for him."

I laughed out loud as I imagined him scything some poor bugger's legs from under him.

Ben continued, "We also had musketry competitions and athletics competitions. I enjoyed all of it, but it was the football and the boxing I did best."

"Apart from sport, some of the lads also put on little shows, some of which were quite good. I suppose they should have been. The brigade was full of people who before the war had been musicians, actors and singers. They should have been performing in a London theatre, not in some muddy field.

"There was plenty of music, military music mostly, but plenty of other stuff as well. The military bands would put on regular performances in the camps and in the local towns. There always seemed to be a band playing in 'Pops' and the camps to the rear of Arras."

"When you say 'Pops,' do you mean Poperinghe?" I asked.

"Yes," Ben replied, adding, "Sometimes the bands would play in the town at 'Pops', but other times you could hear the music and couldn't tell where it was coming from, until we discovered it was usually coming from Toc H, so sometimes we would go there."

"Talbot House is still there. I stayed there last year, 2017," I said.

Ben shook his head, before saying, "2017! I was there in October 1917 – not long after we'd moved to Flanders."

"It's good that you had things to occupy you and take your mind off the war, if only for a short time," I said.

Ben nodded and went on, "Yes, most of the time it was good, but there were some other things that didn't do much for my spirits. I once received a letter from our Florence. Apparently, after the fighting on the Somme in June 1916 there were moving picture shows of the battle in theatres all over Britain. They set up screens on vehicles and drove them out to small villages that didn't have a theatre. When it was shown it caused a massive increase in men coming forward to enlist.

"Can you believe that? After seeing it, more people enlisted. That means that the moving pictures couldn't have shown what really happened – maybe it just wasn't possible to show what it was really like. I suppose that watching men being mown down by machine guns to the sound of some chap tinkling away on a bloody piano doesn't allow you to experience the true horror, but then again, short of being there, nothing could. Can you imagine it? Thousands of men being mown down to the accompaniment of a pianist; it would probably have been quite comedic, if it wasn't so bleedin' tragic."

I cut in, "I didn't know that. I thought it was odd enough that Charlie Chaplin made a recruitment film for the cinemas. It was in 1918, a film called ‘Shoulder Arms’. The French soldiers loved it, I think it was called ‘The Little Soldier’ in French.

“That’s not French,” said Ben.

“What’s not French?” I asked.

“‘The Little Soldier’. That’s English, not French,” said Ben.

“Alright, ‘Le Petit Soldat’, or something like that,” I replied.

“That’s better,” said Ben. “Charlie Chaplin, eh? I bet he never came over here to act in it, it was probably made in America, or some other place that even the railway guns couldn’t reach.

“I don’t ever remember Z Company being filmed, but we were always seeing the Frenchies being filmed; they bloody well loved it. One time we had just handed over and left the trenches, and because of Jerry shelling we had to march about 5 miles to reach our transport. 5 miles isn’t much of a march, but after a week living in filth and getting by on a few hours of sleep each day we weren’t really in parade order.

“There were a group of French soldiers being filmed larking about, playing up for the cameras. They looked remarkably clean and smart for ‘Poilus’ so close to the front. As we marched by, one of the camera operators turned his big camera towards us, only for him to be knocked over like a skittle by a water bottle slung at him by one of our lads. He went down with a thump. We thought it was hilarious and everyone, even the Frenchies, howled with laughter.”

“One of our officers shouted; ‘Sar’nt Major. Find that man and sort him out!’

‘Who threw that water bottle?’ The CSM shouted.

“One of the lads answered, ‘It was me Sir, it was an accident. I was taking a drink and it slipped through my fingers and when I tried to catch it I accidentally flipped it up in the air... quite a long way into the air!’

‘Well try to be more careful in future, there’s a good chap. Now go and fetch it... them water bottles don’t grow on trees you know,’ the CSM said quietly.”

*****

“Anyway, where were we? Autumn 1916. Yes, the quiet time in the trenches stayed that way until late October when we launched a large-scale raid on Jerry in J sector. Our company, Z Company, was detailed to provide fire support from the left flank. Although the weather had turned wet and made conditions under foot difficult, for once the plan seemed to go well, with the initial bombardment hitting all the Jerry trenches and then, just as the attack went in, switching away from the trenches they planned to hit, but continuing to pin down the Jerry support trenches.

"A big chunk of both belts of Jerry barbed wire had been breached and the lads went through almost unscathed and into the Jerry lines, where they made short work of anyone in front of them, before returning with a single prisoner... the poor bugger.

"One of the officers from another platoon was wounded and fell somewhere in no man's land. He was recovered a couple of hours after the raid by one of his own lads. It was a good night all round, but despite the success of the raid, we knew the Jerries in that sector weren't really up for a decent scrap and most of us were still worried about the calibre of our own recent replacements. From the CO down to the Tommy in the trench, everyone's fears were soon going to be justified.

"The weather that November was horrible – it rained constantly. The ragbag Jerries opposite us in the Arras sector were replaced with fresh, well motived chaps, and they certainly did their best to bring the fight to us. It was now our lines being raided. They became the aggressors and we were on the back foot. At the end of the month they launched three big raids in a single day and our division fared badly in its response – apart from the Foresters... our lads held on, but only by the skin of our teeth.

"Our lines were hit with a mine detonation, which smashed our fire trenches and some support trenches. Then came wave after wave of the fresh Jerry troops. On at least three raids they came within grenade-throwing distance of our fire trench before we drove them back. We fully expected them to get in amongst us and we held back several Lewis gunners to cover us in case we needed escape routes through the communication trenches to the second-line trenches.

"Time and again we drove them back. It helped that the Lee Enfield was a good, accurate rifle and we trained all the time to master it and use it effectively. An infantryman was expected to be able to get off a minimum of 12 rounds a minute. That's aimed shots – not eyes closed and yank on the trigger.

"Most of the experienced lads could manage fifteen, even in the middle of a scrap. It helped that it had a 10-round magazine, where the Jerry Mauser only had a 5-rounder. Most of the other nationalities' rifles were 5-round or 6-round magazines, except the Frenchies, they had an 8-round magazine, but ours was the only 10-rounder.

"Our rifle weighed about a pound lighter than the Jerry rifle and all the others. I know that doesn't sound like much, but when you are carrying it for 10 miles that's something to be grateful for.

"If you kept the firing parts clean and dry it was reliable, although that was easier said than done in the mud around Wipers. Whenever I was 'Stood To' I would drape my scarf over the bolt to keep the working parts dry and to keep as much muck off them as possible. It must have worked because mine never once let me down when it mattered.

"It did jam when I was in training, but that was down to me not working the bolt properly when we were practising rapid fire. I learned the lesson from that and I always worked a tiny bit slower than I could, just to make sure I didn't jam it up.

"Anyway, I was telling you about the scrap... despite our best efforts, part of the line to our right flank was breached, and Jerry got in amongst one of the other companies. The fellows pulled back to their secondary positions and managed to contain Jerry in a sort of box, which he couldn't break out from. He was held and eventually driven back after losing a dozen men.

"That night was a real life-and-death scrap, with each company fighting desperately along the whole of our line. There were no reserve infantry sections left to provide support where our line had been breached and it was only when the battalion cooks, storemen and signallers were chucked in as a last desperate effort, that the balance tipped in our favour.

"By the time the last raid had been fought off every man in my section had been wounded... apart from me – not a scratch. Of the others, none of the wounds were likely to kill anyone, and most had been caused by fragments of Jerry potato mashers, which had rained down on us at times. My mate Jim, and Harry, our corporal, were the most seriously hurt. Both had wounds to the chest received when showing themselves over the top of the trench to throw back potato mashers that had landed on the rim of our trench, threatening to roll in and take someone's head off. Both were bloody lucky not to have been killed. I suppose we all were.

"Once we had secured our lines, both were taken back to the rear to have their shrapnel removed, whilst the other chaps were treated by our orderlies.

"In December we moved off the line and on to Beaufort, where we remained over Christmas. It was good to be off the line at Christmas. We spent much of our time training, but we were also forced to do a lot of reorganisation."

"Why was that?" I asked

"Well after the Jerry raids at the end of November many of the wounded still hadn't returned to the battalion. Harry was back with us, but not Jim. His injuries turned out to be a bit more serious than first thought, but the main reason for the re-organisation was due to the poor performance by some of the other Bantam battalions during those raids. It was the end for the 35th as a Bantam division, and in December over 2,500 soldiers were removed from the 35th due to their unsuitability for front-line duties; they were replaced in January 1917 by normal-height soldiers.

"Our battalion shed fewer than most, but it was still a fair few. Not one of the original Bantams though," said Ben, shaking his head, "not a single one of us."

*****

"You said you were the only soldier in your section to escape being wounded. Were you ever wounded? I asked.

"Only once," Ben replied, thinking for a moment before adding, "I suppose being wounded was a bit of a mixed blessing. If the wound was serious enough to get you off the line, but not serious enough to leave you permanently crippled or in danger of dying, it was quite good."

"What were you treated for?" I asked.

"Nothing terribly exciting really. Like most, I'd had a few visits to the orderlies for my feet, but they were never really bad, as being on the short side I could generally keep out of the water and on the boards, without my napper sticking over the top of the bags. The only Jerry-inflicted injury was caused by a shell splinter," he replied.

"What happened?" I asked.

"A single shell came over and exploded above our trench. I threw myself against the trench wall, but a sliver of shrapnel hit me in the fleshy part of my shoulder and sliced it open, nice and clean, before embedding itself in the ground. The rest of the trench was properly torn up, but I was the only one in the open, so I was the only one hit. It was nothing more than a flesh wound that needed a bit of needlework and I wouldn't have usually gone for treatment, but the CSM wanted to make sure it was cleaned properly, which I suppose was wise – no point having a lucky escape only to die from lockjaw a week later. I was only away from the line for a couple of hours, but it was worth the journey just for the tea.

"Lads used to say how lucky it was to get a 'Blighty Wound', but those kinds of wound usually involved being maimed for the rest of your life, however long that might be. Me, I would have been happy enough with something that got me back to the rear for a week or so. Clean sheets, good grub and a few pretty nurses."

"Do you know what? Once when I visited Jim at a casualty clearing station, during one of his frequent stays, the thing I remember most was the nurses. But not how they looked, how they smelled. They smelled clean. I couldn't tell you what any of them looked like, apart from being pretty – but I can remember exactly how they smelled. The whole place smelled clean, but the nurses smelled even cleaner.

"None of the treatment I ever had involved anything more than being treated in one of the aid posts, which were only a few hundred yards back from the forward trenches, but that few hundred yards was enough to give you a break. The fellows dishing out the treatment there did a good job, and they always seemed to give you the hottest, strongest and sweetest tea. It was worth going back just to get a brew from them. Sad to say, unlike Jim's nurses, all of our orderlies had faces like a bag of spanners and ponged every bit as bad as the rest of us.

"Our company commander was good at spotting the fellows who needed a break and would ask to see their feet, which were invariably manky. He would then send them back to the nearest aid post, knowing that not only would they get their feet cleaned and dried, but the time away from the line would give them a much-needed break. Sometimes that was just enough, for a chap who was close to breaking.

"A fellow who was more seriously hurt would be sent to a nearby dressing station where they would be treated and returned to the company, or if the injury was more serious they'd be sent on to a casualty clearing station, which was usually a safe distance behind the front line... but not always.

"More often than not, the fellows received treatment for their feet or some other sickness, rather than wounds received from Jerry. For a more serious injury requiring a visit to the clearing station, if you were lucky you'd be sent by light railway, but if you were unlucky it would be by a horse-drawn ambulance or motorised truck. It wasn't that the ambulances or the trucks were bad, but the bloody roads, or what was left of them, were lethal. Little more than a series of craters, which would rattle you to death if your wounds were serious. The risk of hitting an unexploded Jerry shell was always present, so even if your wounds didn't kill you, the journey might!"

Chapter 6

Trenches

"You haven't said much about the trenches themselves and what it was like for all of you. I've visited preserved trenches, but they are just a sanitized version of what it must have been like," I said.

"What do you want to know?" Ben replied.

"I suppose I'd like to try and understand what it was like on an average day. Not the times when you were being raided, or raiding the German trenches, but the mundane stuff," I explained.

Ben thought for a moment and took a drag on his latest Black Cat before responding. "Well, I suppose all in all life was bearable, in France at least, but in all honesty, most days I would have rather been on the beach at Meggies chucking sticks for our Nan. It's hard to know where to start trying to describe what it was like, but I'll try and tell you everything I can remember about them. Stop me if I'm boring you.

"You'd be surprised at how few of the Tommies in France actually manned the trenches. Most of the army never spent any time in a frontline trench. They were the home of the infantry, mortar crews, machine gunners, pioneers, some engineers and medical staff. The rest of the army wasn't usually on the front line.

"I don't know how many miles they covered, but they stretched from Belgian sea ports on the North Sea coast, through Flanders and all the way across the top right-hand corner of France to the border with Switzerland. The only stretches I was on were from the area around Wipers following the line south-west as far as the region around Albert, in Picardy.

"The trenches weren't just in farmer's fields as you might think, they ran through towns and villages, often on either side of a road passing through the middle. They went through industrial areas, across rivers, canals, railway tracks. Nothing could stand in the way and if a trench couldn't be dug around something, it would often go right through the middle of it.

"Our time in the trenches wasn't always spent in the main fire trench, the one you would call the front-line trench. Time was also spent as part of the close reserve in one of the support trenches, which were set back just behind the main fire trench, and then the reserve trench was set some way back. We could move between them in reasonable safety, apart from the risk of shelling, through the communications trenches.

"We would rotate from the main fire trench, to close support and then to rest every four or five days or so, depending on the weather and having sufficient manpower to do it. Towards the end of 1916 our casualty rate meant that we had little chance to rotate like that, so we went from main fire trench to support and back again, with only the occasional day at rest.

"Trench life was ruled by routine. I bet Jerry had an almost identical one. We would 'Stand To' about half an hour before first light and remain so until about half an hour after the sun was up. Whilst at post we would get our rum ration. It was bloody horrible at first, but you soon got used to it. It was funny watching the new lads, particularly the younger ones, getting their first tot. Most of them would cough it straight back up.

"After 'Stand To' it would be time for breakfast and then the routine tasks would begin. The trench would be scoured for anything that might attract rats. Once rats got into your trenches, getting rid of them was almost impossible, so prevention was definitely better than cure.

"If a rat had the chance of a meal you couldn't shift the bugger by smacking it over the head with an entrenching tool. In fact, some of them were so big, whacking it over the head was likely to annoy it so much that it would take it off you and whack you right back with your own spade.

"They would chew at anything. We were really strict on keeping the trench free of accessible food, but they would still do their best to get in. It wasn't just food – if you put your webbing or clothing down they would gnaw on that as well. I don't know whether it was because they were able to eat just about anything, or because they associated human equipment with food, or even more worryingly associated humans themselves with food. After all they'd had years of feasting on human flesh. I wonder who tasted better, Jerry or Tommy?

"The only good thing about the rats was that they were impartial. They would happily move from our trenches to the Jerry trenches. They were like the animal equivalent of the Swiss Red Cross, being allowed unobstructed access to all aspects of the war.

"While the little bleeders were horrible and annoying, the biggest problem was them spreading disease from having contact with a thousand rotting bodies and then weeing all over our stuff and in the water. This wasn't a great problem with the drinking water as our water supply had long been secured and made safe. But having water splashed up into your mouth by shell fire, or tripping and falling into the water meant the risk of catching Weil's disease from their pee. Bloody horrible.

"After clean-ups we'd carry out maintenance to the duck boards, fire steps and revetments. When it was wet, which was almost always, the chalky soil would be eroded and there was a risk of collapse if the trench walls weren't shored up properly.

"We would check ammunition stocks and if any ammunition had been fired during the night, you would replenish to bring you up to the right amount.

"Every now and then you would catch latrine duties, which was bloody well horrible, and it was generally given to anyone who had committed some sort of transgression and fallen foul of the CSM. I was quite lucky, I kept my nose clean – avoiding latrine duties was a good reason to keep out of the shit, in more ways than one.

"Keeping the latrines in good order helped stop them overflowing in times of heavy or prolonged rain and flooding the area around the trenches in waste. Life in the trenches was bad enough, without adding to it by wading through pools of shit. Few latrines were anything more than a hole in the ground with a plank over it to sit on. If you were lucky, or an officer, you might have a metal sheet for a roof... rank has its privileges.

"If we were in a reserve trench, after routine maintenance we might take the opportunity for a bit of delousing. I think the lice were worse than the rats, because you couldn't ever get any relief from them. Just like the rats, as well as the constant discomfort the lice also caused disease – how is it that these bloody things are never just horrible in one way, but always have to spread disease as well?

"When we were relieved from the line and moved back to a camp, the first thing most of us wanted to do was delouse. Sometimes we were dusted down with some sort of chemical powder, which was a horrible experience, but at least it gave relief from the itching, even if only for a short time. We were then allowed a hot bath, which was one of the most fantastic feelings ever. When you have lived in squalor and experienced the feeling of disgust at the ingrained dirt that gets into every single pore of your skin, you really appreciate feeling the cleanliness of a hot bath and soap.

"Back there we could get our uniforms steam-cleaned and that sorted the lice out. In the trenches we would have to make do with picking them off ourselves and scraping them from the seams of our uniforms, then crunch the little bastards between the nails of both thumbs until they cracked, and we knew then that they were dead. The best way to remove them from the seams of your uniform was with a lighted candle. You would turn your uniform inside out and then run the flame all along the seams. That would kill the eggs and give a couple of days' relief." Ben shuddered a bit as you do when you get a shiver down your spine, and he had a scratch under his left arm pit, just like you do when you think of something creepy. As he lifted his left arm I saw a large dark patch of what looked like dried blood.

He continued: "During the day whilst all the other stuff was going on we kept a minimum number on the fire step. The rest of the lads would have a couple of hours' sleep in strict rotation, either side of dinner whenever possible.

"You'd think that being on the step during the day would be easy, but I hated it, as being so tired all the time it was just too easy to drift off to sleep. Falling asleep on post was a court martial offence and you could be shot for it, and although I don't know if that ever happened, we were constantly warned about it.

"At least one officer was always on duty and they would constantly walk the length of our company lines both day and night, checking that all was well, but more importantly that we were awake at out posts. None of us minded being regularly checked on, and I was always happy to have the boredom broken by a short, whispered chat.

"'Good morning, Leeman... anything interesting to report?' asks the Lieutenant.

'Yes, sir. It's been all go. The Saxon Regiment played a football match against the Uhlans. It was a great game, which the Uhlans won 2-1, although it didn't help the Saxons when one of the Cheshires bagged their centre-forward with a head shot just after half-time. Cleaned his clock, good and proper!' says I.

"Obviously, I didn't really say that, I just thought it. 'No, Sir – all quiet,' I would reply."

"When not on the step we would take turns to strip and clean our rifles before getting the first sleep. If you were lucky, or unlucky enough to be detailed for something like a trench raid or barbed wiring party, you might be allowed a second kip in the afternoon, before 'Stand To' thirty minutes before dusk until thirty minutes after dark. Depending on the time of year, tea was either just after evening 'Stand To' in winter, or at about 5 o'clock during the lighter evenings of spring and summer.

"When night fell, the trenches came to life.

"You would think that keeping silent would be a natural thing at night in the trenches and sometimes it was, but often it was very noisy. I heard that sometimes our lads and theirs would call out to each other and even got to know each other by name. I don't know if it was true – I just know that we didn't do it in Z Company.

"The time when you are at most risk at the front is when you first move on to the line and relieve the battalion in place – this was always done in darkness. Jerry knew that it took time to become familiar with the layout of your trench and get a routine established, even down to knowing where the best cover was during shelling. If he knew that you were fresh and unfamiliar, that would be the best time to send some whizz-bangs or mortars over. That was when the incoming company would get caught out, not knowing instinctively where the best cover was. In some places the lines were so close together that a big lad had a chance to throw a grenade into the other side's fire trench.

"I heard of a caper near Pozieres when the Aussies and Jerry spent hours chucking grenades at each other from their own trenches. I don't know if that was true or not, but it certainly could be. You might not be able to get one straight in, but it was certainly possible for one to bounce the extra ten yards or so when the ground was firm. I reckon the Aussies would have been at an advantage that day. Our Mills bombs bounced and rolled much better due to their shape, whereas the Jerry potato masher didn't bounce so well. Most of the Aussies were bloody great cricketers and lobbing a Mills was very similar to bowling a cricket ball. Me, I was a footballer, which wouldn't have been much help, as I wouldn't have been keen on trying to kick or head a Mills bomb over – but a good bowler, he'd have been a real asset.

"No, our NCOs made sure that we kept our voices down and never got into conversation with the Jerry soldiers opposing us. But sometimes Jerry wasn't quite so clever.

"Once, when we were on the line near Arras, there was a Jerry with a big, booming, oafish voice. We heard him every day as regular as clockwork 'Herman the German' we called him. One day his voice was missing, it was all quiet. We knew that his company had been replaced by fresh troops. That night we went over, a couple of sections of us, to raid the Jerry trench. We hit them good and proper before they had established their routine, finishing off half a dozen of them and scattering the rest. We blew their comfortable dug-outs to bits, grabbed a prisoner and were back safely in our own lines before they had the chance to regroup.

"The poor bloke who we grabbed looked absolutely terror struck when we got him back, his eyes were bulging, and he was jabbering like a lunatic; well he was jabbering once we took the gag out of his mouth. He was taken away for interrogation and we never saw him again. Yes, keeping your voice down was a good tactic.

"Occasionally, Jerry would shout across to us, wanting to trade our cans of corned beef for some of their sausage. I had tasted their sausage a few times when we had driven them out of their trenches, and it was really tasty, but I wasn't about to eat something that they wanted to trade. God knows what they might have done to it. At least with our bully beef it was sealed in a tin, so if the tin was sealed it was most likely safe.

"Sometimes on quiet nights the sound really carried. You could hear every little clink and rustle from the trenches on the other side. Daytime in the trenches was quite a lonely time and it was a time for thinking, but that could be dangerous, because taking your mind off the job could cost you your life.

"Bad weather was miserable, but safer. In bad weather when you were on the fire step you would keep movement to a minimum, because you didn't want to let the cold in or leave a gap where your waterproof sheet fitted around the collar of your tunic for the rain to run in and soak you even more. You would try and get comfortable, keep still, warm and dry. Being miserable always kept your mind on the job – there wasn't much to distract you. Keeping still was a good tactic to keep you safe, as movement was easily spotted from across the line of trenches. Anything that told Jerry where you were standing was a dangerous mistake to make. You might get away with it the first time, but he would be ready when you made the next movement and you'd be topped off before you knew it.

"In good weather it was much too easy for your mind to drift. On some days, when the sun was shining and the birds were singing it was almost possible to forget there was a war on. You would look out towards the Jerry trenches, with the grass growing and the wild flowers swaying in the breeze, butterflies flitting back and forth, and it was easy to drift away from the trenches and let your thoughts take you to a better, happier place. That happy thought was probably the last thing that went through many a lad's head. Well, the second-to-last thing; the last thing being the round from the Jerry Mauser, that cleaned his clock."

*****

"Darkness was a time for trench raids and it was always better to be the raider than the raided.

"Preparing for the raid meant ensuring no item of our equipment rattled, clanked or gave off any shine. We often had to cover a couple of hundred yards across open ground, so it was important to be silent and well concealed. You were a long way from cover if discovered in no man's land and any noise would result in Jerry firing off a barrage of flares. If one of us made an obvious noise and no flare was sent up, it probably meant that there was a Jerry patrol out and they thought the noise had been made by their own boys.

"Even on dark, overcast nights there was always a risk of a break in the cloud illuminating you. We would dump our tin hats and I usually just tied some hessian sacking around my head and blacked my face, neck and hands with burnt cork. Not like a blackface minstrel from the music hall – just patches and lines to break up the shape. I was lucky because I had a flat snout, but Jim had a long beak that reflected the moonlight. I would always tell him to keep well away from me in case the light reflecting off his beak lit me up.

"We always carried plenty of Mills bombs as well as our rifles and bayonets. One of the officers in our company had bought a supply of Webley revolvers, which would be broken out and issued to several of us going on a raid – and I don't mean just the officers and NCOs. Bayonets were carried, not fixed to rifles as there was no room for a rifle fitted with a bayonet. The revolvers and the Mills bombs were really effective and many of the fellows carried a trench knife rather than a bayonet, thinking it was more usable in confined spaces. I preferred my bayonet.

"Bayonet practice in training had been a great way to get rid of your frustration and aggression. The instructors tried to make training as realistic as possible, but sticking a foot and a half of steel through a scarecrow never prepared us for the reality and the complete bloody horror of it.

"When you stab the dummy, the bayonet goes in quickly and smoothly. It's not like that in real life. It isn't smooth, it hits bone, it's hard to push it through the ribs and there's always the chance it will glance off them.

"Even if you get it right, unless you smash it in, it goes in slowly and you can feel it cracking the bones. Once through the ribs it passes through the guts easily and quickly, before striking the ribs again on the way out the back. I always thought of it as slow, quick, slow... like a dance...not that I was much of a dancer.

"After the first time I used it I never wanted to do it again and would use my rifle, until we got our hands on the extra revolvers. I knew a fellow who was the same, you know? Reluctant to use his bayonet, even though he fitted it to his rifle.

"A couple of things happened that changed my mind, and both happened within minutes of each other. One of my section fired a round from his rifle at close range that went straight through a particularly scrawny Jerry and killed one of our own lads. The Jerry survived because the bullet missed everything important and passed right through. When the bullet hit our lad in the bottom of his spine it was moving slowly enough to lodge inside him, but fast enough to shatter his backbone. He screamed in agony for nearly 10 minutes, until he died. When he died it was a relief for him and the rest of us.

"Then as we were pulling back to our own lines another Tommy died for his reluctance to use the bayonet. Face to face with a Jerry he fired his rifle once and knocked the Jerry down. He moved in – the Jerry was all but dead, but he had to make sure he wasn't going to get back up again. But instead of using the bayonet he fired into him again, at close range, killing him instantly. It was the last round in his magazine, and before he changed magazines he was dead. He took a Jerry bayonet right through his chest as he tried to reload.

"After that I used my bayonet. I rammed it in with all my strength. Never again did I feel the resistance of the ribs on the way in, or the softness of the belly, or the ribs and spine on the way out of his back. The bayonet went in with such force it was like ramming it in and out of a tin of bully beef... no mucking about, I just got on with it.

"Raids were carried out for many reasons; you'd think that the main reason was to kill Jerry troops, but usually that wasn't it. It was far more important to try and capture a couple of prisoners to gain information, and to grab maps and documents that might be of value. Maps containing artillery positions and documents detailing unit names and locations and numbers of reserve troops were particularly valuable; especially if we could get them back for our own artillery to fire on them before their gunners were aware we had the information.

"The capture of a Jerry officer was always a big goal, but I was never on a raid when we got our hands on one. They were hardly ever in the main front-line trenches and their dug-outs were usually heavily defended. We managed to kill quite a few, by getting a few Mills bombs into a dug-out, but winkling them out would have taken too long.

"Some of the best intelligence was other stuff. A lot of the time it was what we saw with our eyes. Going into a trench and seeing hardly a scrap of food and what there was being stale and covered in weevils told us how desperate Jerry was in the trenches. I remember taking some of their black bread. It smelled awful. I didn't eat it, but when I broke it open it looked like it was made of sawdust, because that's exactly what they had baked into their bread.

"One of our companies grabbed a load of cinema film cannisters and brought them back. They went well back to the Divisional HQ, but we got to see them a while later when we were resting in camp. They showed Jerry soldiers handing out great big round loaves of bread to the local French population in the territory they had captured. I wonder what the Jerry soldiers in the trenches thought of that. Watching that load of nonsense while they were eating sawdust."

"Suddenly a Charlie Chaplin film doesn't seem so bad." I said.

"I suppose not," said Ben, before continuing: "On one of our raids, one of the corporals took a loaf of bread and a lump of bully beef. After we cleared out the trench and scattered Jerry, he left them on a table with a note telling them to enjoy it. I bet that bashed their spirits as much as the actual raid."

"Did officers go on trench raids? I asked.

"Sometimes, although when they did it was usually a very junior officer or a replacement officer who knew next to nothing; we were going out to collect intelligence, not deliver it, gift-wrapped, to Jerry. Yes, sometimes a young subaltern came with us to gain a bit of experience. They never led the raid, they were with us to learn and get 'blooded'."

"We were all nervous before our first raid, but there was one occasion when a young subaltern was so panicky before setting out on a raid that he accused me of pinching his Webley.

"During final preparations to move he checked his holster and it was empty. He started looking on the ground, on the fire step, he ran back into the dug-out to look for it. He was getting into a right state when he saw me checking the rounds in the revolver I had collected for the raid and demanded I hand his Webley over to him.

"I told him it wasn't his, that he had his own, at which point he pulled open the flap to show me an empty holster.

"It was at this point one of the corporals came up and said quietly, 'Sir, the reason your holster is empty, is cos you are holding your revolver in your right hand. Now, why don't we take a pew and check your ammunition?' Do you know what? None of us laughed or thought any the less of him. Every one of us knew what he was going through. At one time or other we'd all felt that tide of panic rising up from our chest into our throat, until it felt like we were choking.

"He completed the raid with no problem and went on to become a good officer. He was badly wounded near Wipers in 1917 and went back to Blighty. I don't know what became of him, but he never came back to the battalion," Ben explained.

"Do you think the trench raids really achieved anything?" I asked.

"If you asked one of the officers, particularly the less experienced ones, they would agree with the officers of field rank that the raids were useful for keeping us all alert and motivated. It helped keep us sharp and aggressive. Not many of us went along with that. Most raids simply resulted in the death of a few men on both sides and there were hardly any gains, only losses. Most of the experienced lieutenants and captains felt the same way we did... a pointless waste of life," Ben replied.

*****

Ben took out his smokes and offered me one, which I declined... again. He lit his Black Cat and continued. "The weather could help conceal noise or give the game away. Obviously, wind carries sound, and it will carry it further on a stronger wind, unless of course the wind is strong enough for its own noise to drown your sound out. On a light wind, sound will travel in both directions, more so towards those downwind, but it also comes the other way.

"Weather affects how far sound will travel and understanding that gives you a good idea about how far away the source of the sound is. It might not be highly accurate, but any little bit of information can be important especially when it fits in with other bits.

"In cold weather, or in the evening when the temperature drops after a warm day, sound carries a fair distance further, especially low to the ground, which is useful as that is where we all were. But in warm weather the sound seems to rise on the warm air, so it doesn't carry so well, or if it does it rises and goes over your head. Sticking your head up and cocking an ear towards Jerry isn't good for your long-term survival prospects.

"Sound doesn't travel so well in the snow, it seems to get drawn in and soaked up by it. Sound carries for much shorter distances in the snow and always appears muffled, so it's much harder to make out exactly what is causing it and where it's coming from.

"Fog is really odd. In a real pea-souper it's easy to get disorientated or become complacent when moving, which can be fatal when a small clear patch suddenly appears. In fog some sounds seem to travel further, and other sounds don't. The deeper the sound, the more it seems to carry. I remember hearing the foghorns warning shipping off the coast back at home and when I asked why they sounded like they did, our Charlie told me it was because low-pitched sounds travel further than high-pitched sounds in fog. Always trust an engineer.

"There used to be a bit of nonsense that anyone taking a third light for their fag would collect their iron rations. You know? A quick injection to the napper. I reckon that old wives' tale must have cost hundreds of lives. Jerry certainly didn't need three chances to take his shot. Any speck of light would be an invitation to a Jerry sniper. That might be a lucifer being struck, a drag on a fag, or even the glint of light on a pair of spectacles or cap badge, so you had to be on your toes all the time. One mistake was likely to be your last, never mind three.

"One of our snipers told me that the light from a lucifer or a fag being dragged on could be seen from about two miles away and the distance between the lines was always much less than that. I don't think I was ever in a forward trench that was more than five hundred yards from Jerry and nearly always much less than half of that. Even our second line of trenches was well within 500 yards, so you weren't safe there either.

"You always had to be aware of the wind direction, which wasn't always easy. Wind carried sounds between the lines and in the case of smoking or the smell of cooking, it gave away a lot of information. I could tell who was in the trench opposite by the smell of the pipe tobacco and I could also tell when he was on duty and when he was resting, just by the smell of the tobacco smoke. That sort of stuff was useful when planning trench raids. It gave information on trench routine and the absence of a regular smoker might let you know that Jerry had moved troops off the line and brought in fresh troops who had not yet established a routine.

"Course, telling wind direction wasn't always easy from down inside a trench and sticking a wet finger up in the air to check wasn't really an option... not if you planned any future use for that finger!" And he held up his right hand, with the back of it facing me and his middle finger bent over into the palm of his hand as if it had gone missing in action, before laughing.

"Bloody hell Ben, I wasn't expecting a science lecture," I said.

"Wait until I get started on ballistics and the trajectory of trench mortar bombs," he replied.

"I can hardly wait," I replied with a hint of sarcasm. "Don't you know any funny stories about rats? Or trench foot? This is like being back in school with the world's youngest teacher."

"Alright, I'll tell you a funny one," he said, before going on without a pause: "There's a Tommy on sentry duty near Albert and he hears the sound of troops approaching, so calls out; 'Halt! Who goes there?' The response comes back, 'Scots Guards.' And the sentry replies, 'Pass, Scots Guards.' 10 minutes later the sentry hears more soldiers approaching and calls out; 'Halt! Who goes there?' A voice comes back, 'The Buffs.' And the sentry replies, 'Pass, Buffs.' About 20 minutes later the sentry hears more footsteps approaching so calls out; 'Halt, who goes there?' The response comes back, 'Mind your own bloody business!' And the sentry replies 'Pass, Diggers!'" And at this hilarious punchline Ben collapsed onto his back, laughing fit to bust!

"You know you're not supposed to laugh at your own jokes?" I said.

"I know," Ben replied, "But you've got to cut me a bit of slack, I haven't heard that one in years."

*****

After composing himself, Ben went on: "So what else can I tell you about the trenches? I know, 'Snipers', or rather how to avoid them.

"Most of the lads were afraid of snipers. Even our own snipers were viewed with a mixture of admiration and fear. I don't think anyone that wasn't a sniper could understand them... not really understand them.

"I don't think there was any one type of person who became a sniper. You'd think that anyone who became one would be a bit of a loner, and I'm sure some were, but the ones I knew were just like the rest of us – until it was time for work. I knew a couple of them in Z Company. When I say I knew them, I'm not sure that's the right word. I knew the bit they shared with the rest of us, but I'm sure there was more to them.

"Arthur, the older of them, was like 2 people rolled into one. When he wasn't doing his job he was relaxed, affable and friendly, but in the couple of hours before he went to work his whole manner changed; he became quiet and went into his own private world.

"It was as though he was praying; like when our old neighbour in Fildes Street would pray using her rosary beads, except he was praying in complete silence – but his position was the same, sort of hunched over his beads, but his rosary wasn't designed for praying, it was designed for something completely different. His beads were the rounds of ammunition he was preparing for use and the parts of his rifle which he stripped, checked, cleaned, put back together and checked again.

"Once he had done that, he would do the whole thing again, sitting, head bowed in his own thoughts as he checked every round for a second time, then stripped and cleaned every part of his rifle before re-assembling it and checking every single part worked smoothly and silently.

"His final check was a third check of every single round. He would look again for any tiny marks or imperfections, which were then polished with carborundum paste, until the head and the whole case was perfect, reducing any risk of a stoppage and ensuring that each round flew straight. If after polishing it wasn't perfect, he would discard it into a bucket.

"Each day, before preparing his rifle and ammunition, he would inspect the vegetation around the trenches with a small mirror. He did this religiously. If he was going to be firing from a trench he would use a periscope or take a mirror on a stick and examine the area around his firing point. But he would be checking the area slightly along from where he put the mirror, he never put the mirror out too close to the exact location just in case he was being watched by Jerry. He would always recce half a dozen locations, partly because he was looking for the one that gave him the best concealment, but also because checking a single location would give his position away. Even if he knew the first location was going to be an ideal spot, he would still recce several others.

"He would match his personal concealment and that on his rifle to the vegetation in his chosen place. He would head back to the rear trenches to gather it to ensure it would be fresh, and so blend in perfectly. It was something I copied if I was ever going on a patrol to just observe Jerry. I thought it best to watch and learn my lessons from him, rather than the hard and final way.

"He always followed the same pattern – one minute he would be playing cards, chatting, laughing and joking, and exactly 2 hours before he went to work he would fold his hand and leave the game, then move a few paces away and sit quietly preparing himself mentally and physically along with all his kit for the job ahead.

"At some point we'd look up from the game and he would be gone. One minute preparing, and the next gone. Most of the time nobody would see or hear him leave. Even when the floor of the trench was filled with water and nobody could move without the duck boards flexing and sloshing the water about, Arthur still managed to depart like a ghost. Sometimes we didn't notice his absence until the silence was shattered by a single shot.

"We could often judge how experienced the Jerries were in the trenches opposite by the amount of noise coming from their trench after one of their lads had been taken by a sniper. If they were experienced troops there would be nothing – no noise. They would remove the dead man in complete silence. If they were inexperienced there would be a lot of shouting and cursing, which was quite reassuring for us, although not for the poor bugger on the receiving end. I can't ever remember hearing a sniper's shot then hearing the person at the other end crying in pain. It was one shot and then gone – no crying out, no pain, just... gone.

"I once asked him how we could calmly take another man's life without any warning and without any provocation. He replied that the provocation was the helmet and the location. Had the helmet remained in Germany, the wearer would have been safe.

"If aiming at a helmet he would use the rim of the coal scuttle as his aiming point. There was no chance that the bullet would ricochet – a Jerry helmet could never withstand a direct hit from a bullet. It didn't matter if the round went slightly low into the face or slightly high and through the head. Jerry helmets were quite brittle, and when hit would often disintegrate, so even a glancing hit could result in death for the Jerry inside it. Our tin hat was a little bit more robust and tended to stay in one piece. It wouldn't give any protection against anything other than shrapnel, or a glancing rifle shot... an accurate round would clean your clock, good and proper.

"Arthur was particularly fond of the Jerry field cap, describing the two distinctive little roundels on the front of the hat as near-perfect bull's eyes – top roundel for distances over 300 hundred yards – lower roundel for anything under 300.

"Reg, the younger of the snipers, was a very different sort, and he had a completely different way of preparing – not quite so meticulous, and a different way of justifying his job.

"When I asked him how he felt about killing Jerry he simply replied; 'Rabbits! I think of them as rabbits.' Apparently, as a kid he'd spent hours with a shotgun, taking rabbits from the local fields, collecting them, paunching them before taking them home for his Mam to put in the pot. And that's how he looked at it; Jerry or rabbit, it was all the same. Just as he wished the rabbit no ill will and didn't want to injure it and leave it to suffer, it was the same with Jerry, his wish was a clean kill.

"The only similarity between them was that they both worked alone, rather than as a pair. Both reckoned that two people were easier to spot than a single person.

"I don't think I could ever have done their job. I had to think of Jerry as a threat, not just a chap wearing a different uniform. When we were under attack I had no problem firing at Jerry without hesitation.

Similarly, when going forward, it was him or me. There was no choice and I was quick. I fired without hesitation because it was him or me, and better his mother crying than our Mam. That's not to say I didn't feel sympathy afterwards, of course I did. Every single time I fired my rifle I aimed to take my enemy as quickly and painlessly as possible, but give him no quarter. But as soon as the fight was over I would retreat into my own thoughts. I held no hatred for Jerry – it was simply kill or be killed.

"When you were on the fire step you often saw Jerry come out of the trench, keeping low to repair the barbed wire or telephone wire and that was when I struggled to fire. I couldn't see that man as a real threat to my life in that moment. But then you'd think that he was repairing the barbed wire that might just snag you or one of your mates and hold you up in full view of their rifles and machine gunners. And they would have no hesitation firing.

"So, with some reluctance, I would line up my sights, steady my breathing and take up the pressure on my trigger. Just before releasing the shot I would breathe out and then hold it when my lungs were half-empty, then gently squeeze my trigger. The thump of the round and the recoil in my shoulder mixed with the drop of Jerry's head. I never needed to fire a second time.

"It was never an easy decision, but it was something that had to be done. It was the right thing to do. The right thing to do! I can't believe I've even said those words. Millions of us trying to kill each other because it was the right thing to do. For God's sake, none of this was the right thing to do. The right thing to do was to carry on working into old age at the sleeper mill before retiring with a gold watch.

"The right thing to do was to grow up in my own good time, start courting, get married and have children. That was the right thing to do, there was nothing right about being in a country far from home and killing another fellow in a different suit in a country that was just as far from his home." When Ben finished speaking, he took out a fag and offered me one.

"No thanks, Ben, I still don't smoke," I said, declining his kind offer... again.

"Suit yourself," he said, before continuing: "The mad thing is that once a Jerry had surrendered, he stopped being an enemy. We treated him fairly and we looked after him, just as we hoped we would be treated if we ever had the misfortune to be taken by Jerry. After one scrap we moved some wounded Jerries back to one of our aid stations.

Most of them made it, but it was obvious that one of them wasn't going to, so we put the stretcher down.

"He knew he hadn't long left and we knew it too. One of the lads unscrewed the cap from his water bottle and gave him a few sips of water. Then he took out a fag, lit it and gave him a couple of puffs on it. The lad was so weak that he could hardly take a proper drag on it, and when he did, and breathed it in, he wheezed as he blew the smoke out.

"After a couple of little drags on the fag he turned his eyes towards the water bottle again. The bottle was lifted to his lips and just enough water was poured to wet them. The Jerry put out his left hand to me and I took it. Jerry gave my hand a little, weak squeeze. I held on to it. The last time my hand had been squeezed like that was the last time I was with our Dad, so I knew what was coming soon.

"Jerry said nothing – he was too weak. He just turned his eyes to each of us in turn and gave the tiniest little nod and then he was gone. The little nod and the little squeeze just faded away to nothing... and so did he.

"His gestures said what he couldn't say out loud, thanking us for what we had done for him at the end. It wasn't much, just a bit of kindness, but at least that was the last thing that happened to him in life. In the middle of all the bad stuff, his last seconds were filled with a little bit of kindness.

"We picked up the stretcher and took him further back. There were three or four lines of bodies; Tommies and Jerries lying side by side. We lifted him off the stretcher and laid him alongside another German lad.

"A medical orderly was checking each in turn to ensure that none were still alive, and on another line a chaplain was going to each body in turn, giving the last rites. I don't know how many of them were religious in life, but it was probably better to bless someone who wasn't religious than to neglect someone who was – so they all got the same blessing. All were treated equally, Jerry and Tommy alike. It was the right thing to do. None of us had a problem with that.

"Burying the dead was a horrible job, but a necessary one. It gave them some respect and at least their graves would be marked. I remember passing a burial party near one of the casualty centres. There were about 40 bodies laid out on the ground. One was covered in a union flag. The others were covered in their greatcoats or issue blankets. At least those who died at the clearing stations had their graves properly marked."

It was at this point I said something I immediately regretted; "I've seen photographs of British soldiers posing for photographs wearing

German helmets, and other stuff, although I can't really think what the other bits of kit were. Maybe it was just helmets or field caps. I just wondered how they came by them," I said.

"Well, they took them from the Germans. What are you getting at?" Ben asked. "You don't think we took them from the dead, do you?"

I knew the question was a mistake. Ben almost recoiled in horror. He didn't speak – he didn't need to. His expression was one of disappointment and I saw him lean backwards away from me to increase the distance between us. It was only a matter of a couple of inches, but it was enough. He went from leaning forward towards me to leaning back, taking his weight on his arms behind him. I knew the question had hurt him and in turn, his response had hurt me. We sat in silence for about a minute, with Ben looking in my direction, but not at me, he looked past me. After a short time he leaned forward again, but didn't turn his eyes to me, he looked down towards the ground... towards his feet.

Then he spoke. "The lads would pick discarded things up if it was safe, but more often they would exchange bits of food or a few fags with Jerry prisoners to get hold of a helmet or something like that. I don't think I ever saw someone take a helmet or any piece of kit, like a belt buckle, from a Jerry prisoner without paying him for it in some way. And the Jerry was always happy to make the trade. I mean he was going to need food or a smoke long before he was going to need his helmet again.

"Guns were different. Obviously, we couldn't leave the prisoner with his rifle or pistol, so they would always be taken as soon as a soldier surrendered. A Jerry pistol was a valuable souvenir, so it was quite common for the lad who'd taken the prisoner to hold on to it as a keepsake; either to take home, or to trade on again. Strictly speaking stuff like that should have been handed over, but it seldom was, and a blind eye was usually turned.

"By the time I got to France it was very rare to see one of those spiked helmets, let alone capture anyone who was wearing one. Most of them had long since gone and I'm sure that by 1916 those helmets were only being worn by the higher-ranking Jerry officers, most of whom were never to be seen near the front line. On the line Jerry was mostly wearing his field cap, without the peak, and then we started to see more and more of the big coal-scuttle-type helmets. They were the only ones I usually saw.

"I remember the first time I saw a Jerry in one of those field caps without the peak. I thought he was a sailor, not a soldier, because all our caps had peaks. The only people I had ever seen wearing a cap without a peak were in the navy, so I stupidly assumed that the Kaiser's fleet had taken up positions in the nearby trenches. Mind you, when you saw how deep the water was in some of those trenches after heavy rain, perhaps the navy would have been more at home than the army. Sometimes the ground was so wet and trenches so full of water that both fleets could have fought a battle without any risk of running aground." Ben smiled, and I was relieved to see it.

He continued: "I was never tempted to take anything personal from a prisoner or a dead Jerry and I never saw any of my mates do it either. I know it happened, but it wasn't commonplace and those who did it were never approved of – quite the opposite really.

"I remember one day when we were walking into Poperinghe, I think it was. There were about half a dozen of us walking from a camp nearby. During a break in the training we had a day to ourselves and we had permission to leave the camp and head into the town.

"We were walking through one of the streets leading towards the Market Square when we were approached by a soldier from another regiment. He beckoned us into a doorway, acting all suspiciously. As we walked towards him he checked all around him to make sure no one was watching and as we closed in he rolled up his left sleeve to reveal about three or four wristwatches strapped to his arm. He was also holding a handful of pocket watches. 'Good morning gentlemen. Would either of you like to buy a quality German watch, all still ticking, which is more than can be said for their previous owners!' he announced.

"Wristwatches were usually worn by officers, not many of the lads had them. We went to walk on past, when he jumped out of the doorway and blocked the narrow pavement as we tried to pass. A big, stupid grin on his fat face, with his left arm outstretched so we could see the watches. As we pushed past him, Albert reached out his right hand and grabbed the fat-faced bugger by the throat and shoved him hard back against the wall of the building, cracking his head on the wall, before walking on without breaking step. None of us glanced back, none of us spoke. Actions speak louder than words, and Bert had spoken for all of us – none of us had any time for stuff like that.

"Many of us would take things from our friends who had clicked it; but that wasn't the same. They were our friends who we had always shared things with and there was no reason why that should end after they'd gone. I don't mean personal items, obviously. Personal items were always parcelled up and sent back home to family and loved ones, but pieces of equipment, particularly ones in good condition, would often be taken from a friend to replace a piece of your own worn-out equipment.

"Ammunition pouches, knives, entrenching tools, that sort of stuff. A good coat and particularly waterproofs or oil skins were valuable, as were Wellington boots, or even good-quality ammo boots. If your boots were falling apart a pair of good-quality boots taken from a mate might just keep you alive. I reckon we all looked on stuff like that as being gifts from those boys we served with that would be given willingly had they known the circumstances. The only personal item I ever took was that knitted scarf, the one I told you about." As Ben finished speaking, I thought it only right to apologise.

"I'm sorry, Ben." I said.

"What for?" he asked.

"For asking you that stupid, bloody question. I know it hurt you."

Ben replied, "Thanks. I know you meant no offence. He paused for a few seconds before continuing. "There was one time when this young Tommy from Y Company saw one of those big fancy Jerry officer's helmets lying out in no man's land. Against orders, he crawled out from the trench and grabbed the helmet. As he pulled the helmet he realised there was still a head inside it."

"Bloody hell. That must have been horrible," I said.

Ben continued; "It's worse than you'd think. The head then opened its eyes and spoke to him, saying 'Help me out of this mud and I will let you have my helmet and my sword as well if you want. Just don't leave me to die in this mud.'

"So, Tommy pulls and pulls. He pulls for ages and eventually manages to get the Jerry's shoulder out of the mud.

"Now both sides realised he was trying to save this Jerry officer, so no one fired at him. He dug with his hands, pulled some more and dug some more. After what seemed like hours of graft he had managed to get the Jerry out to just below his chest.

"Tommy says, 'Bloody hell, Fritz, I'm exhausted. You're just too heavy, I just don't think I'm strong enough to pull you out.'

"Jerry replies; 'Would it help if I took my feet out of the stirrups?' "

And with that Ben fell backwards, laughing hysterically – I joined in, but I was laughing more at him laughing than at the story.

When we stopped laughing, I said: "I told you before that you're not supposed to laugh at your own jokes... and another thing, I first heard that one about 40 years ago."

"So what? I first told it about a hundred years ago," Ben replied.

I was relieved to hear him joking after I'd been such a tit by asking such a stupid question. Imagine waiting so long to speak with someone and then falling out with them.

Ben was on a bit of a roll now and he went on: "I once spent the day in a shell hole with a dead Jerry, waiting for darkness, before I could move back to my own lines without being killed."

"This isn't another crappy joke is it?" I asked.

"No, this is true, not a joke," he replied. "We'd gone out at night to repair a section of wire when something alerted Jerry. It wasn't any of us, but that didn't stop all hell breaking loose. Fortunately, we were on our bellies when it all kicked off and we just kept low. We had a small ridge between us and Jerry, so we kept low and began to make our way along the gulley from left to right. We moved slowly, but steadily. Then we started to get a few mortars dropping around us and it was then that I was separated from the rest of my section.

"A mortar shell landed about three or four yards ahead, between me and the rest of the lads. I buried my head in the ground and when I lifted it, not only had my mates disappeared, so had the little ridge, which meant that the route they had just taken was now in clear view of the Jerry fire trench. Jerry fired a couple of pistol flares up, the kind that just lit up for about 15 seconds, but during those 15 seconds they raked the ground all around with one of their heavy machine guns, one of the 08s. There was nothing to do but breathe out and press myself as flat as possible, trying to bury myself in the earth, which was difficult while trying not to attract attention by moving. What was left of the ridge might hold when hit by a sweeping burst, but if they concentrated fire on a particular area, they would soon blast it to bits.

"I lay absolutely still for what seemed like ages, just taking tiny sips of air, so if anyone could see me they wouldn't see me breathing. From the earth that was landing on my back I knew they couldn't see me, and they obviously didn't know exactly where I was because they swept their fire all over the place. I just lay there praying that the ridge would hold up.

"Just when I thought they had given up they sent up a flare on a rocket, one of those that then drift down slowly on a parachute. It was like bloody daylight and it stayed lit for over a minute. I was expecting another burst from the 08 when there were a couple of rifle cracks from our lines. The two shots were so close together it was almost like a single shot, and what followed was pandemonium in the Jerry lines. I found out later that the Jerry 08 crew had thrown caution to the wind in order to kill us and a couple of our snipers had put paid to their little game.

"As soon as the shouting began in the Jerry trench I made a quick right turn and was over the ridge to my right and down the gentle slope, crawling as fast as I could towards our own lines. I had covered about twenty or thirty yards before Jerry recovered and put up another parachute flare, which was followed by a couple of mortars.

"Everything seemed to be heading in my direction, so I thought that the rest of the section had either made good their escape or were dead – it was just me they were trying to kill now. I hadn't heard anyone cry out, so I hoped the rest of the lads had made it to safety.

"I looked towards our lines, which were still a long way off, and I knew there was no way I could cover that distance. There was a deep crater to my right, so I slipped over the edge and rolled down into it. At least now I was safe from direct fire and relatively safe from mortar fire, unless one dropped in alongside me.

"I lay on my back looking up at the sky, which was lit up by yet another flare, and for the first time in ages took a big gulp of air, safe from Jerry eyes. I was gasping like a fish out of water, trying not to suffocate. After a few minutes, I started to recover, my breathing slowed, and my chest stopped heaving as if it was going to burst. I rolled to my left and came face to face with another soldier, wearing a coal-scuttle helmet, staring wide-eyed as though in shock, directly in my face. I grabbed him by the throat with my right hand and as I did so, his helmet came off and rolled away down into the crater.

"His eyes remained wide open and he didn't make a sound. He just rocked backwards and lay there as I threw my right leg over him and rolled hard to land on top of him, still clutching his throat with my right hand whilst grabbing for my bayonet with my left hand. I fumbled, trying to pull it clear of its scabbard and then I realised that this wasn't much of a scrap as my new-found friend was already dead.

"I stayed on top of him, straddling him for a few moments before rolling back off him, away to my left, onto my back again. I pulled my bayonet out, then did a quick recce of the rest of the crater to make sure there were no other surprise occupants. It was just the two of us.

"I fully expected to get my bearings and then be on my way back to our lines, but for the next half an hour Jerry seemed determined to light up the whole of no man's land for hundreds of yards either side of me. I didn't know if they were hunting me, the rest of my section, or if they were trying to draw fire from our snipers, to pinpoint their positions. Either way, the light thrown up by the flares was soon replaced by daylight.

"The sun came up and began to warm the ground. I checked my rifle and ammunition. The crater was big enough for me to follow the sun as it moved around, in order to keep warm. As it warmed up I began to get thirsty, so started on my water. By midday I was trying to avoid the sun and find a little shade, but with the sun directly overhead there was none to be found. I took off my stripped-down webbing and tunic, then covered my head with the tunic.

"Late in the afternoon, it began to cool down, so my tunic and my webbing went back on. My water bottle was getting low, so I crawled over to Jerry and rolled him onto his side to get at his water bottle. When I rolled him over I saw he had a decent sized hole in the back of his neck, with a few flies crawling in and out of it, but I couldn't see another hole anywhere else – not that I spent very long looking. It looked like a shrapnel wound, and judging by his wound, his colour and the fact that he hadn't really started to pong, he hadn't been dead for very long. I had no idea how he got there, but I reckon he had probably been with a bunch of his mates, doing what me and mine had been doing.

"I used my folding knife to cut through the straps and removed his water bottle, which was almost full. I poured a little into my hand and smelled it. It smelled OK, but not like our water, so it was either fresh and not treated with chemicals, or dirty and not treated with chemicals. I decided not to risk it... not yet anyway.

"Jerry had a little map case slung around him, which I found when I was looking for his water bottle. There was nothing much in it. I went through his pockets and found his pay book and a few photographs, which I put inside the map case. He only had one identity tag, so I left it on him. His pay book would be enough for our side to let his side know he was dead and the tag would be enough to ensure he had a marked grave. He had a pipe and some pipe tobacco and some lucifers. They went in the case as well. I was gasping for a smoke, but there was no way I could light up, the smoke would bring all hell down on me.

"And then we just lay there together, looking up at a clear blue sky." As he said this, Ben lay back with his hands folded behind his neck and looked up at our clear, dark sky.

"Did you speak to him?" I asked.

"What would have been the point of that, he didn't give the impression of being very chatty, and my German was a bit on the rusty side," Ben replied, before going on; "No, I didn't talk to him... not until I was about to slip out of the hole when it was fully dark.

"I put the map case with his personal effects inside my tunic. I may have told him I would get his stuff back to his family before slipping away over the lip of the crater and back towards our lines.

"In the darkness I made slow progress, keeping silent until I was close enough to hear voices coming from our fire trench. I managed to crawl to within about ten yards and could clearly hear a conversation going on, so I hissed to them; 'Lads, it's Private Leeman from Z Company. I'm out to the right of you. Tell me when you want me to crawl towards you.' "

A reply came back, "Who the bloody hell said that?"

"A second voice in the trench said, 'Well I hope to hell it's Private Leeman from Z Company!' followed by some muffled sniggering from the trench."

"I thought it was quite funny too, but I didn't dare laugh. Not yet anyway.

"Then a voice from the trench hissed; 'Leeman, start crawling in as slowly as possible and slide over the bags. Don't lift your head, or it'll be the last thing you do.' I did exactly as I was told."

"It took me about 2 minutes to cover the last 10 yards, before sliding head first down into the trench and landing amongst X Company. I was taken to their company dug-out and I handed over the map case and before reporting what had happened to me. I was told that the rest of my section had made it back to X Company lines the night before and they had been expecting me this evening. Sadly, no one had bothered to prepare tea and cakes for me, which was a bit disappointing.

"I never got to find out if the Jerry was ever recovered by his side or ours and given a decent burial, or whether he just slowly rotted and disappeared into the earth in the crater. A few months later I had a similar experience with a dead Tommy. He was a Cheshire... a private soldier – just a little older than me.

"The thing is, the feelings I had towards both fellows were the same. I never thought one a friend and the other an enemy. The dead are the dead. It's a great leveller... everyone's equal. I might have felt differently had I been the one who had killed my Jerry, or if I had seen him kill one of my mates, but I probably wouldn't have. He was just doing his job the same as the Cheshire and the same as me."

When Ben appeared to have finished speaking, I asked; "What were the Jerry's chances of being recovered and buried properly?"

Ben replied; "In that sector... not very good. It was hard to recover a body from no man's land and it only took a few shells to bury the remains. It was different on those occasions when we had advanced and held some ground, which didn't seem to happen too often, but when it did, once the wounded had been checked by the medical orderlies they were then moved by the field ambulance to the dressing stations, Jerry and Tommy alike. Then the dead would be gathered for removal or burial, again Jerry and Tommy alike; sometimes side by side, sometimes in separate lines, but always close to each other.

"The packs and the equipment of our lads would be checked. Personal effects and treasured items were kept together to be shipped home to the family. We had a sergeant who would ensure that any letters found in a soldier's kit that hadn't been opened were opened and rustled up, folded and re-folded a few times.

"The same with any letter that arrived within a day or two of death. He would open it and fold it and refold it, so that when it was returned to the family, they would at least have the comfort of believing that their son or husband had received it and read it. I don't know if he was supposed to do that, but he reckoned it would bring a bit of comfort to them – as if anything we did could ever bring any sort of comfort or consolation to a wife or mother, or a dad or a brother. But it showed he cared and that, despite everything, some good remained.

"Even though he opened them and crumpled and re-folded them, he never read the letters, because they were personal, not meant for anyone else. He was a good man. I saw him die not 10 feet from me during the advance on Houthulst Forest in October 1917. After the fighting there we had the chance to recover him and the others. One of the corporals in the platoon did the same for him and his family and then assumed the letter-opening job for the other lads who drew the full issue after the sergeant had gone.

"Any military equipment that was in good order was shared out, as was any food. Over the next few weeks, before the family back home had been given the word, parcels would keep arriving from home for the lads who had clicked it. If they obviously contained food, it was shared out amongst the lads who had received no parcels. Personal items were returned to the family, but any letters arriving after the soldier's death was entered in the regimental records were returned unopened.

"Most of the lads who received no parcels were recent replacements. I wonder how it affected them, knowing they were eating the food of a dead man. Lads who had come in as replacements from other battalions after recovering from wounds took it in their stride, but not the new lads. Some just couldn't eat the stuff. We were happy to take it off their hands. We knew that they would get used to it, but if they didn't live long enough to get used to it... well, we just hoped that their Mams were good at baking.

"Course, there were some who never received a parcel. Some had no family, others were under age and hadn't told their families where they were. I was glad that our Mam knew. It was bad enough deceiving her before enlisting, I couldn't continue with the deceit, but I could understand and sympathise with those who did.

"Much of the time everything I just told you about didn't happen, we just didn't have the time, because the ground taken wasn't held for long enough to do all that stuff. Men were recovered months later, unrecognisable, or in many cases simply never found at all.

"During the months we were around Wipers, the crump holes were often littered with dead. If he was one of ours we would try and recover him, but that was easier said than done. Some of the holes were so deep that anyone slipping into one would stand a good chance of never getting out again.

"Often the dead became quite familiar to us and you almost looked out for them. They were like route markers and when one of them finally disappeared it was something you missed. Does that sound cruel?" Ben asked.

I thought for a second or two before responding, "Not really. Things have changed a bit and these days people your age class a tragedy as a bad haircut, or not being able to get a phone signal. If you were to grieve over every dead soldier you saw, you would just crack up and go mad. We have the same now – black humour amongst people who see tragedies day in, day out. Policemen, firemen, paramedics – you know the medics that go out to treat badly injured people; they make light of it and crack jokes, because the alternative is not to be able to function and do their job. It's often the only way to cope without going around the bend."

"What's a phone signal?" Ben asked.

"I'll tell you later," I replied.

Ben nodded and then went on: "Usually it was the colour of a body that changed. When the body was fresh, I mean recently dead, it was white. Not the sort of white of a living person, but a pale white, almost transparent, so you could see the veins. It changed from this white colour to a yellowy colour, before going from yellow to green. Finally, the flesh would turn black. If it was warm, or anything other than freezing cold, they would also bloat up. It was a horrible sight.

"I remember one body that was different, within days it turned from a body into a deflated sort of thing, like the bladder from a football. It went from being a man, to just a skin, almost flat; as though completely deflated. I don't know why that was, because there were other bodies all around him and they did the usual colour change and bloating thing. It was really odd.

"It was a terrible thing to leave them there, as though we didn't care. I wonder what their families would have thought had they known, but the truth is recovering them was often simply too dangerous. It still didn't sit right, though.

"Until I'd seen death right in front of me, close-up, I don't think I'd ever appreciated how special it was to be alive. To see, hear, touch, taste and smell all the things around me. If I had, if more of us had, then we'd have realised that there had to be better alternatives to fighting wars. If we'd put as much thought in to avoiding the war as we did to winning it, things would have turned out better."

For the first time, Ben looked straight into my eyes, made eye contact and held it, for more than just the odd second that he had done up to this point.

He asked: "Do you realise how special you are? How special I was? Everyone is one of a kind – unique. Nobody else is you, or even close to being you, not even your brother or your sister.

"If people really thought about that and understood it, they'd be much more careful about how they used the life that they've been given. It's a gift, a privilege that has been given to so few. When you think about it, since the beginning of time, there are so few people who have ever lived – who ever had a life.

"Life is the only thing that any of us really own, a thing that belongs to just us and nobody else. It's short enough even for those living to old age. When it's gone it's gone forever and it never comes back. Surely something that valuable should be cared for, never wasted."

I said nothing in response, just nodded in agreement and inwardly despaired at just how little we had learned in a hundred years.

Chapter 7

From France to Flanders

"In January 1917 we moved from Schools Camp, but instead of going back to the trenches we moved to Dainville for training and to take in a whole load of replacements. With our time off the line before Christmas and this additional training, it meant we had a decent spell away from the trenches – well over a month.

"Our battalion had been reduced in numbers quite heavily during our time in the line from July up to Christmas 1916. Just like many other battalions in the division we had been reduced to a level where we were struggling, with most of our companies at not much more than half-strength. Even so, we were luckier than many who had been involved in the fighting along the Somme front. It wasn't just the deaths and the high numbers of wounded; even those not physically wounded were chin strapped. It took so much out of all of us, and some had been pushed to breaking point in body and in spirit.

"If the Somme campaign had such an effect on our lads, it makes you wonder what effect it had on Jerry. After all, we supposedly came out on top, even though the terrible losses made sure that we didn't really feel like we had, but it had to be better than being driven back after all that suffering and loss.

"After Christmas the weather was freezing cold but dry, and it was a relief to be able to walk across ground not littered with munitions and human remains. We had a week when we just rested. Most of us didn't know what to do. Many of the fellows spent some time visiting the local towns and enjoying the beer and, whenever possible, a bit of female company.

"I had a few trips into the local towns by bike along with a few of the lads in my section. It was enough to feel clean and to escape the constant tension you felt in the trenches. Some of the officers took leave and went to Paris. At least one of them managed to get back home across the channel. For me, just being able to sleep through a whole night, rather than snatching a few hours in daytime – to be away from the risk of shelling and trench raids – to lie in a clean bed and put on a clean, louse-free uniform was the height of luxury.

"Towards the end of our week as gentlemen of leisure, we received a consignment of replacement equipment; uniforms, weapons and manpower, ready for our training starting up again. The manpower was desperately needed, but many of the chaps were a bit put out when they saw the replacements.

"From July 1916 onwards, there had been a drip-drip of replacements in most of the Bantam battalions. We were luckier than most, as we were still recruiting from the mines and off the land, so were still getting tough, strong, fit lads, but some of the other battalions weren't so lucky. Many of their "Bantam" replacements were just weedy little runts, who had never done a day's hard graft in their lives. After the poor performance of some battalions during Jerry's raids in late 1916, as soon as the 35th Division came off the line just before Christmas, hundreds of soldiers were removed from the division – deemed unfit for frontline duties. They were sent off to serve in labour units and at service depots, well away from any fighting. As I said, we were luckier than most and we didn't have too many of those types to shed.

"Most, well, just about all of the replacements that joined us in January 1917 were regular-height soldiers, rather than little 'uns recruited as Bantams. It didn't bother me too much, but there was a noticeable change in the battalion, both in appearance and spirit. What do the Frenchies call it? Esprit de Corps."

"Great pronunciation, Ben," I chipped in.

Ben continued without pausing, "That's not meant to be disrespectful to the new lads, most of who were great fellows, but it did change us. Funnily enough, my spirit was dented not so much by the taller soldiers coming in, but by the fact that we lost our divisional emblem, the bantam cockerel. It was replaced by a bunch of number fives bolted together in the shape of a wheel. Seven of them so it added up to thirty-five. I bet it took a high-ranking officer to come up with that load of tosh.

"Many of the replacements were experienced soldiers from other regiments who had been wounded, or dismounted cavalrymen from disbanded units. They were good soldiers who we had confidence in. As well as these experienced replacements our section corporal, Harry, returned to us, fully fit, just after Christmas. It was great to have him back.

"The remainder of the replacements were newly recruited, regular-height soldiers. Most of them didn't seem to have had much training before joining us. Being with the battalion from the very beginning meant that we'd all had many months to train together and become friends before setting off for France. These new chaps had just a few weeks training under their belts before coming to join us. They were coming into an established unit and had to build friendships and earn respect quickly.

"The big advantage they had was that they were joining a seasoned battalion and would be fighting alongside proven lads. When we all shipped over together, experienced soldiers were thin on the ground. These new lads were joining experienced Tommies at a time when we were having an extended training period away from the trenches. It was lucky for them, and lucky for the rest of us who would have to rely on them.

"The new fellows were allocated to their companies, platoons and sections. We got two of them in my section, one of whom was a replacement for Jim, who still hadn't returned to the battalion after being wounded in the Arras sector before Christmas. Imagine that! Wounded in the Arras!" Ben laughed.

He continued; "We'd been given bits of news about Jim being taken to the dressing station and later we got word that he was recovering well; his wound hadn't been serious enough to get him back to Blighty for treatment and convalescence, but we'd heard nothing more about him. I thought he'd probably been sent to a different regiment, after all that was how we were getting many of our replacements.

"We did our best to get the new lads welcomed into the company. One day when we were carrying out musketry practice I was helping a young lad who was struggling. He could hit the target at a good distance, but his rate of fire was well down on what it was going to have to be if he was going to have any chance in a scrap.

"We were practising dry firing. Letting him handle his weapon, use the sights, get his breathing right, slowly applying pressure to the trigger to release the shot, finding the bolt with his right hand instead of groping for it like a blind man, and working it smoothly instead of trying to batter it into submission – when I heard a familiar voice behind me: 'Don't be listening to anything Leeman tells you son, he couldn't hit a cow's arse with a cricket bat'."

"I recognised the voice immediately and rolled on my right side and looked up into the sunshine to see the silhouette of my best mate standing over me. I wanted to jump up and shake his hand, but I didn't want him to know how much I'd missed him. 'That sunlight has travelled millions of miles to get here and warm me up, and you've gone and blocked out the last six feet of it – so shift your arse, you bleedin' idiot!' I replied."

'Couldn't you spend your time teaching him something a bit more useful, like how to get a brew on for a returning hero?' says Jim.

'He already knows how to brew up, so when a returning hero turns up, be sure to let us know and he'll be happy to oblige,' I said."

'It's good to see you haven't lost your sense of humour. I was worried you wouldn't survive without me,' Jim said."

'Well, it's been hard, but I've scraped through.' I tapped my student on the shoulder. 'Come on mate, practice is over. Let's go and make a brew for the hero.' I put up my right hand and Jim pulled me to my feet. 'It's good to see you mate. In fact, it's bloody fantastic,' I said.

'I'd like to say the same Ben, but the truth is, seeing you again is at best slightly above average.' Jim joked.

"We walked back towards the tents leaving the new bloke to gather his equipment, both rifles, helmets and the sandbag he was using as a firing support. As we talked and mucked about together it was as though a part of me that had been missing had grown back. It was the best day I'd had in a long time." Ben smiled at the memory of getting his mate back that day.

*****

"By March the new chaps were bedded in and we were billeted near the Chilly sector, moving on and off the line in a regular routine, when in the middle of March Jerry surprised us all by making a withdrawal and pulling back, allowing us to advance and occupy their positions.

"We weren't too keen on moving in, thinking it was some sort of ruse, and so were all expecting to take a hammering from their guns, but the expected shelling didn't happen. We advanced more in one day than we ever had done before, and more than we ever did afterwards. We were all for chasing him as far as we could. Jerry had pulled back to the other side of the river at Peronne and destroyed the crossing points behind him to prevent us chasing him down.

"We weren't at all happy when we were stopped from following before the bridges were blown, but soon after we were withdrawn, along with the rest of the brigade, to the area around Chaulnes to work on the railway. We repaired and replaced tracks from Chaulnes to Rosiers and then from Chaulnes to Nesle. It was hard graft, but at least it kept the boredom at bay. I would rather have been chasing Jerry though!

"I found it funny that our Dad had spent years as the foreman in a sleeper mill, cutting the sleepers for the railways... I did the same when I left school, and now during my time in France I was employed repairing rail tracks and roads, and building a new light railway, when we weren't on the line or training. I left a sleeper mill, joined the army and became a navvy.

"It was hard graft, and most didn't like it, but I didn't mind. Being younger and fitter than most, the daily routine in the trenches bored me to the point of madness if I was there for too long. I enjoyed anything to break the routine, and laying the rail tracks kept me active and helped the time pass quickly. It was also relatively safe... well as safe as you could ever be that close to the front line."

I interrupted. "I didn't realise how much trains were used. I have seen photographs of trucks and even London buses being used to ferry troops, but I didn't know that you used trains so much, especially getting to and from the trenches."

Ben thought for a while, then went on: "I'm sure that in the early part of the war omnibuses were used a lot. But during the battles of 1916 the roads just about disappeared under the rain, mud and shell fire. It was almost impossible to move soldiers and supplies to the trenches by omnibus and truck. Once you were within about seven or eight miles of the frontline trenches it became far more difficult to move on what was left of the roads, and shortages of ammunition, food and soldiers nearly led to a Jerry breakthrough – it doesn't matter how good you are at soldiering, if you are starving and have no ammunition you can't hold the line.

"Anywhere within about 7 miles of the front and our ammunition and supply dumps were in the range of the Jerry guns. Trucks were in short supply, and due to the state of the roads, moving supplies by horse-drawn transport couldn't be done. Horse transport couldn't carry enough, and they couldn't make the round trip from the supply dumps to the front and back again in a day. The fodder for the horses had to be carried on the transport and that took up more room than the food and ammunition for the soldiers. Laying a new railway was the solution they came up with.

"Us Tommies must have laid hundreds of miles. We had military engineers in charge, advising. Most of those fellows were experienced railway workers, but the rest of us had never done anything like it before."

"You must have been bolloxed," I said.

"What does that mean?" Ben asked.

"Exhausted, I mean," I replied.

"Yes, it was tiring, but it wasn't as bad as you'd think. It wasn't full-size tracks that we were laying, it was what they called narrow gauge. The tracks were just about two feet apart and were fairly light in weight, because the trains themselves weren't full size. They were much smaller. Most of the carriages were just flat carts with sides and an open roof.

"When moving on to the line, or when we'd been relieved and were moving back, we were carried the few miles closest to the front on these small trains, which linked up with proper railheads and stations where we transferred to the bigger trains, you know, proper trains with proper carriages like back at home... the ones with steam engines," Ben explained.

"Didn't the narrow-gauge trains have steam engines?" I asked.

Ben replied, "I'm sure they were run on different fuel. I think it was paraffin or petroleum, I'm not sure, but I know it wasn't steam. Even at night the noise from a steam engine would be heard and the steam from an engine was visible from miles away – certainly visible from the Jerry positions, and they would have had a great time blowing the trains and us to bits. No, whatever fuel it was made the trains run much more quietly than the steam engines and they didn't spew out great clouds of steam. I'm quite sure that they were running on paraffin or petroleum.

"When we laid the tracks, we laid individual sleepers, and when we had enough sleepers down, sections of rail were laid across them and fixed in place. If you were new to the job progress was slow, but we soon got the hang of it and could lay a good length of track in a single day.

"Most of the tracks and sleepers we were laying were supplied by the Yanks. The rumour was that we weren't getting the stuff from Blighty because the French had realised the importance of the railways before we did, and they placed orders with British companies, getting first dibs on the available stuff.

"We began to split into teams. One team would assemble the tracks; you know, the sleepers and the rails, while the others would clear and level the ground where the track was going to be laid, and yet another team would lay the assembled track. It was far quicker and worked well when we got it going properly. Some lads liked one job or the other and liked to stay in the same role. Me, I liked to change. It prevented me from getting bored.

"The railway was a real lifesaver. As well as bringing in supplies and fresh troops it allowed the wounded to be moved back to casualty clearing stations and hospitals more quickly and safely than in ambulances travelling by road.

"I think I might have told you before that the roads were almost invisible; full of water-filled craters, which regularly caused vehicles to tip over – bad enough whenever you were travelling by truck, but deadly if you were strapped on to a stretcher. Then there was always the risk of hitting a half-buried unexploded shell. It might not have worked first time, but whacking one with a fully loaded ambulance would usually do the trick.

"At least on our track you knew that the ground had been dug over and levelled before the tracks went down. We were always careful when we were preparing the ground because swinging a pick onto the end of a shell was just as effective as whacking it with an ambulance and if you were the Tommy holding the pick there wouldn't be very much left to collect and box up. I was always careful," Ben said.

I cut in, "I would have thought that laying a railway was really precision work, yet it sounds like you were really chucking it down."

Ben went on: "We did our best to be careful and accurate, but the speed of getting it down was more important. Our Charlie would have been in tears; him being an engineer, he'd have had a bloody seizure if he'd seen us lot banging and hammering away. But we got the job done. And don't forget those tracks weren't going to stay down forever. When positions moved we would tear up the tracks and move them somewhere else and lay them again.

"The engine drivers were all experienced and knew that as long as they kept the speed down, and the chairs were properly fixed to the sleepers, so the tracks didn't spread apart due to the weight going over them, then the sleepers would bed down after a few days. It's surprising what you can get away with!

"It must have been late spring 1917 when we started to get a lot of Labour Corps men from all over the world coming to help lay and operate the railway, which took much of the work away from us; Africans, Chinese, Indians – they all came. Most of the lads were glad to pass the work on to them, but it was a mixed blessing for me, because I'd enjoyed the work.

"As the light railways expanded they began to get shelled more frequently, so much of the movement was done at night. They also tended to stop a bit further from the trenches. Horses pulled any cargo for most of the last mile or two and then we would work in relays to carry supplies by hand over the last half mile or so, in pitch darkness.

"Anyway, where was I? Once we had finished on the light railway we started on the road to Ham, trying to get that into decent order. One of the lads joked that Jerry had only pulled back to allow us to repair the roads and tracks ready for them when they returned. In the middle of April, much to the relief of the workshy, we moved back to the frontline, where we took over from the Lancashires.

"Once back on the line we spent a lot of time patrolling aggressively to keep Jerry on the back foot and give him no peace. We were very successful, and it certainly raised our spirits. Our battalion built a bit of a reputation for our aggression and Jerry became quite reluctant to carry out raids against our positions.

"This continued into the following month and on the night of the 9th of May took the fight to him for most of the night. We took the lead, along with Y Company, and were supported by elements of the other companies. We hit the Jerry trenches hard and they wanted no part of the scrap. We chased them down through a rabbit warren of support trenches. We took a lot of casualties, about twenty in total, but fortunately most were wounded not dead, with a couple missing.

"Jerry wasn't so lucky, and we finished a good few of them off that night, but I think the previous months' work and the reputation we were building had made Jerry wary of going toe to toe with us and most legged it. If it hadn't been for the break in the clouds exposing us to bright moonlight, we would have got away with it very lightly because most of our casualties were suffered at distance while we were moving over open ground, not while we were in their trenches.

"We all felt that the replacements received in January had done a great job and the disappointment of losing the 'Bantam' title started to fade, just a little. As a battalion our spirits were sky high, but a day or two later we lost our CO, when Colonel Gordon fell ill and was rushed to a field hospital and invalided back to Blighty. Major Crellin stepped in as acting CO and continued the aggressive tactics. We all liked and respected Major Crellin – he had been with the battalion since we formed in Nottingham.

"A week after our first big raid a second was mounted, with W and X Companies taking the lead and getting the same good result. Seven or eight days later we marched to Peronne. It really felt like at long last we were gaining the upper hand... in France at least."

*****

"As spring turned to summer the Cheshires were occupying a long, advanced trench and we spent time providing patrols to give them cover and protection. Most of the patrols were quiet, and in the warm weather, really quite pleasant. The sort of weather when you really should have been walking with a girl you liked or chucking a stick for your dog. Our Nan would have loved it – until one night in the middle of June when we came face to face with a Jerry patrol. Neither of us expected to bump into the other, but we were the quickest to react and saw them off, dropping four of them and taking one uninjured prisoner; well, uninjured apart from the gashed head and concussion when Harry nearly removed the top of his skull with his rifle butt.

"On the 18th of June we marched off the line and back to Heudecourt. The weather remained warm and sunny, and we enjoyed a week of sport and concerts. A football tournament was held and we beat teams from the Cheshires, Artillery and the Machine Gun Corps to win it.

"Several battalion bands got their instruments back for the week and there were regular music recitals taking place all over. The Cheshires had a couple of fellows who were very good singers and they accompanied the bands. It was a happy time. The whole battalion was in good spirits and we felt we were up to any task. As a division our spirit was unrecognisable from the low point of the end of 1916.

"In late June we returned to the trenches for a few days and then moved by train to Villers Faucon, where we were given the unpopular task of setting up camp for the whole of 105th Brigade. We weren't happy, but our mood improved when the RSM told us to get a move on as our billets in the village wouldn't wait forever. The village billets weren't exactly luxurious, but many of us slept in a real bed in a proper brick building, with a roof and everything, for the first time since Tidworth.

"July saw the division moved to the Epehy Sector, relieving the Cavalry Corps. This was a dangerous sector – in many places little more than a group of separate strongholds linked by barbed-wire defences, which we set about reinforcing as soon as possible. One of the posts known as The Birdcage was nothing short of a bloody death trap. In the middle of the month we were holding The Birdcage when we were attacked by Jerry. He was serious about shifting us and pasted us with an accurate shelling before the infantry appeared close behind a creeping barrage to assault our positions.

"We drove him off and he withdrew, taking most of his dead and wounded with him, apart from a few who were left hanging on the wire. One Jerry was alive for about an hour, crying out for help. No one could see him, and no one would raise their head to look, until one of the lads from another section spotted him and put him out of his misery with a single shot.

"As the fighting tailed off we could see that there were three or four Jerry dead tangled in the barbed wire. The raid had cost us half a dozen dead and about twenty-five wounded. All the dead had been killed by the barrage, not the Jerry infantry.

"The following morning Jerry put up a white flag and eight of their stretcher bearers came out under the cover of the flag and recovered their dead. We watched in silence as they struggled to untangle their boys from the wire. It took a long time to get the bodies free.

"Not only did Jerry get his dead back, no doubt he reported back that the wire linking our positions was almost impenetrable. There were no further attempts to shift us and a couple of days later we left the line and had almost a week of training and sport. We took part in an inter-brigade musketry competition and the Foresters took first and second place."

*****

"In August the brigade was given orders for a major raid on the Jerry lines at Gillemont Farm and our battalion was tasked with seizing a position known as The Knoll.

"The importance of the task became obvious when we were taken completely out of the line to prepare. We were sent to Aizecourt Le Bas, where a full-size reproduction of The Knoll trench complex was built for us to practise our assault alongside the 15th Cheshires. We had often trained for different types of assault, but this was the first time we'd been put through a full rehearsal with replica trenches. We were well into our training and were all confident in our objectives when the date of the assault was suddenly brought forward.

"The artillery supporting the operation was impressive and we watched the gunners go through their drills. In all there were about 50 howitzers in different calibres and more than dozen 60-pounders.

"It would have been about three in the morning when we assembled. Our guns had been shelling Jerry for some time, giving him a right battering. We could see the explosions as the gunners hit the Jerry trenches and the barbed-wire defences standing between us and those trenches.

"Even the Flying Corps had aircraft up in the air, observing and dropping bombs on The Knoll, and at four o'clock we went over the bags. Our company and Y Company advanced behind a creeping barrage and we covered the open ground with hardly a shot being fired towards us due to the artillery and the Flying Corps keeping Jerry well pinned down. When we reached the wire, it had been well and truly smashed and we were through it as the barrage ended.

"We cleared the parapet of the fire trench and were in by the time Jerry was scrambling out from cover. We moved down the trench from left to right, a Lewis gunner led the way with two of us supporting him, and a couple more lads carrying spare pans for him. He just rattled away blasting everything that appeared in front of him. When he changed magazines, he dropped behind us and we continued to fire until he had re-loaded and we dropped in behind him and advanced again.

"One of the bombers caught up with us and as we moved along the trench he lobbed his Mills bombs into any places of concealment. As we approached any new fire bays he lobbed them over the top before the Lewis gunner rounded the corner.

"By the time we had cleared three or four bays we met up with another section coming the other way. It was all over in about 15 minutes and we were quickly joined by W and X Companies, who secured the position while we escorted about a dozen prisoners and helped the stretcher bearers tend and remove the wounded.

"Even though everything had gone to plan in the initial attack we still had over 25 lads killed and twice that number wounded or missing. 3 of the wounded were machine-gunned by the Flying Corps who hadn't expected us to capture the position so quickly."

I cut in; "Things like that still happen today – it's called 'Blue on Blue' or 'Friendly Fire.' But as we all know, 'Friendly Fire' is anything but friendly."

Ben nodded, then continued: "W and X Companies held The Knoll throughout the day. They were shelled heavily, but no counter-attack came, and Z and Y Companies took over as soon as darkness fell. We spent most of the night digging communication trenches and repairing the position. As daylight came we could see the whole of the German defences laid out to our front and our defences laid out to our rear. This dominating view of the whole area was the reason for the position's importance to both sides. We handed over to the Gloucesters a day later.

"After a period of rest, we moved back onto the Knoll on the 25th of August and the following day we were shelled constantly by Jerry. We waited for him to make an assault on our position – but it never came, more's the pity. A good scrap would have meant a break in the shelling. As it was, there was nothing for it but to go to ground and hope for the best. On that day alone, we lost about 20 men killed and twice as many were wounded. A few of the lads were showing the effects of the bombardment, but all held up and the following day we were relieved and returned to camp at St Emilie. A few days later Jerry recaptured The Knoll again; he'd already re-taken Gillemont Farm a little earlier.

"September was spent skirmishing around The Knoll and The Birdcage. Nights were spent on working parties, most of which involved barbed wiring in the darkness.

"There were regular rotations and turns in the camp, training and playing sport. We remained in good spirits despite the losses we'd taken over the previous few months, and perhaps we became a little complacent when off the line. Lance Corporal Nicholson was killed near St Emilie, while he was in a rear area. It was a warm evening and he was taking a couple of horses out to pasture, much like hundreds of people were doing back in Blighty that very evening. Unfortunately, he was spotted by a Jerry aeroplane, which dropped a couple of bombs, killing him and one of the horses – nowhere was truly safe.

"A couple of days later an identical Jerry aeroplane made a forced landing nearby. Although the thing was spluttering and smoking they got down safely and shut down the engine. Before the crew emerged from the aeroplane a Lewis gunner who was a mate of Nicholson emptied a full pan into the crew, then walked off without saying a word. We all understood exactly how he felt."

*****

"As October began we were withdrawn to Arras for a refit and a short training period. We packed all our kit and said goodbye to France for the time being as we boarded trains for Flanders.

"When I say boarded our trains for Flanders, it wasn't quite that simple, which shouldn't really have surprised any of us. Our first move was by truck to Peronne and from there we moved by train to Arras, a place we were familiar with. We were billeted on the edge of the town.

"We spent our time training and re-equipping with kit to replace stuff that had been worn out and lost. Our initial happiness at the re-fit waned a bit when we found out where we were soon to be heading – Wipers.

"Much of our training was to prepare us for the different ground conditions we would find in Flanders, where most of our soldiering wouldn't be in the same kind of trenches that we had grown used to, as the ground there just wasn't capable of supporting effective trenches. We spent a lot of time training to make effective use of cover and practising assaults on block houses, so we had a good idea what we were getting into.

"We practised the tactic of making small advances and then consolidating, before doing the same again, rather than making longer advances and becoming overstretched; they called it 'Bite and Hold'.

"We also had a re-organisation of the companies. We were all worried as no one wanted to leave lads who they had fought alongside for a couple of years. Even though a move would be to another company within the battalion, no one wanted it. It was bad enough being moved to another section or platoon, but not another company. I'd been in the same section since Masham; just me and Jim. The rest of the section manning had changed a few times, apart from Harry, our corporal, who joined us in about May 1916, but me and Jim were the only originals. That's why I'd been so relieved when he came back in January. I didn't want to be the only original. Apart from missing your mates, it would have meant the other fellows starting to look at you as if you were some sort of lucky charm, indestructible or something, when all you really were was lucky.

"We even managed a day off to head out for a coffee and a few beers. The sun was shining and even though the temperature was getting cooler, sitting outside having a drink it was almost possible to forget about the war for a few hours. As I said earlier, a few hours or a day being human again was often the only thing keeping you from going bonkers.

"After about ten days we were on our way to Flanders. After breakfast we marched from the camp to the railway station at Arras for a train due to leave just before one o'clock. When the train arrived, it was a couple of carriages short. After much shoving and heaving it was clear that you couldn't get a quart into a pint pot and the decision was made to leave our company behind to catch a later train. The rest of the battalion rolled out just before one o'clock as planned, while we made ourselves comfortable at the railway station.

"As we sat on the floor of the station a choir of schoolgirls together with a group of nuns from a local convent arrived and spent about an hour singing for us. I don't think I had ever seen our company so quiet. We sat in complete silence for a whole hour and listened. I had never heard a choir sing like that; it was almost enough to turn you religious. Before they left a couple of the girls moved amongst the fellows carrying wicker baskets and gave to each of the lads a tiny posy of wild flowers and a little cross made of woven grass or something.

"Before they left the CSM walked over to them and thanked the nun who had led the choir into the station. He put out his hand to shake hers, but she put her hands on his arms and kissed him on both cheeks. When he turned back to face us he was blushing and had tears running down his face.

"He saw me looking at him as he wiped his face, before kicking my outstretched foot, saying; 'What are you looking at Leeman? Have you never seen someone with an allergy before?'

'Yes, I have Sir. Just not anyone with an allergy to nuns,' I replied, then quickly lay back with my head on my pack and closed my eyes, before he closed them for me."

"We eventually moved off just before 9 o'clock that evening and arrived at Cassel in French Flanders at three the following morning, before marching from the railhead to the village of Arneke, about 5 miles away. Under normal conditions we would have been hacked off, but after 6 hours being cooped up on a train we were glad to stretch our legs. Arriving just before 5, we managed a couple of hours' kip, before being woken and marching back to the station at Arneke a few hours later. There was a lot of moaning in our company about this. We had slogged for 10 miles and 3 hours, not getting more than an hour's kip, only to be back exactly where we started. Even after 3 years of war the army could still be relied upon to bugger us about," said Ben.

"They're still buggering us about a hundred years on, Ben, so you've got nowt to complain about," I said.

"Really?" Ben replied.

"Yes, mate. It's still a cake and arse party at the best of times." And I laughed thinking about the time I had flown three-quarters of the way to Afghanistan, only for the aircraft to be turned around and land back at Brize Norton – then be sent home a hundred miles away, only to receive a call before arriving home telling me to turn around and head back to Brize and get back on a C-17 to fly back to Afghanistan. (It wasn't funny at the time though.)

Ben went on: "Our train set off from Arneke at about midday for a small town named Proven, just a few miles from Poperinghe. This train had plenty of carriages and plenty of room, which was unusual, so I bedded down and slept for the whole journey. When I woke up, I was alone in the carriage. Every other bugger had gotten off and left me there. I had to run to catch up with the lads as they marched off towards our overnight camp.

"The following day, which would have been about the 15th or 16th, we moved by train from Proven to Elverdinghe where we relieved the

Scots Guards at Rugby Camp. A bit of a fracas broke out when one of the Jocks thought it funny to call one of us Bantams a midget. The matter was soon ended when the 'midget' punched the big bloke right in his balls, leaving him writhing on the ground making noises like a chicken being strangled. As one of the Jocks stepped forward to take matters further, the CSM stepped forward and said, 'You don't want to go doing anything like that, old son – you'd do better helping your friend lay that egg. It sounds like he's got it stuck.' Even the Guards laughed at that and we carried on the handover without further punch-ups." When he finished speaking, Ben took out his Black Cats and offered me one. Again, I declined, so he lit up his own fag and took a deep drag.

*****

"You must have been familiar with the frontline trenches in France and now you were coming to somewhere completely unfamiliar. How did it feel moving to Flanders after so long in France?" I asked.

"We all knew we were about to be sent forward to the fighting. Most of the fellows claimed to be keen to get involved, but we had heard a lot of horror stories about the fighting around Wipers and especially about the swamp-like conditions. I think a lot of the talk was bravado; most of us were worried, you know, apprehensive, not afraid.

"We knew the move would be soon, we just didn't know exactly when, or where, but we knew it was coming. I was surprised that we hadn't marched straight in to the fighting from the trains, but had been given a few days to attend briefings about the field conditions and the lie of the land, regarding Jerry positions. The briefings gave us a lot of information that had been gathered by recce, both on the ground and from the air.

"While we were waiting for our orders, most of the companies spent time on working parties for the Field Artillery sorting out their gun positions. As we all knew that these were the guns that would be supporting us, we made sure we did a good job.

"It would have been about the 20th of October when we moved forward to Gouvy Farm, which was close to Boesinghe. We set off late afternoon, about 5 o'clock, shortly after tea and moved in just after dark.

"We all settled down for a night's sleep. Usually before going into a scrap I never slept particularly well, having a million thoughts going through my head, but that night I slept like a baby. One of the lads thought I had died in my sleep when he tried to wake me the following morning.

"We brewed up and ate a hot breakfast, which we all appreciated, and filled our water bottles with tea before moving out to take up our assembly position. It was slow going, moving in single file, and it was hard trying to keep your feet and keep an eye on the last man in the section in front so you kept to a safe path. We didn't want to bunch up and present an attractive target, but we didn't want to get lost either and stray on to ground that would just suck you down, so we made regular stops to stay in touch with the other sections.

"When we eventually arrived at our assembly positions the weather, which had been good, turned bitterly cold. We were exposed to the sleet and freezing rain with little shelter other than our waterproof sheets as we settled down to await the order to advance towards the Jerry positions. It was bloody miserable.

"Our battalion was to provide support for 2 battalions of the Cheshires – one directly to our front, the other on the left flank – and the 17th Lancashires, who were to our right.

"Before dawn the barrage started up – a short but heavy initial barrage that then started to creep, with the infantry following close behind. At first it went well, but the ground was proving hard to cover with any speed. As everywhere else, the ground was pitted with crump holes and the overnight rain and sleet had again turned everywhere into a swamp, slowing the advancing troops – but the barrage kept creeping forward, getting away from us.

"On the far left of the line beyond the Cheshires, the Gloucesters and the Frenchies were going well, having little difficulty following the barrage. The only thing that slowed them was trying to stay in touch with the battalions in the centre of the advance.

"A block house directly ahead of the 16th Cheshires and our lads was causing problems. But after some fierce scrapping the bunker was overrun and captured. Once past it we made quick progress towards a second bunker, and this time it was impossible to capture the position, but we were able to pin down the Jerries inside it while the Cheshires moved around it to the left and we went around it to the right.

"The 17th Lancashires had quite a straightforward run to Marechal Farm and were giving the place a right pasting from the right flank. They delayed a final assault until we had passed the second block house and were able link up and hit the farm from the left as they hit it from the right – it was a good plan and Jerry was soon in full retreat from the farm.

"We met up with the Lancashires at the far side of the farm and set up defensive positions in and around some outbuildings about thirty yards beyond the main farm. Support positions were established in the remains of the main farm buildings. Once prepared, we settled down and waited for the counter-attack that we knew would soon come.

"Apart from the second block house the attack had achieved all objectives to the left flank and centre as far as Marechal Farm, but the line was supposed to stretch out further on the right flank from the farm, eastwards to a point called Six Roads, and this didn't happen – which meant that we were left with no defences of note to our right-hand side.

"We didn't have long to wait. Jerry launched several counter-attacks to shift us from the farm, but we were having none of it and all were driven back with relative ease. On a couple of occasions, they got in close, but we had prepared by fixing bayonets. The counter-attacks were co-ordinated and getting stronger, when things took a turn in our favour. Apparently, the Jerry attacks were being directed by a couple of officers further back in the forest. Unfortunately for them they were spotted by one of our sniper teams and relieved of their command, you know? Topped 'em off and no messing about. As soon as that happened, the counter-attacks became less effective and weren't pressed home with any real determination.

"Jerry switched his attention to pounding the farm with his guns, but we just got down low and kept our heads. There was some discussion amongst the officers about how well prepared we were to hold on after dark. It was agreed that it would be impossible to hold the farm in darkness with our right flank completely unprotected. The inevitable flanking movement there would leave us cut off and surrounded.

"Our withdrawal was silent and calm, just as dusk gave sufficient cover to move without being exposed to direct fire. After all the effort to take the farm, none of us wanted to leave, we had fought hard to take it and it might sound daft, but we knew that even though it was derelict, it gave us a bit of shelter from the rain and sleet, which again started to belt down as the light began to fade.

"The CSM gave us our orders. Our company, supported by a couple of additional Vickers crews and several Lewis gunners, would cover the withdrawal. As the rest of the lads left us we knew there was a chance we would be cut off, but to be honest I wasn't thinking any further ahead than the next Jerry attack, which came as soon as it was dark enough to give him cover.

"We chucked everything we had at Jerry as he attacked. A dozen or so got within ten yards of our positions before we drove them back.

And as they retreated into cover the command to 'Cease Fire!' was given as loud as possible.

"This was the agreed signal for those of us acting as rear guard to leave our positions and slip away from the farm. As we left it behind and quietly disappeared into the darkness, the farm was hit by about twenty heavy Jerry shells – we had been seconds away from being smashed to pieces. In the darkness we couldn't see the damage, but there couldn't have been much left. We continued silently on our way to our new positions and began helping to prepare a new defensive line as best we could.

"The next few hours were spent taking stock of our casualties, which were high. As we were digging in, one of the sergeants asked Jim why he was limping. Jim tried to bluff it out, but he was sent to a medical orderly who discovered that he had been shot in the top of his right thigh. The bullet was still in his leg, but luckily it hadn't hit the bone. He said he couldn't remember being hit but thought it had happened during the initial assault on the farm that morning – so it had been in his leg for most of the day.

"He was moved back for treatment and ended up in the field hospital. Bloody hell I thought, this bloke's got a girlfriend in the field hospital. Once again, I was unhurt, but without my best mate.

"We held our new positions until the 24th. Jerry launched half-hearted attacks at regular intervals, but to be honest they were less of a bother than the bloody freezing, wet, horrible weather. Shortly before we were relieved I was so cold I had lost all feeling in my hands and feet and had begun to shiver uncontrollably for stretches of about 10 minutes at a time. Even scalding hot tea, being gulped down so quickly it burned my mouth and throat, couldn't warm me up.

"We were relieved by the Durham Light Infantry and I was never so happy to be moving off the line. I felt bloody awful and as we marched to a camp near to Elverdinghe, I wondered if I had been hit without knowing it. I felt icy cold and had no strength at all. When we got to the camp I spent the next three days in my bed trying to thaw out. They were planning on moving me back by the field ambulance, but an orderly convinced them I was suffering from exposure and wasn't contagious. I just needed to warm up.

"On the fourth day at camp I felt much better and was up and about. On the evening of the 29th we were back on the line, replacing the Jocks, just in time for Jerry to zero in on our lines and spend the night having some target practice.

"Just before dawn the following morning the intensity of the shelling increased, and we were all 'Stood To' waiting for an attack that never came, although some of our snipers managed to get in a bit of target practice of their own and top off a few careless Jerries, who thought themselves safe.

"Over the next few days back on the line we had a steady stream of casualties, both killed and wounded, and as a parting gift on the 31st Jerry dropped a load of gas shells on us, so we spent hours and hours in our gas kit.

"We were relieved by the Highlanders on the 1st of November, but even as we moved back towards the railway we were shelled again and suffered more casualties. We slipped and slid over the duckboards, under shelling and gas attack, before eventually reaching the narrow-gauge railhead and being moved by train to Dykes Camp, where we rested for five days, by the end of which I was fully fit and well again.

"I must have been in a bad way, because I remember hardly anything from the time when we withdrew from the edge of the forest until arriving at Dykes Camp and it was only on about the 4th of November that I began asking about Jim – until then I had been working in a sort of daze."

Ben paused for a second, giving me the chance to ask him the question I already knew the answer to: "Was it at Houthulst Forest that you were awarded your Military Medal?" I asked.

"Yes, it was," Ben replied.

"In that case you seem to have missed out a big part of what happened at Houthulst and the capture of the farm. Would you tell me what happened and what you got the medal for?" I asked.

"Well it was nothing special. I just did the same sort of thing that many other fellows did, the only difference is that it worked out well and an officer saw it happen and wrote it up," Ben replied.

"That must have been an unusual citation, Ben, 'The Military Medal is awarded to Private Ben Leeman, for doing not very much whilst the 'Box-heads' legged it, with Lieutenant Cholmondeley-Warner looking on, pencil in hand'," I said.

Ben laughed and asked, "What's a Box-Head?"

"I'll tell you later," I replied, adding, "If you don't want to tell me about the medal I understand. I won't be offended. Just being here and speaking with you has been more than enough.

"I don't want you to feel obliged, just because I've waited a hundred years and travelled hundreds of miles to be here – really, don't feel bad about hurting my feelings," I continued, laying it on with a trowel.

"Bugger off – you daft sod," he said, before chucking a small lump of earth, which bounced off my head, adding, "I suppose I'd better tell you then. We don't want any tears, do we?"

*****

Ben sat in silence as he gathered his thoughts and prepared to re-tell his account of the fighting at Houthulst – this time without glossing over his own actions, "It was during the first part of the advance at Houthulst. The attack moved quickly at first, but then parts of the advance got bogged down in places by the ground conditions and the Jerry block houses right in the middle of the advance. Despite the heavy fire coming from the first bunker the lads battled through.

"The place was being given a right pasting while we skirted around to the right of it. We pressed forward and as we approached the second block house we could see lads to our left flank – Cheshires, not Foresters. I think my company was the closest to the middle of the advance and the line began to straighten up – but the approach towards the second bunker gave hardly any cover and Jerry was able to get accurate fire on all of us and we had to go to ground.

"We hit back as best we could, but we had no Stokes mortars with us because the ground was so boggy they couldn't be fired without burying themselves. The Cheshires went up the middle and to the left of the bunker and we were pushing around to the right, but our progress almost stopped dead due to the lack of cover and the heavy fire from the Jerry bunker.

"Up ahead of me, towards the bunker, I saw a Lewis gunner and his pan carrier get hit and go down into a deep crump hole. I think I was the only one who saw them get hit because I was the last man furthest to the left. I called to them to keep down and lie still.

"There was a bit of cover due to the crump holes between me and them, so I dashed forward, only about 10 steps and then down into a hole, moved to the furthest edge of the hole, then up and forward a few yards again. In about 3 short runs I was into the hole with them.

"I called out to the rest of my section and looked to my right for them, I was sure that they had moved forward alongside me, or had gone on ahead of me, but it turns out that I had moved about 30 yards ahead of them – it certainly wasn't deliberate though.

"As soon as I was in their hole I saw that the gunner was dead, the whole top of his head was missing. I reached the pan man. He had been hit at the top of his chest on the left side, just where his chest met the front of his shoulder. The bullet had gone through the strap of his webbing and out of his back near the shoulder blade.

"We were in a natural defilade, well, natural if you regard the site of a bloody big explosion as natural, below the lip of a deep crump hole. I used his own field dressing for the exit wound which was big and still bleeding, and my own dressing on the front entry wound. The front wound was easier to deal with as I could push the dressing inside his tunic and the pressure from his webbing strap held it in place. I got him to hold the webbing in place with his right hand.

"The back one, the exit hole, was more difficult, and I ended up jamming the dressing into the hole. I found an empty hessian sandbag in his webbing and cut it into strips with my folding knife and wrapped it around him like a sort of reversed Sam Browne. Then, half sitting him up, I lay him with his back pressed against the side of the crater to keep the pressure on the dressing and help keep it in place.

"He was able to talk, and I told him to keep as still as possible and no matter how much pain he was in, to keep quiet.

"I grabbed his 2 bags of pans and made my way forward to his mate. I knew his name, although he was hard to recognise due to the damage to his head, so I didn't take his identification with me. I took the Lewis and his satchel of pans, then took his unused field dressings and shoved them in my tunic pockets."

"Are 'pans' the magazines for the Lewis gun?" I asked.

"Yes, that's what we called them," Ben replied.

"I always thought they were drums," I said.

"No, they were pans. Drums and pans have the ammunition inserted in a completely different way," Ben explained.

He went on: "Once I had the gun and the pans I eased forwards, keeping my face in the mud. I was able to look around the right-hand edge of the thick rim of the crump hole. There was a small gap, which I could see through. There were a lot of dead tree stumps and shattered tree trunks and branches, some of them large and heavy, which gave a decent amount of concealment and protection. I had a small window through it all and from where I was lying I could see the front firing slit of the bunker, which was facing south towards the Cheshires and us, and the one to the right of the bunker which faced eastwards towards our fellows and the 17th Lancs, who were trying to outflank the bunker.

"I could see the muzzle flash of the 08s coming from inside both slits, but the gun crews were deeper inside, so I assumed that if I couldn't see them, then they couldn't see me. I knew that I could get rounds into the bunker, which would make their lives a lot less comfortable when they were bouncing off the walls inside.

"And that was it really, nothing more exciting than that. I spent about 15 minutes firing into the block house. I fired in short bursts, no more than 4 or 5 rounds at a time. I had about 15 pans and it would have been easy to get carried away and empty each one in about 6 seconds. I also knew that a long burst was going to be seen much more easily by Jerry in the bunker, or even worse, by the snipers who were always out there – if one of those fellows saw my muzzle flash I wouldn't stand a chance.

"I just lay there; 5 rounds to my left, into the south-facing slit – short burst to my right, into the far side of the east-facing slit – and repeat. It didn't stop the 08 crews firing, but every time I put a burst in, I could hear them shouting and cursing. A Jerry pushed a mirror on a pole through the slit; it didn't last very long. I nearly began laughing at the thought of them scrambling around inside trying to avoid the ricochets – and while they were cursing, they weren't putting down the same amount of fire on our lads.

"I fired until I had no more ammunition. I considered carrying on with my rifle, but that would have been a waste of time.

"Before following the advance, I went back to the dead gunner and took his water bottle, which was full, and a packet of fags from his breast pocket. I crawled back to the pan man, who looked to be in good nick, all things considered. I gave him the canteen and the fags. He must have been OK because the cheeky bugger asked if I could leave him my lucifers. I gave him them and slipped off to join the rest of our lads, wherever they had gone.

"I wrapped a piece of hessian around the firing parts of my rifle to prevent it clogging with mud and crawled on my belly with my rifle pushed out in front of me in my left hand, dragging the Lewis gun with my right. The Lewis weighed a couple of stones without a pan fitted and I was considering dismantling it and dumping the parts when I heard one of the officers from another company call out, telling me to get over to his position with the gun.

"I slipped from hole to hole until I reached him and flopped down next to him, telling him I was out of ammunition for the Lewis and that we had a wounded fellow back where I had come from. He asked me my name and section, so I told him. It turns out it was him that wrote me up. He saw it and wrote it up – nothing more, nothing less.

"I managed to get rid of the Lewis to one of his lads and I stayed with his crew as we moved forward towards the farm. The rest of our advance was fairly straightforward and by the time we arrived at the farm, Z Company had already linked up with the 17th Lancs, and between them they had secured it.

"As soon as I got to the farm, I moved to join my own section, at which point Jim shouted, 'Hey up lads, Leeman's arrived back from leave and he's brought tea and crumpets!' He was a bloody annoying sod. But I was relieved to see him and be back with my own mates. It's bad enough being shit-scared when you are with mates, being shit-scared and with strangers or alone is much worse.

"As soon as the position at the farm was secure I led a couple of stretcher bearers back to collect the ammunition man, who was still alive and looking remarkably perky, and the Lewis gunner who was still dead and not looking perky at all. But at least we got him back, despite the fact the Jerry bunker had still not been taken.

"A couple of days later I was called in front of our Company Commander. He had received the report from the lieutenant who had recommended me for an award. He asked me what happened, and I suppose I gave him a shorter version of what I just told you.

"He said nothing to me, just nodded and then signed a sheet of paper in front of him on the desk. Then he told me he was endorsing the recommendation and dismissed me. As I left the Company HQ, he added, 'You saved an awful lot of your friends that morning, Mr Leeman. Well done!' I was disappointed that when I got my medal that wasn't what was written on the citation – it was one of the best things anyone ever said to me," Ben reflected.

"I'm sure it was, Ben. I think I would have felt the same way, although I don't know if I'd have had the guts to do anything brave enough to earn it," I replied.

*****

"What were we talking about before the medal?" Ben asked, anxious to change the subject.

"You were at Dykes camp for five days and had just fully recovered from your illness," I answered.

Ben thought for a few seconds, "That would have been the first week in November 1917 then. That's right, as soon as I was fully recovered we were on the move again, this time to Proven, by train, before marching from the village to Paddington Camp.

"A few days later we had another large intake of replacements, and this time regardless of height we really needed them. Fortunately, most of the replacements were experienced soldiers drafted in from other regiments following convalescence, so it was just a question of getting them settled in rather than training them up, as was the case with those arriving straight from basic training, although we still received a small number of those.

"Shortly after the replacements arrived there was the presentation of medal ribbons. A few of the new lads were issued their 1914 Star ribbons as were a few of our earlier replacements... those who were still alive. None of us Bantams were eligible for that award, as we hadn't been in France in 1914.

"In Mid-November about half of the battalion moved out to Kempton Park, where they formed a working party preparing firing positions for the Artillery. The day after the working party left, the rest of us were transported to a camp near to Vlamiertinghe, to get those lads who had arrived straight from Blighty up to scratch before moving back on to the line.

"In the last week of November, we moved from the camp to join up with the rest of the battalion at Kempton Park and after a decent night's kip, we moved back on to the line at Poelkapelle and there we sat for about 3 days, in the rain and the bloody freezing weather, until relieved and moved back by train to Siege camp, near Elverdinghe. Those few miserable days cost us a dozen of our lads, including a few of the replacements, to artillery and mortars in exchange for 2 Jerry prisoners – it wasn't a good deal.

"I know our guns were doling out the same treatment to the Jerry trenches, but it didn't seem that way towards the end of the year – everything seemed to be heading our way. We just seemed to sit in our gas kit and wait for the next shell to take a few more of our lads. The gas was more of a nuisance than a real threat, but wearing gas kit for hours and hours at a time didn't do our spirits any good.

"Still, at least we were being moved to and from the trenches on a regular turnaround, seldom more than about 4 days, and with the ground conditions in Flanders being so bad, that was the only thing that kept most of us from going around the bend." Ben finished speaking and took out a Black Cat, offering me the pack. This time I took one and his bloody face was a picture!

"I thought you didn't smoke!" He spluttered.

"I don't, but I might start," I replied.

Ben sat open mouthed, staring at me, before I threw the smoke back to him. "Here, I'm only kidding. And close your mouth, you look like you're trying to catch flies." He quickly recovered his composure at the prospect of almost losing one of his precious fags before lighting up.

*****

Ben continued: "We had a lance corporal who had been in the army when the war broke out. He had been wounded and then, after recovering from his wounds, instead of returning to his old unit, he was sent to us in January 1917 as a replacement. He was far too big to be a 'Bantam'. He was an old-looking chap. A creased face, dark, sombre eyes and a droopy moustache. He always looked as if he had been working for too long in the sun. He looked like a bit of a tinker and I always expected him to be flogging pegs or pots every time I saw him.

"He smoked a pipe and on the first day back on the line he would be fine, but within a day or so, he would develop a nervous tic in his face and his right hand, the one holding the pipe. At first the hand would just jump a bit every minute or so. As the days passed the jump would get more obvious, until by the time we were due for relief he would almost be taking his eye out with the mouthpiece of his pipe every five seconds or so

"I remember someone once saying that smoking would be the death of us – even if we believed that, none of us expected to live long enough for it to do any harm, but in his case, there was a real risk of smoking making him go blind!" Ben smiled briefly before going on.

"After a few days out of the trenches, his tic would disappear, only to return the next time we moved back in. When he was killed in late 1917 one of the lads cleaned out his pipe and wrapped it with the rest of his personal stuff to be sent back to his family – he kept the tobacco. In amongst his personal stuff was a photograph dated 1916. In the photo was a young man proudly displaying a new, white lance corporal stripe on his pressed uniform. He was arm-in-arm with a pretty woman who looked to be his wife. Just a year before joining us he hadn't looked like an old tinker, but was a smooth-faced, handsome young man, before the shitty war slowly crushed his spirit and dragged the life out of him."

*****

"After a short time in reserve, at the start of December we moved back on to the line at Langemarcke. The front line there had few trenches but was kept secure by thick belts of barbed wire and a series of fortified pillboxes. During daylight we kept no man's land under observation and changed over at night. During the night we carried out almost constant patrols to ensure Jerry wasn't up to mischief. Jerry did much the same thing and by and large we avoided each other, apart from a few skirmishes in which both sides suffered a few casualties.

"The weather was bloody freezing, cold and foggy, but at least the ground was hard and dry, which was a great relief after the months of constant wetness. Patrolling might have been risky, but at least it kept you a bit warmer. The pillboxes were icy cold.

"Shortly before Christmas we moved back to Schools Camp near Pops. We stayed there right through Christmas. That was a big boost to our spirits, and it was much needed.

"Just before Christmas there was a lecture – which I mostly slept through, from the Corps Commander about enjoying the festive season but maintaining our discipline. We were all looking forward to Christmas and took advantage of a fair amount of drink circulating around the camp. A few of the lads had a bit too much, but as it was mostly confined to camp, the RSM and the officers turned a blind eye, only delivering a gypsy's warning when things got a bit too raucous.

"Everyone got a gift from Players; a packet of twenty fags and a bar of Cadbury's chocolate along with a card. We were very grateful. I wasn't sure if we got them because we were a Nottinghamshire regiment and Players was a Nottingham company, or if everyone in the division got them. I didn't much care. My bar of chocolate lasted the whole of Christmas day. I kept one small piece back for the first night back on the line, wrapping it carefully in one of my ammunition pouches – I thought it might melt in a pocket.

"Christmas was carols, games, beer and chocolate. We all received a load of mail from home. It was a good one. The only thing missing was Jim, who was still recovering from his annual wound and Christmas holiday in the hospital. I'd had word that he was making a good recovery, which eased my worries, but I was still concerned that he would be sent back to a different company, or even worse, to a different regiment.

"By way of a festive celebration, just before New Year's Eve W Company decided to have an outbreak of diphtheria and were evacuated to a nearby camp to prevent them spreading their germs to the rest of us.

"The rest of us celebrated with a mass delousing in big tin baths, so hot they almost took our skin off, but it was the first time I had felt warm all the way to my insides for so long that I didn't care. I stayed in the bath for as long as I possibly could. We all had our uniforms and kit fumigated as well, which was even more welcome than the fags and chocolate."

When Ben finished giving me his account of 1917, he sat quietly for a few seconds before going on; "You said something before when we were talking about the medal citation. What's a Box-Head?"

I burst out laughing and Ben joined in.

"It's how some British servicemen affectionately refer to the Germans these days," I replied.

"Box-Heads! That's a good name for them," he replied, grinning from ear to ear.

I went on: "It's better or worse than that, depending on how you look at it. We are on the same side now. I served alongside the German Army in Afghanistan – mostly their engineers – we had Belgian Infantry, Royal Air Force and German Army Engineers all serving side by side."

Ben thought for a moment and then spoke; "It's definitely better, not worse. Much better than everything that went on here." And he swept his hand towards the dark, silent countryside, which had once been his battlefield.

"I'm glad you feel that way, Ben, because you have a couple of great-great nieces; Charlotte and Emily, who were both born in Germany and hold German and British papers. I call them "the Baby Box-Heads!" and with that we both laughed again. But this time it was a proper laugh – not one to cover the tracks of sadness.

Chapter 8

Comparisons

I broke the silence. "By the end of 1917 you'd experienced the war in France and Flanders and it sounds as if you experienced terrible things in both places. In what way were they similar and in what way were they different?" I asked.

"Are you asking me which I preferred?" Ben enquired.

"I'm not sure, Ben. I suppose I am," I replied.

Ben thought for a moment, as he usually did, before speaking, "That's really difficult to give you a proper answer to, because I've never thought about it before. I've never had to. It's hard to describe what I liked and disliked about both places, because what I experienced was war, not France, or rather Picardy and Flanders. I am sure that both places were as pleasant in peace time as they were horrific in war time.

"I suppose if I was to give a short answer then I would say our time in the trenches was less terrible in France, but time away from the front was more pleasant in Flanders.

"Aside from the fighting, the trenches in France were, for the most part, just about bearable. The earth of the Somme was chalky and drained much better, so while the weather may not have been so different, the result of the rain was very different. In France the floor of the trenches would fill up, but at least it did drain reasonably quickly. The sides of the trenches would get worn when it rained heavily for a long time, but we shored them up with sandbags and wooden planking, so those trenches were more substantial and better constructed. You wouldn't ever describe them as comfortable, but they were at least habitable.

"The chalk in the ground that allowed the ground to drain the rain water away had the disadvantage of making the trenches clearly visible, because the spoil that had been dug out could be seen over long distances on the ground – not that we ever had much trouble finding each other. Once both sides got better at dropping bombs on each other from aeroplanes the chalky spoil made the target far easier to find and hit.

"It's easy to compare the trenches in France with those in Flanders, because trenches in Flanders didn't exist. The earth was just fine-grained clay with nothing but a thin coating of sand or loam. Much of it had no top-soil at all. The clay fields were called 'clyttes' and they were at their worst north of Wipers and particularly around Houthulst Forest.

"So rather than digging down into the ground the defences were built up above ground level using sandbags and wood into what were called breastworks.

"Before the war the land in that part of Flanders was marshy and liable to flood so the land had lots of drainage cuttings, in the same way that parts of Lincolnshire did. Within months of the war starting the constant shelling destroyed all the drainage pumps, gates and cuttings in no time at all. As well as the damage caused by shelling the Belgian Army deliberately flooded large areas in order to stop the Jerry advance to the coast. Faced with being completely overrun it was the only way to stop the advance long enough to prepare effective defences. It worked – the smaller Belgian Army halted a massive and almost unstoppable Jerry advance.

"But getting back to Wipers, whenever it rained the whole place turned into a giant swamp and in the back half of 1917 it rained and rained. It was never ending. Even without the fighting and shelling, the weather and mud were enough to destroy your spirit, but when the rain was accompanied by constant shelling and skirmishing it really was a hell on earth. There's just no other way to describe it. It was horrific in every way.

"The manner of the fighting was different too. Our army was almost surrounded at Wipers for 3 years. We were in a sort of pocket, almost completely encircled and taking daily casualties due to constant skirmishing and shell fire. It was rumoured that we were taking about 7,000 casualties a month, just to hold on to our positions. There wasn't a single inch of ground within that pocket that Jerry wasn't able to shell from all 3 sides.

"Course, the brass never told us about the number of casualties and they certainly didn't tell anyone in Blighty, but I reckon it was true. The never-ending evacuation of casualties by the field ambulance and by trains provided the proof. From everything I'd heard Wipers was awful from beginning to end, but by the time of the 3rd battle, the horror was unimaginable.

"In France, the situation was a bit more stable. Both sides had their positions and were fairly comfortable in them. There were large battles and offensives along the Somme and around other objectives like Arras, but apart from those, the daily routine could be almost bearable.

"For long periods the trenches would be quiet, with neither side wanting to antagonise the other any more than we had to, and if it hadn't been for the HQs on both sides demanding intelligence and prisoners, even the trench raiding would have died out. But as I've told you, we were regularly ordered to carry out trench raids, so we did. I suppose the same thing happened on the other side. But if it was left to the soldiers in the trenches, we would have just rubbed along together in relative peace and just-about-bearable conditions."

*****

"But Flanders was different. What do you know about the 3rd Battle of Wipers?" Ben asked.

"You mean Passchendaele?" I replied.

"Is that what they've called it?" Ben asked.

"Yes. All I know is what I have read and seen in photographs in historical books. It looks like something that doesn't belong on earth. I suppose that unless you were there you couldn't possibly get an idea what it was really like," I replied.

Ben thought for a moment, then asked; "How can I best describe it? I could talk about the bodies of men, horses and a mixture of both that littered the ground, apart from when they'd dissolved into crump holes and become some sort of soup? A soup that dragged in everything around it.

"I can describe what I saw, which was bad enough, but have you ever heard a man drowning in a cesspool? How do you describe that sound?

"How do you describe the smell? The surface water suppressed much of it, but when the water is disturbed the smell gets released – like farting in a bathtub, only a million times worse. It was worse still when you knew that you weren't just inhaling the remains of your dinner in a fart, you were inhaling all that might be left of a man or a horse; life and death reduced to slime and stench.

"I could talk for hours about how it felt to go through all we lived through. Us, Jerry, the French and the Belgian lads. It was the same miserable existence trying to cling to life, no matter how painful life had become. Almost every second on the line in those months leading up to Christmas 1917 was painful, physically painful. Everything hurt – every limb, every joint – the only thing that let you know your feet hadn't completely rotted away was the constant pain in them. Cold, hungry, wet and thirsty.

"You wouldn't believe that you could feel so thirsty, despite the water all around. But the water was so rank it would kill you. It must have been like being in a lifeboat after a ship wreck, needing water to survive and being surrounded by it, but knowing that to drink it would kill you. I never even opened my mouth to swallow the rain. I drank only from the disinfected stuff in my water bottle, which I always made into weak, cold tea – the chemically treated water was too disgusting to drink on its own.

"I was almost permanently disorientated. Most of the time I didn't know which way was up, never mind anything else. It was impossible to judge distance. In France the trenches had defined lines and apart from in the dark or the fog it was reasonably easy to navigate.

"Not around Wipers. There was nothing apart from the skeleton remains of trees to navigate by. That worked until the shape of the trees changed due to shellfire or simply disappeared during a bombardment. We were taught to navigate or take measurements from something fixed – the problem was that nothing there was fixed. Not trees, not pieces of wreckage, not bodies, not craters, not even villages. Everything was destroyable. And anything that appeared not to be destroyable seemed to present both sides with a challenge, to set out and prove it was. The only thing that was unbreakable was the sky and the sky seemed to be doing its very best to break us. My God, how were we ever reduced to that?

"I felt completely and utterly exhausted all the time. Physically and mentally empty. I don't know how every one of us didn't crack up. I know lots did. The only thing that is surprising is that they were relatively few.

"Along with the cold, wet and thirst was the constant fear. Fear of being raided, of straying into a Jerry position, fear of being sniped, of being shelled, of having an aeroplane drop bombs on us, of just waiting for death to come from anywhere, until it all changes one day.

"That's the day when you just give in... when you've had enough. The day when my fear of being killed was replaced by something much worse, the fear that I wouldn't be killed – but I'd have to keep going day after day, week after week, month after month – the fear that there would be no end." As Ben finished speaking he put his face into his hands and rubbed his eyes.

I wanted to speak, but what could I say to him? 'Don't worry Ben, it'll all work out,' when he knew that to be total bollocks. Ben resolved my dilemma.

"Do you want to hear a funny story?" Ben asked.

"I'd settle for anything a bit more cheerful than what you've just told me." I replied.

"Remember when I told you about me seeing the first black sailors when I was a kid near the docks in Grimsby?" Ben asked.

"Yes, I remember... hang on, is this a true story or another one of your terrible jokes?" I asked.

"If I knew that many jokes I'd be in the music hall. No, this is a true story," Ben assured me, before going on: "One day shortly after we had completed our first stint in the trenches at Laventie we moved well back from the front and had been given a few days off, before starting training.

"We got off the omnibus that was moving us and as we marched through a village towards our billets there was a group of Poilus sitting, leaning up against a fountain, and almost all of them had black faces. Some of the lads who I was marching with had never seen anyone who was black before and they didn't know that it was really the colour of their skin – that it really was black, that they didn't just have dirty hands and faces.

"The German High Command didn't like the black and brown colonial troops, calling them 'cut throats' and 'cannibals' and complained that it was unfair to use them in battle. Unfair! Can you believe that? They invade France and Belgium, destroying half of both countries, fire poison gas and kill and maim millions, then have the barefaced cheek to come out with that nonsense. You'd have to laugh if it wasn't so bloody sad.

"Anyway, we gave them a wave and marched onwards to the camp. A few days later, when given permission to leave camp, me and Jim borrowed a couple of bikes and rode into the local town. We nipped into a small bar and while we were standing at the bar drinking beer, there were two French colonial soldiers sitting at a small table next to the door drinking that French drink, the aniseed one, I can't remember what it was called."

"Pernod," I said, helpfully.

"That's it, Pernod. I remember now. I never tasted any of it. The smell of it used to make me feel sick. Anyway, we drank a couple of glasses of beer at the bar, neither me nor Jim were drinkers, it was all quite new to us. I remember Jim staring at the two black-faced soldiers. We finished our second or third drinks, and by this time I was a bit worse for wear, and I'm sure Jim was the same.

"We were leaving the bar when suddenly Jim moved towards the

Frenchies and put out his right hand, to touch the skin on the back of the bloke's right hand. As his hand stretched out towards the Frenchie, the fellow, thinking Jim wanted to shake hands, took hold of Jim's hand, in a firm grip. Jim almost filled his pants and recoiled back in fright.

"The Frenchie didn't have time to let go and as Jim shot back, the Frenchie was yanked up to his feet. He looked to be about seven feet tall. It was the funniest thing I'd seen in ages. I don't know who was more shocked, Jim or the Frenchie, but after the initial shock, one of them let go, and Jim went flying backwards, sliding backwards across the wooden floor and cracking his head against the bar. I laughed so much I thought I would choke, and after the initial shock, within seconds the Frenchies and me were laughing fit to burst.

"Jim climbed slowly to his feet and dusted himself off with his cap, rubbing the back of his head with his left hand, at the same time offering his right hand to the French soldier, who shook it firmly and gave Jim a big grin. We left the bar and walked out on to the street. We never saw the those Frenchies again, but as we walked away I could still hear them laughing until we were out of earshot.

"As we walked up the road pushing our bikes, Jim stopped walking and began rubbing his head with his left hand and his arse with his right hand.

'What's the matter?' I asked him.

'I've cut the back of my head. Look, it's bleeding,' he said, showing me a tiny smudge of blood on the palm of his left hand. Then he added, 'And I don't know what's worse, the cut on my 'ead, or the splinters in my arse.'

'The splinters,' I said. 'I don't mind sorting out the cut on your head, but you're on your own with the bloody splinters!'" And Ben and I both laughed at the thought of his mate's splintered bum, before we fell silent and Ben became a bit quieter and more serious.

He continued: "I never really gave much thought until now about how far I came from my home to finish up here in France. I wonder how far those two lads came to fight in France and if they are still here? I wonder if they survived the war and stayed in France? Or if they didn't survive the war and stayed in France? Perhaps they survived the war and went back home to their families in whatever country they came from. I hope they did – that would be the best ending to this tale, don't you think?"

"Yes, mate. That would be the best ending," I replied.

*****

Ben continued: "If the ground conditions in Flanders were terrible, our time away from the front was less so; it was quite nice at times.

"Poperinghe was the closest town to the front line that sort of wrapped itself around the town of Wipers, which was about 5 or 6 miles away. I think every Tommy who served at Wipers must've passed through 'Pops' at some time or other. The town was at the centre of a big hub for our troops. When I say ours, I mean us, the Tommies, Aussies, Canadians, South Africans, New Zealanders and Indian troops. There were lots of Chinese men from the Labour Corps and black soldiers from South Africa there as well. It was like the whole of the Empire had been picked up and dropped from a balloon on to some little Flanders town.

"The railway station was always busy even though there were only a couple of platforms. It never seemed to be quiet, with trains coming and going all day and most of the night. Even in the middle of the night, from our camp nearby, you could hear the trains coming and going at all hours. The station building wasn't all that grand. It was just a big wooden hall, more of a long shed really – well that's how it looked from the outside, I never went inside it.

"It wasn't anything like the railway stations in the towns at home and certainly nothing like any of the London stations we passed through, but it seemed to be just as busy as any London station. I don't think the tracks went right through the town. As far as I can remember the station was the end of the line and trains came out the same way as they went in.

"Every soldier in Flanders must've come through Pops, arriving at the railway station before climbing aboard a long line of omnibuses to carry on towards their camps and regimental billets. I had never visited London before the war, but I'd seen pictures of places like Piccadilly Circus with the big London omnibuses carrying people to and from their places of work. That's what Pops looked like after the trains arrived. If you were lucky enough, you would board one of the omnibuses. If you were to be billeted close by, it was time for a bit of footslogging, but after hours of being cooped up on a train, a stretch of the legs wasn't such a chore, particularly in decent weather.

"The countryside all around the town was filled with headquarters, divisional camps and training areas where the soldiers would be billeted, trained and rested when not at the front. It seemed that half of the army was camped in those fields for miles around.

"Many of the camps were close enough to be able to walk into the town when we were given time for recreation, and if you could scrounge a few bicycles, it wasn't very far at all. I mean it wasn't exactly Paris, but at least it had a few small cafes and open-air public houses where you could sit at a table outside and enjoy a beer, not that we had too many days off when we could sit outside at that time of year... sometimes it was as cold as Grimsby.

"I was never a great drinker. Don't get me wrong, I had the odd beer, but it really was the odd beer in my case. Before the army I think I'd only ever tasted beer on about 4 or 5 occasions and then it was just a mouthful from our Dad's glass. Charlie and George, being a bit older, liked the occasional glass of beer and they would give me a sip. I didn't really enjoy it. It was quite bitter – in fact, it was horrible. Even our George used to pull a face when he swallowed it, so I'm not sure he enjoyed it that much either. I asked him why he drank it, if it made him pull a face every time he tried to swallow it. He told me it was an acquired taste. I never had enough time or opportunity to acquire it.

"I had my first full glass of beer on the day I enlisted. I paid for it myself and sat in the public house, on my own, drinking my beer. I remember looking at it in the glass. How dark and thick it looked. The froth stuck to the inside of the glass as I slowly worked my way through it. I drank a couple of glasses and felt very shaky afterwards and a little bit sickly. As I drank I remembered my first attempt at enlistment in Lincoln and the tea and cake I'd bought with the sergeant's shilling before travelling home.

"I next drank beer in a small bar in France, with Jim and a few other lads from our platoon; a million miles and a lifetime away from all I'd ever known. I preferred the French beer to English beer. It was colder and much less bitter; but like I said, I wasn't much of a drinker.

"I did like coffee though. Coffee was exotic. I'd never tasted it before I arrived over here. It was always tea at home; I don't think I'd even smelled coffee before arriving here.

"In France, when we could get into a local town I used to like taking time to sit at a street bar and read a book or a few letters from home for half an hour and drink coffee. I think it was the smell as much as the taste."

I looked at Ben as he closed his eyes, leaned back on his hands and raised his face towards the sky. He looked like one of the Bisto Kids, following the smell of the gravy, but in his case, it was the smell of the coffee as his memory took him back to his little café, his coffee, book and a bit of sunshine.

"They say that the sense of smell is the sense that is most closely linked to memory," I said.

Ben didn't answer, but went on: "I remember one day in a small French town near Arras. It must have been in the late spring or very early summer. A few of us went into the town. We all had a few bob in our pockets and would be off the line for a few days. We'd been deloused, cut our hair and had our uniforms laundered with steam. It seemed like such a long time since I actually felt clean – like a human being instead of a walking colony of lice and other parasites.

"Our uniforms were clean and looking smart. My boots were polished, and my cap had been brushed and cleaned. For the first time in months I felt like a soldier rather than a tinker. We caught the omnibus from the camp into the town. It was a lovely day, what you would imagine a typical spring day to be; warm sunshine with a light breeze blowing. We sat on the top deck of the omnibus as it drove into the town.

"The town was busy and not just with the usual soldiers from all the different countries, but with people from the town as well. Quite a few local people still lived there. The town was occasionally shelled by Jerry, but this was something the locals were prepared to live with in order to remain in their own town, in their own homes. You might wonder how anyone could remain living in a place that was sometimes shelled, but by comparison with the complete misery you saw on the faces of refugees fleeing from their homes it was a small price to pay.

"Whenever we went through a town or village – or what was left of one – it made you want to weep for the poor buggers who once lived there. Imagine how terrifying it must have been to have been forced to leave everything, carrying just a small bundle of possessions. Everything abandoned apart from what could be bundled into a bedsheet, tied up to make a sack, and carried on your back. Old men and women, young women with babies and young kids, all carrying their sad little bundles.

"The lucky ones, if you could ever use the word lucky, had a small handcart, which sometimes carried a few pieces of furniture. I once saw an old lady pushing a tiny cart with a few items in it. She had a single dining chair, standing in the middle of the cart on its four legs – just one chair... one bloody chair! I don't know if she could only fit one chair in the cart, if she'd lost the others, or if she was all alone in the world and so only needed the one chair.

"Her whole world was in that cart; well, what was left of her world. The rest of her world, which she had spent her whole life building, lay in ruins a few miles behind her. It was a world she might never see again. It was a world me and my mates would march through without giving her another thought, not until I next closed my eyes to sleep – then I'd see her again. Not her face, but her little cart and single dining chair. How could anyone carry everything of importance on their back in a bedsheet, or in a handcart?

"I often thought about what my family would have put into our small cart if we had to abandon our home. I mean, how do you choose what to carry with you? I have no idea now those poor souls coped, or where they went. We only saw the destruction they walked away from. Presumably they found somewhere else to live away from the fighting, but with so many people having to flee their homes with almost no possessions... where did they sleep? Where did they go to live? How many of them ever came back to their homes once the fighting stopped?

"What would they have come back to? Most of the towns and villages were hardly recognisable as places where people had lived, with barely a dozen bricks left cemented together. Whole villages were flattened, with nothing for anyone to return to after the war; and how would they know where to begin rebuilding their town and how to rebuild their lives?

"Maybe this was at the back of our minds and was why so many of us fought so hard. We'd seen with our own eyes what had become of so many towns in France and Flanders and the people driven out by the fighting. I know at times, when I felt so tired that the will to fight was draining out of me, I pictured Fildes Street flattened into rubble and our Mam and my sisters, packing up a few belongings before heading north after we had failed them. That was more than enough to give me a kick up the arse – as if the memory of the old lady with her cart and chair wasn't enough." Ben paused, staring into the distance at nothing, but seeing the refugee and her cart once again.

He suddenly came back to me and our conversation. "Sorry, I lost track of where I was," he said.

"You were telling me about a day in town with some mates from your section," I replied.

"Thanks. As I was telling you, the group of us travelled on the top deck of an omnibus into town. When we got off the bus we walked through the streets. Although they weren't busy by comparison with home, compared with what I had seen everywhere else it was like a bit of normal life. There were lots of soldiers, but there were real people too. Going about their business like there was no war on. It felt nice to walk upright. I felt about 6 inches taller... because I was 6 inches taller, there being no need to fear having the top of your head taken off by Jerry.

"We walked down the sunny side of the street to a small bar with tables set out in the afternoon sunshine. The four or five small round tables were covered with matching red and white chequered tablecloths, all pressed and spotlessly clean. The owner had a matching cloth folded over his arm and as soon as a group left their table he would quickly gather up the used cloth and replace it with a new one.

"As he saw us approach he prepared a table and welcomed us, showed us to our seats, and wrote down our order in his little book. It was a long time since I'd felt like a real person, doing what a real person would do in the real world, or at least what I imagined a real person in the real world would do. But really, I was just a visitor, not to the real world, but a pretend world. The real world was the one where I lived in filth, always trying to avoid being killed or maimed; the one I'd return to soon enough.

"But for as long as the visit to the pretend world lasted we all enjoyed it, ordering three beers and a coffee. I had the coffee and we sat upright, not hunched. Up straight – with dry feet – without tin hats – without lice – without scratching – without ears pricked for danger. We just sat like people feeling the sun on our faces and necks. We talked about home, football, girlfriends, wives and families – anything except the war. For a short time there was no war and we were wealthy gentlemen visiting this foreign town, enjoying each other's company, the sun and our drinks. Good mates together, but mates who would never have met had some bloody Archduke and his wife not been done in a few years earlier. None of the four of us even knew what an Archduke was – an Archbishop maybe, but what the hell was an Archduke?"

I wanted to ask Ben a question but didn't want to break his memory of a happy afternoon with mates, so I said nothing.

He went on: "We sat there for the best part of 2 hours until the sun dropped behind the tall buildings across the street and the air quickly cooled. I think it must have been spring, late spring but not quite yet summer; it doesn't cool so quickly in summer. We paid the bill and took a slow walk around the town before making our way back towards the railway station where we could pick up an omnibus and make our way back to camp. Some of the shops had a very dim light in their windows as the sun went down. I remember thinking that those were the first lights I had seen in the dark for such a long time.

"As we rolled out of the town on the omnibus, because we were now ten feet in the air, in the distance I could hear the faint thud of the artillery being fired every now and then, close enough to identify what it was, far enough away to feel safe. But it was a reminder not to forget why we were here – that we were here to do a job, to be soldiers, to fight a war, rather than the gentlemen travellers that we had been for a short time an hour or so earlier."

Ben changed the subject: "Do you know that thing you said about smell being the sense most closely linked to memory? I think you are right. Whenever I remember our Mam, I can remember burying my face into her skirt when I was small and wrapping my arms around her legs to hold on to her. I can remember how she smelled far more strongly than I can remember what she looked like. The same with our house and the street. The smells are still so clear in my memory."

I asked Ben; "The town you just described, was that Poperinghe, or did you say it was a French town?"

"It was in France, west of Arras, probably not a town, more of a big village. I can't remember the name, but it definitely wasn't Pops, I'd have remembered if it was," Ben replied.

"I visited Poperinghe last year. There was a big photograph in the Market Square of how it was in about 1915. The big photograph was positioned exactly where the cameraman must have stood to take the picture. Standing there, looking at the photograph, then looking across the square towards the town hall, it was amazing how little it had changed. Most of the buildings and the church were still the same. You would have no trouble recognising it – the same with the railway station. I have seen photographs of it from the war and it's hardly changed, and you were right. The line does stop at the station, it still doesn't go straight through.

"Did you ever visit Talbot House?" I asked.

Ben replied, "Yes, quite a few times." He paused to gather his thoughts and choose his words carefully, before going on: "Toc H was an odd place, or maybe a place that was out of place; something that didn't belong in the middle of all the madness going on around it. Or maybe it did. Maybe it belonged right there, because without all the madness going on around it, there would have been no reason for it to exist.

"It was a big, high, black and white house, like something from a history book, up one of the side streets leading from the main square in Pops. On one side of the square was the street leading to Toc H with all the good stuff that happened in the house and the gardens around the back, and on the opposite side of the square, the railway station side, no more than 300 yards from Toc H was the town hall, or whatever the

Belgians called a town hall. The courtyard round the back couldn't be any more different than the Toc H gardens.

"I suppose I visited the house about seven or eight times during my time in the camps nearby. Some of the lads liked to listen to the music or watch the shows they put on from time to time, but I liked the books best. It had a decent library. You couldn't take books away, not as far as I can remember. They didn't have library tickets, but when you borrowed a book to take into the garden, you had to take your cap badge off and leave it as a guarantee that you wouldn't pinch the book; it was called 'a book for a badge' or something like that.

"After going there a few times to read I had taken my cap badge off so many times the metal became weak. I broke the back of my badge trying to get it off one day, so when I returned my book and put the badge back on my hat it was hanging off. If you nicked a book you would get into trouble if caught wearing your hat without its badge. It wasn't much better heading back to the camp with the badge dangling half-dead from your cap, but luckily it was getting dark, so there was no one to notice.

"There were a lot of rooms at Toc H, all with different stuff going on in them. There were lots of card games and dominoes games going on. It was a bit weird really. A bit like some of the scenes in Alice's Adventures in Wonderland. She might have seen talking March Hares and Mad Hatters, but she never saw anything as odd as a colonel serving tea to a subaltern, a couple of corporals and a 'Tommy' while he was playing cards with them. There was a sign as you went into the house; 'Abandon Rank All Who Enter Here.' It was an all-ranks club, or rather a no-rank club.

"The house was 3 storeys high. On the ground floor you entered a big hallway. It was high ceilinged with wood-panelled walls on both sides. It was as I imagined a really posh house, or a sort of stately home to look like. I can't be sure though because I was never in a stately home, or anything as grand.

"In the room at the back of the house on the left as you looked towards the garden was a music room with a piano. Every time I visited, someone was playing. Occasionally it was being played badly; but that was rare. Most of the time it sounded as if there was a concert pianist playing, possibly because the player had been a concert pianist before the war.

"The house was run by a captain from the chaplains department. He was a cheery chap – definitely more of a chaplain than a captain. He had a sidekick, called Petty, no, Pettifer, who was his batman, I think, but who seemed to act as the butler or something. Regardless of his rank, or lack of it, he appeared to run the place. He was an older chap with a thin face and moustache. He was quite a nice fellow, but he wouldn't stand any messing. It didn't matter what the rank of the offender was, Pettifer would have a quiet whisper in their ear and there the matter ended – no arguments.

"They even had a few pets there, cats and dogs. This was the first time I had been in the company of a good dog since leaving our Nan. If you sat out in the gardens on a sunny day, the animals would come outside and sit with you, but as soon as it clouded over they were gone, back indoors.

"The garden had seen better days. I bet it was impressive before the war. Don't get me wrong, it was still a nice place to sit and read, listen to the piano, or even a regimental band playing, but it had become a bit threadbare under the boots of a thousand visiting soldiers.

"There would often be groups of the local kids coming in for visits or to see shows put on by the troops. Coming up to Christmas 1917 there was a party for the kids and they were given small gifts and fruit. Nothing much, but they appreciated it. It gave them something, even if only a small thing to unwrap to celebrate Christmas. It was nice to see the kids smile and forget about all the terrible stuff they were living through, if only for a short time. The fellows who had children at home really enjoyed it, it was as though they could see their own kids' faces in the little local kids – almost like a real Christmas.

"On the third floor was a chapel. You had to climb up a steep ladder to get up there. Getting back down was quite a challenge. You would often hear the thump of a falling Tommy who had lost his footing on the way down. I always treated it like a ladder rather than stairs, and went up and down facing the rungs, just like a ladder.

"I was never much of a churchgoer, but I used to like sitting up there, it was a quiet place to read and think. If there was a service beginning I would go downstairs and continue reading in the library, or out into the gardens.

"One day the chaplain came up while I was reading there to set up for a service. He asked if I would stay and do a reading. Apparently, he sometimes struggled to get people to do readings apart from officers and he didn't want it to be that way – so I agreed. After that I did a few readings for him and there was one that seemed to come up every time I happened to do the reading."

I interrupted Ben: "I don't suppose it was Psalm 1? "Blessed is the man who does not walk in the counsel of the wicked... "

Without hesitation Ben continued: "nor stands in the way of sinners, nor sits in the seat of scoffers; but his delight is in the law of the Lord, and on his law, he meditates day and night.

He is like a tree planted by streams of water that yields its fruit in its season, and its leaf does not wither.

In all that he does, he prospers. The wicked are not so, but are like chaff that the wind drives away. Therefore, the wicked will not stand in the judgment, nor sinners in the congregation of the righteous; for the Lord knows the way of the righteous, but the way of the wicked will perish."

"You mean that one?" Ben asked.

"Jesus, Ben! That's bloody creepy," I exclaimed.

"What? In a way that sitting in the middle of a former battlefield holding a conversation with your long-dead great uncle isn't?" Ben laughed.

"No, hang on," I said. "A few days ago before I came here I visited Poperinghe and Talbot House. In fact, I have visited just about every bloody place you have just told me about. But I was a tourist. I was interested, in the history, in you, but I wasn't tracking you down. I wasn't looking for you."

"Are you sure? Do you believe that? That this is all a big coincidence?" Ben asked.

For the first time, I felt a bit rattled, "Look, as far as I know this might not even be happening. It might just be a dream, something I imagined might happen, so I'm dreaming it. In a few hours I will wake up, with Carol telling me I've kept her awake by farting in my sleep all night!" I replied.

Ben laughed, "Do you really think that? Like this is some version of A Christmas Carol? And I'm just a product of an undigested potato? he asked.

Still rattled, I continued: "I have no idea, Ben. I came to visit the Menin Gate, Houthulst Forest and Pozieres. I only went to Talbot House cos I thought it would be interesting and it was 10 Euros a night cheaper than anywhere else. Now I find out it was your private reading rooms and the chapel was where you did your Billy Graham act.

"Jesus, when I was up in that chapel I stood at the lectern and I read an extract from the Psalms, the one which you just happen to know by heart because that was the Psalm that you always read in the same chapel, at the same lectern, from the same bible a hundred years before me?" I replied.

Ben replied: "Well, if what you say is true, and what I say is true, that's exactly what I'm telling you. Of course, I may have memorised every line in the Bible and have been waiting a hundred years in silence for the chance to show off. Perhaps it's all a big coincidence."

"Do you know what, Ben? That whole visit to Talbot House felt strange. Not in a bad way. In a familiar, comfortable way. Don't think me a soft, girly sod, but the first time I sat in that chapel and read that Psalm I just sat quietly and bloody well cried," I said.

"And so did I," Ben replied. "I cried the first time I visited the chapel too."

"Really?" I asked.

"Yes. I swear I did. Mind you that was because I'd almost shattered my knee cap on the rungs of that bloody ladder!" Ben laughed.

"You really are a bloody piss taker, Ben. It must be a family trait," I said.

"Who's Billy Graham?" Ben asked.

"I'll tell you later," I replied.

*****

"Everyone I know really liked Pops, but it wasn't all card games and concerts," Ben said, before going a bit quieter. He diverted his eyes from me and again he looked down towards his crossed feet. Whenever he did that I knew he was feeling uncomfortable about what he was going to tell me.

He went on: "The town hall in Pops wasn't usually somewhere you wanted to visit. That was where the firing squads used to go about their business. There were a couple of cells in the building. They used them for different reasons: drunks, scrappers and other minor stuff which the army came down upon, but in all honesty, not too heavily. Spending the night 'in clink' was generally enough and if you got back to your company without missing a work detail or training it would usually be dealt with by the docking of a day's pay, or latrine duties. As we didn't have much to spend our pay on, it wasn't the end of the world, although latrine duty was unpleasant.

"The cells were also where they confined those lads that had been tried and sentenced to be shot. You had to do something bad to be shot – like trying to mutiny or doing a runner. Anything like that and you were going to be made an example of. I remember our last train journey and seeing the military police standing around the train during rest stops, just in case anyone decided to have it away on their toes.

"I'm sure there were a few bad fellows who were shot and fully deserved it, but most of them didn't. They were probably just worn out and broken by the war. It was enough to break anyone. I honestly don't understand why so few of us broke and refused to soldier on. I think as well as the fear of the consequences, we had other things going on in our heads.

"You would see it in the eyes of a mate. An empty look – not a mad one, and you could see that they'd taken too much. Everyone would rally around them and we looked out for them until they began to come around. I'm sure the poor sods who were shot just reached that depth of despair when they had no one looking out for them.

"When we arrived near Wipers, before going out into the swamp that passed for a battlefield, we were talking with a Yorkshire lad from another division. He told us that about a month earlier, in September, he and a couple of his mates got into a scrape one night in Pops and were thrown in the cells. There were three of them in one cell and in the other cell was a coloured chap from somewhere in the West Indies.

"Yorkie said that he and his mates were getting a bit rowdy in their cell. One of the guards came to the cell, opened it and stepped inside. He thought the guard was going to give one of them a right battering, but he just called them all together and whispered for them to keep the noise down as the chap in the other cell had been sentenced and was going to be shot the following morning.

"He said that none of them spoke another word all night. All he could hear was the poor bugger in the other cell walking the floor of his cell. He listened to him walking the floor all night – shuffling, not walking, mumbling, praying and sobbing.

"Apparently there was one barred window in the thick external wall of the cell he and his mates were in and as soon as it started to get light, through that window they could see the top of the execution post. As the first ray of sunlight crept in through the window, the door to his cell opened and he nearly leapt out of his skin, thinking that there had been a mistake and one of them was going to be taken out instead, but the guard just popped his head in and told them to grab their things and get as far away from the cells as fast as they could manage.

"They didn't need telling twice as they grabbed their boots, tunics, belts and caps and bolted for the door; all getting jammed as they tried to get through it at the same time. As they squeezed through they came out of the short corridor into a wide alley and he turned right to look towards the courtyard. He saw the firing squad checking their rifles and, looking further round to the right, in the corner of the yard just under the cell window was a single, thick wooden post driven into the ground.

"He spun around to his left and saw that the large heavy gate was partly opened. None of them waited for the gates to open further, but dashed through the gap and out into the street. They turned left towards the town square, running like the clappers, keeping their left shoulders close to the walls of the town hall and away from the main square, up the street leading to the railway station, carrying their clothes. They didn't even put their boots on until they reached the railway station.

"As they stopped to dress and put their boots on, he heard a volley of rifle fire. They just sat there with their boots half-laced and said nothing for about 15 minutes as the sun slowly rose in the sky. Then they walked back towards the camp, not speaking a word.

"I remember thinking about what he told me a few days later. I always thought the saying about being 'shot at dawn' was just a saying, but they really did it. They didn't even wait for anything more than the first rays of light; perhaps they were impatient to get it over with.

"I don't know if the story Yorkie told me was true, but I can't think of any reason why he would lie. A few weeks later when I was in Pops I passed the place he told me about and it was exactly as he had described. He wouldn't have been able to give such a lot of detail if he was having me on, would he?" Ben asked, looking up towards me.

I thought for a while before replying: "I'm sure he was telling you the truth, Ben, just like I'm sure that you are absolutely right about the state of mind of most of the lads who were shot. There's been a lot of research and it's now accepted that most of those lads were suffering from mental illness caused by constant shelling and fear of death. A few years ago, they were all given a pardon and exonerated from any blame and their military conduct records restored."

Ben nodded and then spoke: "It took them a hundred years to work out what every Tommy on the line knew all those years ago? And a pardon? For something they couldn't help doing? Bloody hell! It's nothing more than they deserved. It was the least they could do for them; poor bloody lads."

Ben took out a fag and lit it. We sat whilst he had a few drags on it.

"For a minute I thought you had packed in smoking. You haven't had one for ages," I said.

"I was considering giving up after your advice on the health benefits," Ben replied, with a grin.

*****

"Did you ever see a dog pulling a milk cart?" Ben asked.

"No, I haven't, well not in real life anyway. I think I've seen a photograph in a book somewhere," I replied.

Ben went on: "I have. It was in a small Flanders village. I can't remember the name of it, the village, not the dog... I never knew the dog's name in the first place, but bloody hell, it was a strange sight.

"Can you believe that? Your uncle ... sorry, your great uncle goes off to the biggest war in history and one of the things he remembers best was a flippin' dog delivering milk?

"Massive it was. I don't know what sort of dog it was, but it was enormous. I don't mean as big as a small pony or a donkey, but it was bigger than any dog I ever saw. Not so much tall, but strong and muscular. I remember seeing a drawing in one of our Dad's books of a dog that served with the Roman legions and it looked something like one of them. I remember those in the book were called 'war dogs', but this one had more sense and managed to get a job delivering the milk. I always knew that dogs were clever, but that one was cleverer than the thousands of soldiers he must have seen marching past him every day.

"The milk cart was big enough to be pulled by a horse; it was full of straw and about six big milk churns. I think the straw was to prevent the milk getting too warm. It was driven by a lady, about the same age as our Mam.

"One day when she was returning to her farm after making her deliveries she stopped and called us over. She took the top off one of the churns and dipped the ladle into the milk before offering it to us. The milk was cold and very creamy. We each had a few mouthfuls before passing the ladle around 'til we'd all taken a drink and given her back the ladle. Then without saying a word she pushed the dog onwards back towards the farm. It was the best milk I ever tasted, and I never forgot her little bit of kindness."

"Didn't the Belgian Army use dogs to pull their heavy machine guns? I asked. "I'm sure I have seen a photograph of them doing that."

Ben replied, "I don't know. I never saw that, but I'll tell you something: If I'd been a Belgian dog, I'd have been the bugger pulling the milk cart, not the one pulling the bloody machine gun," he laughed.

Chapter 9

Lunatics

"We had been getting ready for a big Jerry attack while we were training near Langemarck. From about the 20th of March the whole division was at 12 hours' notice to move to any point on the front line that we might be needed. It wasn't a question of if we would be moving to the front, just when and where we would be going. The answer to that question would be decided by Jerry generals, not ours. We would be responding to their move. People always say that the waiting was the worst. What a load of nonsense that is. I always preferred to wait 10 miles behind the front line over advancing towards a bloody machine gun. Yes, waiting in relative safety was always preferable in my book.

"Before the sun came up on the 23rd we were on the move from our training billets at Chauny Camp. I'd slept badly as we had been given our orders the night before. In the first glimmers of daylight we were taken by omnibus and any other vehicle capable of carrying soldiers to Roesbrugge and assembled at the railway station for transportation to wherever we would be needed. I think our whole battalion was transported, but we passed columns of men marching in the same direction as us, who had to cover the distance on foot.

"On the way to the station and whilst waiting for our transport that morning it seemed as if the whole of the army was on the move. There were columns of vehicles making their way to Roesbrugge, passing endless columns of marching troops, and when we arrived at the railway station there were trains, all pointing in the same direction on both lines, parked so close together it was hard to tell if they were separate trains or just a big long one – like a giant snake, stretching away into the gloomy distance as far as the eye could see.

"After getting off the vehicles we moved slowly in columns on to the station platform and there we waited. We waited in company order to get on board. All of us were weighted down with equipment and wrapped up against the cold. I was pleased with my inherited scarf as we waited.

"We still had no idea where we would be going. We only knew that something big had happened or was about to happen. I hadn't seen so many soldiers on the move since October the previous year, when thousands were moved forward for the third battle of Wipers, around Passchendaele. This time it was different; when we moved forward that time it was slow and organised, and troops moved in stages, properly prepared – if it was possible to prepare for something like that. This time it was different, it all seemed to be much more hurried. Our battalion had been lucky as we'd been in a training camp, giving us time to reorganise and get our equipment in order. I'm sure most of us felt well rested.

"Some of the other battalions who were recently back from the front line had to do an immediate about-turn and head back to the trains, without rest or the chance to replace or repair damaged equipment. Some of them were dressing each other whilst on the hoof. Many looked like they were missing pieces of equipment and what they had was in poor condition and needed to be serviced. They were turning around to head back into battle without anything other than what they could scrape together on the road or on the train.

"By comparison with those poor sods we were quite lucky, we were organised, and I was ready for what we were about to face. One of the few problems we had was that whilst in training we'd received another batch of replacements. These poor lads had no idea what they were going into, and we'd only had about a week with them to knock them into shape, but I'm sure that a couple of companies had received their replacements the previous evening at about 6 o'clock and at 6 in the morning they were heading off into the middle of God knows what, at God knows where, with a couple of lads who knew bugger all about anything – not even the names of their section. That's a lonely place to be at the best of times, and this was quite possibly the worst of times.

"We usually tried to split up the new lads. We'd learned from experience that it didn't do anyone any good to have 2 or 3 inexperienced replacements serving alongside each other. That was no reflection of how brave the lads were, it's just that two or three Tommies might be responsible for holding or taking quite a large stretch of ground. You'd be surprised at how good Jerry was at finding a weak point created by inexperienced soldiers. They didn't need to see the cleanliness of the uniform or the shiny paint on a tin hat. They could identify a lack of experience purely by the rate and accuracy of fire coming from an area on the line. We knew the same when facing inexperienced Jerries. That was one of the main reasons we split them up and put them alongside seasoned fellows – their rate of fire would keep the new lads safe until they gained the experience needed to keep themselves alive.

"The first time you're in those first shattering seconds of battle is an absolutely terrifying experience. The fear is almost indescribable. That first close engagement when you can feel the heat from the muzzle of a Mauser on your face and are blinded by the flash – in that moment I don't care how brave anyone thinks they are, it makes your blood run cold and it takes valuable seconds to react in the way you have been trained to. In those few seconds you can't have a bunch of lads that hesitates as a group. Having an 'old sweat' either side of you is probably the only thing that will keep you alive. In those moments when you're paralysed with fear, your only hope is to have mates on either side of you meeting fire with fire whilst you shake off the terror and gather your wits about you.

"I remember my first meeting face to face with Jerry, not just being shelled. I was on the line near Albert. I can clearly remember the terror that left me frozen with fear, just for 3 or 4 seconds, and in that time the whole area to my front was filled with enormous Jerry soldiers, so close and so big they blocked out the daylight. Without the steadiness of my mates they'd have been on top of me in seconds, before I'd even had the chance to fire a shot. As it was, the lads either side of me stopped them in their tracks. One Jerry got so close to me before being shot in the head that as he fell forward onto his face, as dead as a nit, his helmet smashed into the earth within a couple of feet from me and the mud, mixed with his blood, splashed up from the ground and hit me in the face.

"It was like the world was moving in slow time, not normal speed. I couldn't hear what was being shouted, the sound of rifle fire was muffled as though my ears were covered. The first thing I remember was our section corporal crawling forward into the gap on my right-hand side and slapping me on the shoulder. He shouted 'There's no point looking down the sights and not pulling the trigger. It's a bleedin' rifle not a 'what-the-butler-saw' machine – Now fire the bloody thing!'"

"I fired my first round. God knows where the shot went. Probably into the mud 3 feet away, or into the dead Jerry right in front of me."

"'Come on Ben, bloody well fire!' Jim shouted to me from the left."

"I did as I was told and gradually I began to lose the numbness in my hands. It was like they were being thawed out, from being frozen solid. As the blood and feeling came back into my hands I worked the bolt and fired again... at nothing in particular – then the bolt – then fire – then the bolt – then fire, going on until my magazine was empty. I needed no telling to reload. I changed magazine quickly if a bit shakily and began firing again, this time looking to the front and firing at moving shapes rather than firing blindly.

"By the next magazine change I was working smoothly and effectively, playing my part. Firing quickly and accurately, taking time to check my mates to my left and my right. I could see them a few feet away, firing a bit faster than me, completely absorbed in what they were doing, and I knew I was in good company. They didn't look to their left or right, to see what I was doing, well not that I could see. Later I was to understand why.

"I noticed that Jim had gone. I saw him appear to my left about ten feet away, next to another young lad, shouting in his ear and directing him where to fire, before moving on to the next area where he was needed. He might not have had the tapes, but that was the first of many times I saw him take the lead when everyone was on their bellies. He was the sort of soldier we all wanted to be.

"As I gained experience I learned that there was no need to look left and right with anything other than a quick flick of the eyes, rather than a head-turn, because the sound of the steady rate of fire by your mates was all you needed to tell you they were alongside you and covering your flanks.

"It was only when the rate of fire to your left or right wasn't there, that you began to worry that they were hit, or in the case of an inexperienced replacement, not firing effectively, and you worried about your flank. When everything was going well, you trusted your mates to play their part, you could feel them there... you didn't need to look. Once I understood this I was proud that my mates had trust in me so quickly.

"Anyway, where was I?" Ben asked.

"You were on the platform, waiting for your train," I replied.

Ben picked up the story. "There we were standing on the platform, waiting and looking to our front. The first train arrived, approaching from the left. One of our officers went forward to speak with an official who appeared to be in charge. The train stopped, but no one moved forward. The train shunted on for about another hundred yards or so and stopped again – none of us moved. I looked to my right and saw the first soldiers climbing aboard. They struggled to pull themselves up; weighed down with their equipment. As soon as they were on board the train was moving. When I say on board, I don't mean on the train and sitting down, I mean hanging on. The last few lads were still being hauled aboard by their mates as the train rolled out.

"As it departed we turned to the right and shuffled down the platform. As we moved, I could see on the other platform similar lines of soldiers facing us. Another train pulled in, but this time it was on the other platform. I couldn't hear the soldiers climbing aboard, just our own shuffling footsteps as we waddled forward. We were packed so tightly that we could only shuffle. I'd seen penguins in one of our Dad's books and that is the only thing I could think of. I must have started grinning at the thought because one of the sergeants sidled up to me and said, 'Don't think that grinning like an idiot will get you to the aid station Mr Leeman. Perhaps if you started drooling it would help.' Then lowering his voice, he added, 'but probably not. If you weren't already a certified lunatic, you wouldn't be here... none of us would!'"

"The train on the other platform to my left was now loaded and pulling out. Another stopped at our platform about 100 yards ahead. Our column ground to a halt, but we didn't turn to our left this time – we continued facing forward. I couldn't see this train being loaded as my face was buried in the pack of the man in front. I could hear a few shouts from the NCOs urging the lads to get aboard quickly.

"A lad in front shouted, 'At least it's not raining!' which resulted in him receiving a shower of abuse and a slap around the back of his head from the soldier to his right. His cap fell off and we were jammed so closely together, he didn't have space to bend over and retrieve it. Almost immediately our column waddled forward. The bare-headed soldier shouted for someone to get his hat, which quickly became a football being kicked forward in the direction of travel. As we shuffled onwards the sodden cap fell further behind and was trampled underfoot as the light rain began to fall.

"'Where's my cap? I've lost me bloody cap!' he shouted.

'That's God's punishment for bringing the rain, you bloody daft sod!' someone replied.

"As our column advanced, another train arrived and departed from the other platform. By now we were caught in the steam from the engine as it departed. We ground to a halt and were given the instruction to 'Left Turn!' and we faced the tracks. Everyone knew that the next train would be taking us to a dark and frightening place, but at that moment all I wanted was to get on the thing and out of the miserable drizzle.

"One of the sergeants shouted, 'Does anyone need to go for a piss?' but before anyone could reply our train was pulling up to the platform. 'Too late, you'll just have to hold it for now! Keep in line lads, keep together.' That was a bit optimistic, I thought.

"It descended into a free-for-all as we scrambled aboard to get out of the rain and tried to get a seat. It was a right scrap with loads of pushing and shoving, and this was to head towards the enemy, not to get away from them! That NCO who spoke to me earlier was absolutely right, I mean who in their right mind would be fighting for the best seat on a train heading towards the battle? What a bunch of lunatics!

"Before I knew it, Jim had got to the front and was up on to the train. He put out his right hand, which I grabbed, and he heaved me aboard and into a couple of first class seats. They really were first class, well, they were at one time. It was still embroidered on the headrest. I don't think I'd ever been in such a posh seat before. I was never in one again, that's for certain.

"Within minutes the train lurched, and we rolled out into the murky morning. It must have been about 9 o'clock when we pulled out of the station, still not knowing where we were headed. I wonder if the driver did, or whether we were simply moving in the right direction, with the destination to be decided by the events of the next few hours.

"Even if the driver knew, we seemed to spend a lot of time standing still or crawling along. The train moved slowly all day. I lost count of the number of times we stopped in the middle of nowhere, when we would be allowed off for a pee break before being herded back on to the train by our NCOs, with a number of military policemen always waiting in the wings, should anyone be daft enough to try to have it away on his toes.

"We seemed to change direction a lot. I'm not sure if this was because our destination hadn't been finalised, or whether part of the intended route was in danger of being overrun by the advancing Jerries. I heard some of the officers talking with the railway staff about whether we were being routed through Arras, or whether it would be safer to pass to the west, whilst continuing to head south towards the Somme.

"After passing Arras we stopped for about an hour. As the sun began to set, the train was very quiet. I had a window seat and as the sun dropped down to the west I pulled down the window and leaned out to have a smoke and watch it slowly turn from day to night. The sunset was fantastic to watch – even the snoring coming from the carriage behind me couldn't take the shine off it.

"In the trenches the sunset wasn't something you watched. At sunset and sunrise, we were always at 'Stand To' so watching the sky wasn't a priority – watching front was. But when we were away from the trenches, in training camps, then I used to like to sit quietly, have a fag and a brew and watch the sunset. Spring and autumn had the best ones; particularly autumn. In summer it took too long and in winter one minute it was day the next it was pitch black. In autumn it set gradually and often coincided with the time when we had finished our duties for the day.

"Sitting at Chauny Camp I would look west towards France, which was only a couple of miles away, and watch some great sunsets. Looking to the west also meant I was looking away from the war – away from the bad stuff and towards places that were still relatively peaceful, and which we were doing our best to keep that way. Looking towards the border I would watch the sky turn from blue to yellow and then orangey-red as the sun dipped. On a calm day the red would spread horizontally from one side of the sky to the other in separate ribbons, with bits of blue sky in between them. Finally, all the ribbons would merge into one thick band of colour. Red closest to the sun and slowly turning more orangey, then yellowy – as the band of colour got further away from it.

"When the single band of colour was complete there would nearly always be a strip of bright blue between the setting sun and the horizon. Not sky blue – a little darker. It looked like the sea... like the colour of the sea on a bright, sunny day, but of course it wasn't.

"It's funny how easy it is to take things for granted. I bet most people have never in their lives just sat and watched a sunset from beginning to end. Perhaps they're scared to think about its meaning. I mean, every sunset is one less, another day gone, a day they'll never get to live again – the sky's way of reminding them that they are another day closer to the last sunset they'll ever see.

"I looked at it differently, maybe from the point of view of a soldier. I thought of each sunset as a milestone to be enjoyed and treasured. For me it wasn't one day less, but one more that I had survived, when so many others hadn't lived to see it. For me, a sunset wasn't a reminder of my own mortality – Jerry reminded me of that every day; sometimes every hour. No, for me each sunset and sunrise were proof that I'd made it through another day, or another night. It meant that I'd survived one more than I had any right to expect.

"Shortly after sunset the train lurched forward, and we continued slowly for another couple of hours. By the time we stopped at the end of the journey it was dark – but at least it was dry. We disembarked at a village called Mericourt, maybe 5 or 6 miles from the town of Albert." Ben finished speaking and took out another Black Cat.

"Smoke?" he asked, whilst offering me a fag.

"No thanks, mate," I replied, "I've still given up, but thanks for the offer, and if I start again, I promise you'll be the first person I tell."

*****

Ben continued: "We filed off the train and began dressing, putting on greatcoats, tying up bootlaces and adjusting puttees. Within a few minutes we were ready to move, when the CSM pointed us to the other side of the tracks where a field kitchen had been set up and was in good order.

"Get yourselves over there lads and get something hot inside you. It's going to be a long night," he said. We didn't need telling twice, we marched over the tracks under the orders of our NCOs and filled up on tea, with lots of sugar and hot stew. Irish stew I think, although I don't know how Irish stew differs from English stew. It had been a long day and I ate too much – my stomach felt hard and swollen under my tunic. After 30 minutes of wolfing down the rations we formed up and set off towards the war.

"The road out of Mericourt led us sort of eastwards... I think, and we were quickly marching up some long, drawn-out inclines. Following the 12-hour journey, we'd all stiffened up, and after filling our stomachs with tea and stew we moved quite sluggishly. There was so much belching and farting going on it was almost like we had a military band keeping time for us.

"It was quite a pleasant, mild evening and we soon began to break into a sweat as we climbed the winding route out of the village. About two miles later we were on the high ground. To our left was the town of Albert and to our right was the Somme valley. We headed on towards the village of Bray-sur-Somme.

"We followed the road towards Bray, or what was left of the road, until we arrived at what was left of the village. It was slow going in the dark and it was a couple of hours later when we took our first break at the rubble of Bray; not the best place to rest on the way to the frontline, right next to the cemetery containing the graves of our lads who were lost along this road in 1916.

"There was a small broken-down farm building, which we used as shelter and cover to get some tea brewed without the light from the flame giving our position away. We were also able to grab a few smokes as we gulped down our tea. The lads were experienced enough not to leave the building without putting out their fags. When one of the new fellows tried to leave holding a lighted fag, one of the corporals picked him up and almost threw him back to the building.

"I finished my fag and went outside. I put my waterproof sheet down and lay on my side with my head propped up on my right hand. Now that we had stopped moving I started to feel the chill. I was looking towards the road from Bray-sur-Somme towards the war. I bet that in the past that road brought good things into the village, but now it just brought soldiers, and whenever the soldiers came, trouble and misery weren't usually far behind.

"The ground was quite bare. There was grass growing, but it was very sparse. Before this whole shitty mess landed on the village, that road would have been lined on both sides with trees; now there was nothing. Any trees that once grew had long since been reduced by shell fire to little more than splinters and dead stumps, but this far into the war those last bits of wood had long since been dug up by the villagers, or soldiers passing through, and been burned in a desperate attempt to keep warm. They even dug the roots out, dried them and burned them.

"Have you ever watched cows lying down on the grass on a cold day and seen all the steam coming from their nostrils?" asked Ben.

"Yes, why?" I replied.

"That's what we must have looked like, drinking our hot tea. We had been there for only a short time when the temperature suddenly dropped, and frost began to form on our uniforms and waterproof sheets.

"Through the steam of my brew I saw them coming out of the darkness; two adults pulling a cart – a handcart stacked with some furniture and what looked like a couple of small suitcases. There was an older man, possibly the grandfather of the family. He was wearing a smart hat and a long overcoat. The woman looked as though she might be his daughter – she was far too young to be his wife. She wore a hat and long winter coat. She had thick grey-coloured stockings on and very smart shoes. Each held one of the handles of the cart; the man closest to me and the woman on the other side. They walked slowly, but it didn't look as though they were walking slowly because of the weight of the cart. It looked as if they were weighed down by the complete destruction of everything that lay behind them.

"Right behind the cart was a tall girl, about 13 years old. She walked purposefully and upright, ramrod straight, about 6 feet behind the cart. She held a piece of thin rope to which was attached a large, athletic, tan-coloured dog, which walked at exactly her pace at her right side.

"I'd seen these dogs when we first arrived in Flanders. They were handsome animals, but not to be mucked about with. They had originally been kept to control and guard sheep, but all the sheep had long since gone. The farmers kept their best ones as guard dogs, and bloody good they were at their new job. Many a Tommy had come off second best to one of those dogs whilst trying to nick a few eggs from a barn. If he was lucky he'd have lost the arse out of his trousers, but more often than not, he lost half of his arse as well.

"Behind the girl and her dog were 3 younger children scampering along. Two were holding hands and half running to keep up, with the third little 'un a short way behind. All of the children were dressed in their best, smart clothes; their Sunday best. The smallest kid was a little boy aged about 4 years old, who scampered, skipped and ran along, trying to keep up – but not trying too hard. He looked like he didn't have a single worry in the world.

"As the family passed us by they kept their eyes fixed firmly on the road ahead; apart from the dog at the older girl's side, as firmly as they kept their eyes forward, he never took his eyes off us. I bet the people didn't want to look at us – didn't want to look at those who were at least partly responsible for them losing everything.

"I know it was the Germans that had invaded their country, but sometimes I wondered if it was worth fighting them. We were fighting to protect families like these in villages just like this one all across France and Flanders and all we had managed to achieve was the destruction of the very things we were trying to save.

"As the little lad ran to catch up with his brothers and sisters, he looked straight towards me. He stopped and looked me right in the eye and then he gave me a wave and a big smile, before scampering after his family, without waiting to see if I would wave back. I watched as they walked on, without a backward glance at the wreckage of the life they were leaving behind, maybe forever. Even the dog now had his eyes front.

"As they disappeared into the remains of Bray-sur-Somme, the road dropped downwards until all that remained of them were the clouds of exhaled breath floating into the air, like a locomotive heading away into the distance, until the steam disappeared, and they were gone, along with their clouds of breath. I closed my eyes, because I was tired... tired of seeing so much bloody misery.

"About 15 minutes later one of the sergeants gave us the news we were heading for Maricourt. Some of the lads thought he'd said Mericourt and became quite cheery about heading back to the railway station... but no such luck.

"We were soon on the march again. In the darkness we followed the road, but we were all aware that we were getting close to being within artillery range – but it was the only way to move quickly in the darkness. By now we could see the moonlight reflecting off the Somme snaking its way through the valley below us to our right. There was the constant sound of fierce fighting ahead of us. It sounded like the whole of the front line was engaged in battle, not the usual small scraps that were commonplace during trench raids, or when one side was probing the other's lines."

"This was different. This was an attack over a massive stretch of the line, just where we were headed. This was a full-scale offensive with everything Jerry could throw at us, and we in turn were throwing everything we could muster right back at him.

"The noise told us that Jerry wasn't having it all his own way. There was an incessant firing of machine guns, providing a co-ordinated defence of our positions. It was almost like some sort of mad conductor was orchestrating them, an orchestra of Vickers, artillery and mortars all playing the same piece – in defence of our ground.

"It was clear we were being rushed in to support any sections of the line in danger of collapsing, or we would be pushed into any gaps, should Jerry succeed in breaking through. As we approached Maricourt we were in ignorance of the exact situation in the valley below, but it was obviously serious.

"We were still slogging onwards as the sun came up at about a quarter past six. A short time after sunrise we made our way into the village of Maricourt – once again passing the village cemetery. I remember thinking, 'does some bugger think it's funny routing us past every cemetery on the Somme?' All we seemed to do was rest and brew up in the company of the dead.

"Our march throughout the night had been accompanied by the constant sound of battle. The sound of the Jerry 08 heavy machine gun was horrible. It was almost unstoppable. It just kept on and on and on; never taking a rest from spewing out death. Over the years they'd taken a terrible toll on us, but when you heard it 'barking' and considered the millions and millions of rounds fired at us it was incredible that even one of us survived. It made a terrifying sound, even at a distance of a few miles... especially when you were marching towards it."

*****

"The artillery hadn't let up all night, neither ours nor theirs. It was like the bass drum of the regimental band keeping us in step. We had kept time with it, moving at a constant pace all night, and the beat wasn't about to be disrupted by daybreak.

"We moved into the centre of the rubble of Maricourt just before half past six in the morning and rested in the remains of the village church, which was positioned at a staggered crossroads. The daylight revealed a thick layer of frost on the fields.

"We must have covered about thirteen or fourteen miles from Mericourt, with only the one break at Bray-sur-Somme before advancing towards Maricourt – although both places sounded alike, they certainly weren't; Mericourt was where we'd come from and Maricourt was where we were. They were different places, and when we arrived any lingering confusion disappeared; the one we had marched out from was a sleepy hamlet and the one we marched into was a pile of rubble providing us with some uncomfortable seating as we awaited the arrival of the Kaiser's finest boys.

"As ever, there was no sign of life in the remains of the village – well, apart from us. The only clue that this was once a place inhabited by the living was the presence of the dead in the local cemetery. It seemed that just about everywhere we went, the living had left the place to their dead forefathers in order to avoid joining them any time soon. I'm pretty sure that with the horror developing in the valley below us, even the dead would have done a runner if they'd been able to. Maricourt... a village occupied by the dead and soon to be dead.

"I remembered the joke the sergeant had made to me about 'lunatics' before we boarded the train 24 hours earlier, and here we were, preparing to head towards almost certain death like a bunch of lunatics.

"Someone had made a good start brewing up, using the water from a load of old fuel cans that were now used to hold clean... well, treated water. Most of us had acquired extra water bottles so we filled up all those we had with the brewed-up tea, which was a lot more drinkable that the chemically purified water. The treated water prevented us getting dysentery, but was foul.

"Breakfast was hard tack biscuits and whatever we had in our packs. More and more troops from our division were arriving by the minute. It seemed as though half the battalions leaving the station at Roesbrugge were assembling in and around the village.

"Breakfast was accompanied by the sound from the front line, which, judging by the noise was only a mile or so away and getting ever closer. There was no let-up, just a never-ending rattle of machine guns, and the roar of the artillery in the mad man's orchestra. We didn't need to see the picture; the music told the story.

"The CSM relayed orders that we should prepare to move and to move light. We removed our packs and any equipment that wouldn't be immediately required when we met up with Jerry. Any weight we were able to shed was immediately replaced with additional ammunition and Mills bombs. Some of the lads were pressganged into assisting the machine gunners – carrying additional ammunition tins, spare barrels and just about any spare parts needed to rebuild a weapon in the middle of a scrap.

"Within about 15 minutes we were ready to go. We weren't just ready to go, we were champing at the bit. Not because any of us had ideas of a glorious outcome or becoming heroes; anyone who ever saw a mate die on a battle field knew full well there's sod all heroic about it, but because the quicker we got into the battle, the quicker it might be over.

"Officers were gathering in briefings, runners were going about their business and the signallers were in demand. We were assembled by company and were ready to go. We waited for our orders.

"We didn't wait long before the 15th Battalion advanced to the high ground alongside the Bray to Perrone road, where we awaited further orders. At about half past eight we were ordered to advance about two miles towards Perrone and hold the ground in and around Curlu Wood, a mile or so beyond the village of Curlu. The village of Curlu was within a sort of loop in the river Somme, so the front line had always been interrupted there by the river.

"The part of the line that met the river would be held by the Cheshires. The Cheshires led off and we followed – moving quickly using the undulations in the land for best use of what little cover was available. We made it to the edge of the wood without incident and pressed on cautiously, deeper into the wood.

"It took us about half an hour to cover the ground from Maricourt to our positions in what was left of the wood. Despite the noise of the fighting, the thing I remember most was the sound – not the sound of guns, but the singing of dozens of skylarks, hovering above us. I mean, how did they do that with everything going on? More to the point, why would they do it? If I'd had wings I'd have used them to get as far away as possible.

"When we made it to the cover of the wood, we set about repairing what was left of any defences and increasing the depth of any natural defilades. We quickly began digging to create some decent cover, particularly for our Vickers crews. We soon had reasonable defences from infantry, but little in the way of overhead cover from artillery fire, which was sure to come. The best we could do was to cover our holes and scrapes with branches and throw our waterproof sheets over them, then cover the sheets with as much earth as they could support, in the hope this would absorb at least some of the shrapnel.

"After preparing as best we could, we waited for the storm we knew would soon arrive. But it didn't arrive, so at about midday the order was given for Z and Y Companies to advance and drive Jerry from his newly occupied positions, before he had the opportunity to strengthen them.

"There were only a couple of hundred yards or so between us and Jerry. The ground undulated and so gave us a small amount of cover – more than we would have expected, but less than we would have hoped for. We drove out hard; the Vickers crews laying down constant support fire to keep their heads down, and we made quick progress overrunning those isolated Jerry positions that had gotten too far in front of their main force.

"The Cheshires to our right flank were also pushing on and taking care of those Jerries that had been pushed sideways by our attack. We could hear the Cheshires' Vickers crews hammering away, so knew they were close alongside us.

"We pressed on slightly beyond were we had hit Jerry and occupied the remains of some ramshackle shallow ditches, which had probably been hastily dug trenches at one time, but they were now little more than shallow dips. Once again, we began digging them out to give us something to defend. We banked earth up at the front and rear edge in the absence of anything to put over us to give protection from artillery.

"We waited. We could hear the Cheshires firing at Jerry from our right flank, but we could hear and see nothing to our left – no movement and no sound of firing. The Company Commander gave the order to hold our positions whilst a runner was sent to the left flank to try and link up with any troops. He returned 15 minutes later as though his backside was on fire and reported that he had been right to the edge of the wood and the only troops he had seen were Jerries, lots of them, and they were only a few hundred yards away.

"Almost immediately we saw movement all along the line about a hundred yards to our front, almost like ghosts moving through patches of sunlight, before disappearing into the shadows.

"Suddenly they emerged, running at full speed towards us, in complete silence, so that the only thing I could hear was their boots thumping the ground and the rattling of their equipment. I don't know if they thought our positions were close by and they could overrun us, or further away and they planned to dash forward before going to cover – either way, it was a mistake. We opened up with every available rifle and Lewis gun and in less than a minute, every single Jerry had been dropped.

"Less than 10 minutes later Jerry did the same thing again, as did we, with the same result. The second wave fell on top of the bodies of the first wave. Unbelievably, within minutes a third wave was sent in the same manner and dispatched with the same ease by our lads.

"The Company Commander realised that Jerry was probably now considering moving around the edge of the wood and either encircling, or just by-passing our position. Even if temporarily exposed to artillery fire when skirting the wood, it was probably a better option than another frontal attack against us in the wood, where we had shown our strength.

"We silently moved much of our company strength to protect the left flank, whilst a few sections, mine included, and the whole of Y Company spread out as best we could. We were now seriously overstretched, and a runner was sent back to request reinforcements for our left flank, or for permission to pull back to link-up with the rest of the battalion. That must have been about 3 o'clock."

"At about 4 o'clock nothing had been heard from the runner sent an hour earlier, so another was sent. Everyone knew this was our last chance to get word back. Nobody wanted to be the runner – no one wanted to leave his mates. One of the lance corporals had a shoulder wound received during our advance and couldn't hold a weapon, never mind fire one. He argued that he could help feed the Vickers, but he couldn't. His legs and mouth were still working and that was all he needed to use. The CSM left him in no doubt he was to go, grabbing him by the scruff of his collar and almost throwing him back towards our Battalion HQ.

"As he left, we hoped he would make it and bring reinforcements, but in all honesty none of us thought he would, and unless the reinforcements were going to arrive sitting on an artillery shell, we knew they were going to be too late. I saw him disappear into the wood taking our hopes with him, and I knew that short of a miracle none of us was ever going to walk out of Curlu Wood."

"Did nobody discuss the possibility of surrendering if you were being overrun?" I asked.

Ben replied without hesitation, "No. And it never even crossed my mind. Not then, nor at any time since arriving in France two years earlier. As long as I was able to fight, I was going to – I never even considered that any of my mates might feel differently. We all knew that the only chance of getting out alive was to keep our hands on our rifles, not in the air."

Ben continued: "I looked across at Jim, who was on my right-hand side. He was busy lining up his magazines on the rim of the shallow defences.

"I said, 'What the hell are you doing, if we have to move you'll lose half of those magazines!' But he just winked at me and then lined about 4 or 5 Mills bombs in the soft earth just below the magazines and said, 'Get your stuff organised Ben, we ain't leaving here, and I'm planning on taking plenty of foreign company with me to the next life.' And then the daft bugger started laughing, pulled out a packet of fags and lit up, before throwing the packet to me.

"As I pulled a fag out and put it in my mouth the CSM came along the line. Jim blew a big cloud of smoke up in the air. When I saw the CSM I nearly filled my pants – expecting a massive telling-off. But he just flopped down on his back next to me and grabbed the packet and lit one up, blowing another big cloud of smoke up in the air. 'Bloody hell Sir, won't Jerry see the smoke?' I said to him.

"The CSM rolled onto his side and propped himself up on his right elbow. 'I reckon Fritz has got a pretty good idea where we are, son. And if he doesn't, as soon as he climbs over the bodies of his mates and shows his ugly mush through the wood he bloody well will.' Then a bit louder, so the rest of our section could hear, he added, 'get your bayonets fixed lads. Keep firing till you've nothing left, then get to work with the bayonet. If we hold on long enough, we might still be here when some support arrives.' He crushed out the stump of his fag and prepared to move.

'Do you reckon we can hold them that long, Sir?' I asked.

'Not a sodding chance, young Leeman, but there's no point letting it get you down – nobody likes a misery guts!' he replied.

"And with that he took off, keeping low towards the left flank and flopping down next to a Vickers crew, where he started to line up his magazines and Mills bombs, just as Jim had done. I did the same, before fixing my bayonet to my rifle."

*****

"Once we were as prepared as we would ever be, there was a bit of a commotion from the right-hand side of the line. A couple of lads from Y Company came moving towards us, keeping low, with a large wooden crate which they were half carrying, half dragging by a couple of rope handles.

"The box was full to the brim with Mills bombs, which they doled out to each of the lads. It was a bit like feeding time in the cookhouse with the cooks doling out dollops of mashed spud, except this time the cooks were doling out dollops of death.

"By the time they got to me they were whacking out about 3 per Tommy. They got to the CSM and the Vickers crew on the left flank, dropped off a load and then began making their way back, giving everyone second helpings... that was a bleedin' novelty I can tell you.

"As I began to arrange my Mills bombs Jim hissed to me; 'Ben! eyes front. I'll be back in a minute!' and off he shot, loping along behind me and the lads to my left and heading towards the CSM. A brief conversation and he was heading back, stopping on the way to clip a few lengths of wire from a big spool he was now carrying and give the pieces to one of the lads. He passed me and kept going; stopping every fourth or fifth man and doing the same.

"A short time later he reappeared and then, as one, about half a dozen of the fellows at regular intervals slipped out of cover and crawled forward about 50 yards, before setting concealed Mills bombs and trip wires every few paces. The pins in each of the bombs were pulled out to the point that the lightest touch on the wire would remove the pin.

"On a signal from Jim, as one, the lads crawled back towards our positions, stopping when signalled to set up another two parallel lines of trip-wired Mills bombs about 40 yards and 30 yards from our position, before scuttling back to cover and picking up their rifles. Their efforts were never going to stop Jerry, but if it slowed him sufficiently it would give us the chance to top him off with some effective fire.

"The lads placed their surprises in the areas where we were spread thinnest and left fewer in those areas covered by Vickers crews or Lewis gunners, so that any assault might be funnelled towards our heaviest firepower – that was the plan anyway, but as I had rarely been involved in a plan that had worked, I wasn't too hopeful this time. It might not have been much, but it was better than nothing.

"And there we lay in wait – not really knowing what we were waiting for. Waiting for reinforcements, or waiting for Jerry? Waiting for death, or waiting for a bloody miracle? We all hoped for the reinforcements or the miracle, but deep down, I reckon we all knew that we were going to get Jerry and death. I slid down from the lip of my position and rolled onto my back, took out a fag and lit it up, then threw it to Jim. I lit another for myself and there we lay, like a couple of toffs, on our backs, hands behind our heads, looking up at the patch of blue sky visible through the skeletons of trees."

*****

"The sun shone down, making me feel warm and comfortable. I looked towards Jim. He slid along the ground to the next man and whispered something in his ear. He lay there whilst that man slid to his right and whispered to the next man, before returning to his original position and the routine continued with each man passing the message along the line.

"Jim returned and slid back into his scrape and peered over the rim and through the undergrowth he had placed there so as not to be clearly seen. He didn't glance towards me, he just kept looking forward to where Jerry was likely to emerge.

"I hissed as loudly as I could, 'Jim! Jim! What the bloody hell was that all about? What were you telling them? Why are you passing it down the line that way?'

'Nowt you don't already know!' he replied.

'What do you mean by that? What do I already know?' I asked.

'I told them not to be alarmed by a cloud of steam rising from the left flank, it's nothing to worry about – Leeman's pissed his pants.' He laughed.

I picked up a lump of earth and threw it and it bounced off Jim's left ear with a thump. 'This is no time to be arsing about!' I hissed.

'You're wrong, Ben. This is exactly the time, because there won't be another,' he replied."

"I made no reply. I knew exactly what he meant."

"For a few seconds we both took in the meaning of his words in silence, before Jim added: 'I passed on those last instructions from the CSM – you'd already heard them. I just wanted to make sure we all had the same brief. Don't worry, your pants pissing secret is safe with me.'"

"I lay there in silence. I should have rolled back on to my front and watched the wood, but I had a feeling that when the attack came, there would be no sneaking up on us – we'd all know soon enough.

"I continued to lie in the sun looking upwards. The wood was completely silent apart from the skylarks singing in the distance. I felt completely at peace. I lay there for about 10 minutes, until the brightness of the sky made me squint, and I got little spots dancing in front of my eyes. I rolled on to my front and looked over the top of my rifle sights, not through them, just looking along the barrel.

"Jim hissed, 'Jesus! Look at that!'

"I took my eye away from my rifle and looked to my front left and there was the most handsome hare I'd seen since leaving Lincolnshire. I reckon he was a big male, moving a few shuffling skips at a time, before sitting up and scenting the air. He remained perfectly still, except for a little twitch of his whiskers and his ears swivelling from front facing to side facing, listening for any sounds signalling danger. He came level with my position, about 5 yards directly in front of me. His coat was beautiful – shiny and thick, the backs of his ears almost white with a sort of black fringe all around the edges – likewise his tail. His tail was bobbed upwards and had the same markings, white with a black fringe. He carried it, stuck up and twitchy, just like a dog's tail before a scrap.

"Suddenly, he stood up on his strong hind legs, as high as he could, his ears swivelled, and he raised his nose to sniff the air. He turned his head to his right and looked straight towards Jim and me just as there was the sound of an incoming shell that made me press my face into the earth. The shell landed with a bang about 20 yards behind us. I raised my eyes towards the hare, but he was gone. He'd been replaced by dark shapes in the distance moving towards us through the trees... and 'Harry the Hare' was forgotten.

"I slowly slid my rifle into my right shoulder and looked down the sights. The foresight was dirty. I licked my left thumb and forefinger and slid my rifle back towards me and cleaned the sight, before sliding it forward again and lining up eye, rear sight and front sight. The front sight's blade sat snugly into the slot of the rear sight. The tiniest gap between them. I gently applied light pressure to the trigger, knowing that the slightest squeeze was all that would be required. I breathed slowly and deeply as I waited for the final part of the picture to arrive and it wasn't long coming.

"A large approaching shape in grey and steel slowly filled in the gap between rear slot and the front blade, sights and soldier perfectly aligned. I breathed in and slowly out, but when the breath was halfway out, I held it and applied the slightest pressure. My rifle kicked back into my shoulder as the round left the barrel.

"My eye held the picture until Jerry dropped like a stone, down on his face, motionless. My right hand moved forward and operated the bolt, ejecting the spent casing and chambering the next round. My eye returned to the sights and once again the same picture was displayed; eye, hand and breathing worked together, as practised again and again on the ranges and again and again in the trenches. Same picture – same breathing – same pressure – same kick – same result. Again, and again and again. A few minutes later silence returned. I had a single round left in my magazine. I fitted a full magazine of ten and slid backwards a couple of inches into my scrape.

"Jerry had been stopped at a range of about 80 to 90 yards and without the use of the Vickers or the mortars – those would be saved for later. Just for a moment I think we all felt that we could hold out against any direct assault on our positions. Even if Jerry got close enough to be engaged with bayonets, I was sure we would have thinned them out enough to deal with any that got through.

"We had several snipers well concealed in the wood behind our line. They still hadn't fired a shot. They'd been briefed that their role was to top off any Jerry who was operating a flame-thrower. They were bloody horrible things and the soldiers using them would get no mercy from us. We'd all seen what they could do close-up and they weren't going to get close enough to use them today. They would be topped off and no messing about. If one was hit, it was likely he would go up in flames, and if past experience was anything to go by our lads wouldn't even fire to put him out of his misery, they'd just let the fire do its business.

"About 10 minutes after the first probe came a second. This was more serious and extended over a wider area of our line. They pressed much closer – they didn't reach the Mills line, but they got within the range of the mortar crews, who dropped about a dozen rounds on them. In 5 minutes we dropped maybe 50 Jerries that I could see from my position. As soon as they turned back, we stopped firing to conserve ammunition. Again, the Vickers crews never engaged and for a few seconds there was complete silence in the wood.

"The silence was broken by the cries of the Jerry wounded, lying out in the wood. Judging by the sound I reckon they'd been hit by our mortars. We could hear them calling for help, but we couldn't see them on the ground. There was no attempt by Jerry to send out stretcher bearers.

"Their cries were soon drowned out as the Jerry artillery opened up, probably 4 or 5 guns. I pressed my face into the soil, making myself as flat as I could. The soil tasted like loam rather than soil, due to the mix of soil and rotted leaves that must have been there for at least 3 years, as I'm sure none of the trees in Curlu Wood had been able to produce leaves since most of the branches had been blown off in 1914.

"What remained of the old woodland was dead – every single adult tree having been blown to bits. But there were a few weedy saplings that had managed to take hold and begin to grow. As I lay there trying to see out the barrage with my right cheek pressed to the loamy earth I saw, growing out of the face of our shallow trench, a little green sapling. From the shape of its leaves it looked like a little oak. I thought that, if by some miracle we both survived the war, that little oak would still be growing hundreds of years after me and my mates were long dead – mind you, I didn't expect to see nightfall, let alone survive long enough to see a tree grow.

"As I lay there I suppose I accepted what was to come. I was grateful that I had seen the sunset the previous evening from the window of the train and had spent a little bit of time with my thoughts, proving that even when surrounded by hundreds of Tommies, it was still possible to find a bit of peace in a quiet moment.

"Why is it that simple things that most people never give a second thought to suddenly become important when there is a war on? I spent more time thinking in France and Flanders than I'd ever done back home. About daft stuff really; sights and sounds and smells that in normal life you would never think about, unless you were some sort of philosopher, not a lad in a sleeper mill.

"This shitty war turned millions of us on both sides into killers. Killers and philosophers... and poets. Bloody hell, every bugger with a pencil and paper thinks they are a poet in wartime! But I admit the things that happened here made me think about small things quite deeply, simply because they became more important.

"You might think that there is nothing important about a sapling growing. But when you know it might be the last living thing you see, it becomes important. You imagine that you can see it breathing, slowly growing into a strong adult tree, if you look hard enough. Of course, you can't see it, but it is growing and living all the same. And that little sapling sticking out of a trench wall is looking at you – watching you die; slowly – right in front of it, so slowly that the sapling doesn't notice, but you're still dying all the same. Of course, there's every chance that a Jerry bullet or shell is going to speed up the dying process by about 50 years.

"I looked at the little oak and wondered what it would become when it grew. Would it be cut down and taken to a wood mill in France, or maybe Grimsby? Would it be cut into railway sleepers for a railway track taking people all over the world, to exotic, faraway places? Or would the tracks still be taking soldiers off to a never-ending war?

"Our Mam probably looked at me that way once, wondering what I would become when I grew. I don't know what she thought that might be, because she never spoke with me about it. But one thing was certain, it wasn't this; lying in a trench, praying that the shells just kept landing twenty yards behind. Whatever her hopes had been for me, I knew that they were never going to happen.

"Suddenly all hell broke loose. Half a dozen shells landed bang on top of our positions. I kept my face down for as long as I dared and then came up to the lip of my position just in time to see hundreds of Jerries charging though the wood.

"Every man in Z and Y Companies fired with everything we had and for a few minutes we held them. The mortars did their job, but still Jerry came, into the line of Mills bombs. The noise from the Vickers crews to my left deafened me, until they were silenced. It ceased firing as the expected flanking move to our left saw it overrun and Jerry was in amongst us. There was nowhere to run... except forward to meet them."

*****

"When the second round hit me, I knew it was the end. I think the absence of pain gave the game away.

"The first round had hurt like hell, but the worst part was the loss of control. It was like being drunk, although that had only happened once, so I'm not speaking as an expert or anything like that, but my mind was telling my body to do something and getting no response.

"It was like being hit hard with something big, like a plank of wood – not a sharp piecing pain, but a dull whack, which knocked me sideways. Maybe the plank of wood is a bad comparison, it was like being kicked full force by a horse. It felt like my insides were being pushed out the other side – there was no sharp pain at all, just a terrible burning sensation that started like a fire but burned itself out in a few seconds.

"The feeling of wetness was horrible. It was a cold wetness, not a warm one. You would think that your own blood would feel warm, wouldn't you? But it didn't – it was cold just as soon as it spilled out of me and into my tunic – a cold, horrible, sticky wetness.

"I managed to get up on to my right elbow. I felt for the wound with my left hand, and I saw my hand was covered with blood. It wasn't a smear or a smudge of blood, it was as though I'd dipped the palm of my hand into a pool of blood. I knew it was bad, but I also knew I had to keep fighting just to stand any sort of chance.

"I used my rifle as a sort of makeshift crutch and got up on to my knees facing the oncoming Jerries. I managed to plant my left foot on the ground and take aim from the kneeling position. I was struggling to operate the bolt, and it seemed like an eternity before I managed to chamber another round. Holding it steady was difficult, but I fired off another shot at an advancing Jerry about 20 yards away. He went down on his face. I worked the bolt and fired again, a different Jerry, but the same result.

"By now I knew I was alone. There was no fire coming from any of my mates. They were either dead or had pulled back. I looked to my left and saw Jim, about three yards away. He was lying face down, with his hands under his body, completely motionless – I knew he was gone. I could see another fellow just to Jim's left, lying in a similar position, but I couldn't tell who he was. As I looked along the trench the Vickers guns had long since fallen silent – their crews were strewn about the ground.

"There was no way back and my legs wouldn't push me forward. Ahead of me I could see figures approaching, crouching as they made their way along the trench. I got off a couple more rounds, both of which dropped their intended targets, until I could no longer chamber another round. My right arm just refused to work.

"Through all of this I wasn't aware of a single round being fired at me. No crack of the shot, no buzzing rounds passing me like a mad wasp, no earth being kicked up by near misses and then... thump.

"Silently and without warning that horse kicked me again, as the second round hit me in the chest, close to where my rifle butt sat in my shoulder. I didn't fall though; when I boxed, I was never knocked down, and I wasn't going down now. I rocked backwards, a long way backwards, but I sort of rebounded forward again and back into the kneeling position, as if on a spring. I didn't fall forward – my rifle butt remained in my shoulder as I gently pitched forward until my bayonet pierced the earth and dug in, my rifle holding me up like the wooden prop held up our Mam's washing line.

"I tried telling my left arm to bring my rifle up to the aim, but nothing happened. It simply refused to move and just hung down at my side. My right arm had already given up and hung there, all limp – leaving me looking like a dangly scarecrow being supported only by my rifle. My head didn't drop – I wouldn't let it – and I tried so hard to lift it, but I couldn't. I just stared at the earth – a rifle and bayonet's length away.

"I knew I was dying and I wasn't afraid. There was no pain, no fear, no sound, just complete peace and quiet as my eyes closed."

Ben looked up towards me and asked, "Did you ever lie under the blankets in a warm bed knowing that you have to get out from the warmth and go into the cold? You try to put it off for as long as you can, because you know it's going to be horrible. You eventually slip out from the warmth of your bed into the cold air – first one leg then the other. Your feet hit the cold floor and the chill creeps into you, right into your bones?"

"Yes, I have," I replied, "I live in a bloody caravan, so it happens every day in winter. Is that what it was like in the final seconds?" I asked.

"No!" Ben replied, "It was the complete opposite. It wasn't warmth giving way to cold, it was the cold giving way to warmth. It was like the moment when you dip your cold foot into a warm bath and slowly sink into it, and as you take the weight on your arms and slowly lower yourself into the water the warmth slowly but surely drives out the cold.

"It was like sitting under thick clouds watching the sun break through ahead of you, hitting the ground like a patch of fire, and as the clouds blow over, the sunshine races towards you. You can either wait for the sun to arrive or run to meet it. I didn't have to make that choice, the sun came quickly, and I just slipped gently into a desperately welcome sleep."

Chapter 10

Reflections

When Ben finished describing his last moments I wanted to give him some kind of meaningful response – but what do you say to someone who has just told you such a story? I was drained just listening to him, so God knows how it must have felt to tell it.

Ben took out his fags and lit one. He'd apparently given up trying to get me to start up again.

"I never imagined that dying would be like that," I said.

"What did you think it would be like?" Ben replied.

"I don't know. I suppose most of the accounts I have ever heard from people who have had 'near death' experiences always seem to involve them walking into a big, bright light, with someone shouting, 'Don't go into the light'," I said.

"I don't know what to say, it wasn't like that for me, but we are talking about something different. I never had one of those 'near death' capers. I suppose I was lucky, because I was never seriously wounded. A few stitches here and there, but never anything more than that. Hardly a bloody scratch and then... finished. As our Mam would have said, 'Our Ben never does anything by half-measures – it's always all or nothing,' he said in a high-pitched voice, mimicking his Mam.

"But remember, I only know how it was for me. I don't know if it would feel the same for everyone else, but there were no bright lights for me.

"As for what it's like afterwards, I am sure that must be different for everyone, in the same way that everyone's life is different. We all live, but we all feel differently about life. Some of us have a happy, content life and some have a sad life. Some of the fellows I served with had miserable lives as kids, and even as men before the war, but I had a happy life and a great childhood, being looked after and loved by my family. If we experience life so differently, surely there's every chance that we experience death differently.

"I don't know if what comes after death is influenced by how we lived our lives – you know, if we led good or bad lives, or whether we were a cheerful or miserable bugger in life. Perhaps the way we die influences it. All I know is my life before the war was a happy one and by and large my time in the army was the same. My life was a good one, if a bit on the short side, and up till now this has been a time of rest.

"I don't know if that is going to change, but I have a feeling that it will. This isn't all there is, I'm sure. Something comes next and I think that this, you know, you and me together tonight is part of it; something is ending so something else can begin. It feels like this is the last conversation on the platform before my train departs.

"I'm not afraid, because I don't think I have anything to fear. Maybe it's because I was always an optimistic lad when I lived, and I am still an optimist, experiencing death just as I experienced life... optimistic and unafraid." He shrugged his shoulders.

"Bloody hell, Ben. If I thought I was going to come away from this with all the answers I was wrong. I'm more confused than ever now. Can't we just go back to talking about football and dogs?" I said.

"There's not much point talking about footy. I haven't kicked a ball in a hundred years. Not a single kick, never mind played a game," he replied.

"What about dogs?" I asked.

"Oh, that's a different matter... as you might be lucky enough to find out one day," he replied.

"What do you mean?" I asked.

"There's no point telling you about things that might be different for you. I wouldn't want to give you false hope," Ben replied, before putting his fag out.

He continued: "I am sure something else is coming next for me, perhaps I'll find out soon, or maybe it'll take another hundred years.

"I'm sorry I haven't really been able to answer your questions about this. If I'd known you were going to be dropping by for a chat I would have been better prepared. I mean look at me – I haven't even had time to polish my boots, never mind prepare an operation order on life after death."

"I understand, Ben. Would it help if next time I pop by I book an appointment a week in advance?" I replied and we both laughed.

I continued: "You've given me such an honest account, although I've a feeling you've played down the importance of some of the things you did. How can you remember all the details of things that happened so long ago? I asked. "The details are so clear, I can almost see the things you describe, like I was alongside you."

Ben thought for a few seconds, then asked, "What do you mean, so long ago?"

"The events you've described happened so long ago, yet you describe them like it was only yesterday," I replied.

"To me it was only yesterday. I don't have years and years of new memories to obscure the things that happened, the good and the bad... and they weren't all bad. Those events are as clear as daylight. There's nothing to obstruct my view. The memory is as fresh as the dew drops on this grass," and he swept the palm of his left hand across the surface of the grass, leaving a sort of swish of dry grass the width of his hand. He looked at his wet hand before cupping it and repeating the sweeping motion, but this time he gathered the dew into the palm of his hand before lifting his hand to his mouth to sip the dew.

"That's the first water that has passed my lips in a hundred years. It tastes much better than I remember it – like real water was when I was a kid, not the treated stuff we had to drink over here," he said, before taking another scoop of the dew from the grass and drinking again.

"You always speak in much more detail and with more feeling about personal things rather than what happened during the fighting," I observed.

Ben paused and then replied: "I suppose that's because they're the things that matter most. The things that I valued and loved, even if I didn't fully appreciate them at the time – I was only a lad, after all. The war was something that just happened to me, so I prefer to think of the good parts, like family and friendships, rather than the painful things. If the war is a 'thing', it's hard to speak with any great feeling about it.

"Most of the things that we care about are the things that stir up strong feelings. Often, they are people; family, friends and even enemies, and how they made you feel – but it's not all about people, you can feel the same about places and the things around you."

"It's really hard to explain and I don't know that I can, because I'm not sure I can find the right words to use. Where are all those aspiring war poets when you need one? I suppose when I think of war, it's like looking at a flat picture; a sort of blurry image of it. Not blurry in a way that means I don't remember it in detail, because sadly, I do – but like I am looking at a picture in a newspaper. I can see it and I can remember it, but I'm not back there, probably because I don't want to be there. I'm looking at it from a distance.

"But when I speak about other stuff, it comes back to feelings. I'm not just seeing a picture in a book or looking on from a distance – it's as though I'm in the middle of the scene, seeing its colours, hearing its sounds and smelling the scent.

"I'm surrounded by it because I want to be there. That's why it's so clear and I can speak about those things in more detail – those are the things in my life that I lived and felt... the war is something that just happened to me."

"How did you feel about the Germans?" I asked.

"When? Before I arrived in France, or afterwards? he replied.

"I don't know... both I suppose," I responded.

Ben gathered his thoughts for longer than usual before speaking: "I'll try and explain things to you, but what I say might come out all confused and I'm sure I'll contradict myself as I'm trying to explain. That's not because I'm thick, or not telling the truth, but because everything was confused and contradictory.

"When the war started I wanted us to beat Germany for what I thought they were doing. But I don't know if I hated the Germans. I probably hated the German Army, or the German government, but I don't think I ever hated an individual Jerry soldier. And yet, I never had any hesitation killing one in battle. Does that make me better or worse than someone who kills in hate?

"At least someone who kills in hate does so for a reason. It may be a stupid reason, or it may be a valid reason – but stupid or justified, at least it is a reason. A soldier kills because someone he has never met tells him to kill another person he has never met. I still don't understand it.

"Does any other creature on earth do things like that? When a fox kills a rabbit, she does it because she has to eat, or feed her young. She doesn't do it because she hates rabbits, and she certainly doesn't do it because another fox she has never met, tells her to. She doesn't kill the rabbit because she's been told that rabbits are bad – she does so to survive.

"She certainly doesn't do it because she's been told that if she doesn't, then the rabbits will kill her and her cubs, or take over her territory and drive her and the rest of the foxes out.

"Both us and Jerry thought we were killing to survive, because if we didn't the other would take everything we had – our homes, our families and our lives. And because we believed that, because we were led to believe that, by politicians and generals, millions of us travelled hundreds of miles from home, to sit in a hole in the ground and kill others who'd been told the same thing. Madness, really.

"It never failed to amaze me how easy it was to change the behaviour of a man and have him do things he wouldn't do before the war; things he would never have imagined doing.

"It must be one of man's greatest talents to be able to adapt so quickly and behave differently, and to feel differently about doing them. Or is it one of man's greatest vices? That we can have our minds, hearts and actions changed so easily. How else do you explain a good man learning that it's acceptable and right to plunge a foot and a half of bayonet right through the body of another man?

"How can you explain how easy it is to train a man to fire a machine gun – slaughtering a thousand men walking towards him across a field; to have him sweep the machine gun in a smooth arc from left to right and back again, mowing down those men. He learns to be at ease with his actions because those other men wear a different uniform and speak a language he doesn't understand. It's insanity isn't it?" Ben looked at me, waiting for a response.

"It is, when you put it like that," I replied.

"Do you know what is even more crazy?" Ben asked.

"No. I can't imagine anything more mental than that," I said.

"Well, you're not thinking hard enough. But you haven't had as much time as me to consider things," Ben replied, before adding: "What's even more crazy is that not only did the man learn to fire the machine gun, but the thousand men learned to walk across that bloody field as he fired, and to keep going as their friends and brothers dropped like flies around them. Now that even tops the madness of the machine gunner.

"Those thousand men; are they brave beyond belief? Or stupid beyond belief? I still don't know the answer. Stupidity or courage, or a mixture of both. If men couldn't learn all this; if they couldn't be trained to overcome their natural survival instinct and their bloody sensible fears, none of this could have happened. It would have been impossible. Can you imagine it?"

Ben put on his best attempt at a posh voice, which wasn't very effective. But he pretended to stick an imaginary monocle into his left eye and squinted as if to hold it in place. He craned his neck, so it seemed to stick higher out of the collar of his coat, which gave him the look of a ventriloquist's dummy as he went into his impersonation of a commissioned officer. I managed not to laugh, as I knew he was making a serious point.

"'Right chaps, today we will be climbing over the bags, so get yourself up those ladders and make your way across that field towards the chap in the funny hat who is going to kill most of you!'

'Sorry, sir, we're not doing that. It's bleedin' suicide!'

'Yes chaps, you're probably right. In that case, Leeman, start making the tea and I'll dig out some cake Mummy has sent me.'"

Ben ceased the Lord Charles act to become Ben again: "I know that conversation sounds mad, but it's not. That would have been a normal, sensible conversation. I'm all for courage; the courage to dive into a river to rescue a drowning kid, but surely that's different from the soldier walking towards a machine gun or firing one. I don't know... maybe you can't have one without the other.

"If we lacked the instinct to be able to fight and kill, would we lack the instinct to dive into that river to save a kid? I only know that we'd have to save a lot of drowning kids to balance the ledger for the millions of lives wasted here," Ben said wearily as he took out another Black Cat and lit it.

As he took a deep drag on his smoke a piece of tobacco stuck to his lip. He did a little spit to remove it and the tobacco landed on my leg.

"Thanks for that," I said.

"Sorry, I'm out of practice with my aim, time was I could have dropped that down a rat's lughole at 10 paces." Ben laughed.

He continued, but it was as though he was thinking aloud, rather than talking directly to me: "Although if you can't have one without the other, how do you explain medical orderlies, stretcher bearers and the conchies – the ones who came over here and served?"

"You mean conscientious objectors?" I asked.

Ben nodded, before going on: "Before we landed in France, I was the same as most people – I couldn't understand them – didn't really want to! I thought they were all cowards, but when the steel started flying I saw that they were anything but. They had the courage to face the machine guns, but also had the resolve not to fire one."

Ben stopped speaking and sat quietly, but with one eye still half-closed as if winking.

"You've still got your monocle in, anyone might mistake you for an officer," I said.

Ben made as though to remove his imaginary monocle and leaned forward to pass it to me, saying, "You should use this instead of your spectacles, it would make you appear very distinguished," before breaking into a wide grin.

We sat quietly for a few minutes whilst Ben finished his Black Cat. He stubbed it out and continued: "Now this is the bit where I make an ass of myself, because despite the futility and stupidity of the whole war, I suppose I felt proud. I had pride in myself and pride in my mates. Pride in our battalion. Even now I don't know if holding on to that pride is right or wrong, good or bad. Surely, it's right to feel pride in helping to free France and Flanders.

"I suppose that kind of pride is different from the pride I felt in things before the war, which, if you went to church, was supposed to be a bad thing. I never paid much attention to anything the parish priest told me about the dangers of pride, but I did listen to our Dad.

"Our Dad would tell me: 'There's nothing wrong in being proud of a job done well, son – just as long as it doesn't lead you to thinking you are better than the other man. Be proud of having given your best, not because you are any better than your friends or neighbours.' So, right or wrong, I am proud of what me and my mates achieved and how we fought our little bit of a big war," Ben concluded.

"Is there anything you regret? Do you regret enlisting? Would you have done it so young, if you'd known how things would turn out?" I asked.

As usual Ben didn't respond immediately, choosing his words carefully: "I think regrets are for those still living... those clinging to life. Once you have let go, I think that you also let go of any regrets. Even in my last moments of life, when I knew how it was going to end, I had no regrets.

"I don't think you can regret the way things turn out unless you have made a conscious decision to steer things in that direction. To be capable of feeling regret, you must have had the opportunity to take a different path. Only then can you say the path you took was the wrong one – course, as you didn't take the other path you have no way of knowing if that would have turned out better, or worse. Although I volunteered, I'm not sure I had a real choice – I'm not sure any of us did.

"There were things I would have regretted, if I'd made a bad choice. I could have taken life needlessly or cheaply or gloated over the dead. I'd have regretted that. But I don't think I ever did. I fought as hard as I could, for me and my mates. I fought like a bloody tiger at times, but I don't believe I ever crossed the line from right to wrong... never did I cross it.

"I held on to the respect I had for myself and my mates. I held on to the respect and sympathy I had for the women and children in the villages, or on the roads, pushing their lives in a cart to escape the war. I even retained respect for Jerry – sometimes that was hard, especially when you saw him as a uniform, or a bloody big square helmet – but I never saw Jerry as a monster; I saw him as a man, and I treated him like one. I took many Jerry lives in battle, and taking any life is a terrible thing to do. But I never broke the rules. I never took a life without thought, or cause, or in hate. My soul remained intact... and for that I am grateful.

"Of course, I wish things had turned out differently. But wishing for something different or better isn't the same as regret. I wish the war had never happened, that's for certain. But once the war had started, what was the alternative to trying as hard as possible to win it?

"Until tonight I didn't even know the war had ended. Now I wish I had lived to see the peace and how it turned out. I wish my best friend, Jim, had done the same. I wish I'd returned home to our Mam and my sisters and brothers and saw them look happy and proud when I walked down Fildes Street.

"I wish I'd met a pretty, funny girl who I wanted to marry and who wanted to marry me back. I wish we'd raised young 'uns together and watched them grow up to have their own kids. I'd never thought about those things before, but now, meeting you... I wish I could have had what our Charlie had, a life spent raising a family. I envy our Charlie that."

Throughout the time discussing regrets Ben's head had slowly dropped until he was looking towards the ground as he added quietly, "I'm sorry for deceiving our Mam and the pain I caused her, by not returning home." He wiped his face on his left sleeve before looking up at me.

I had nothing to say. I just wanted to go and put my arms around him, but instead I simply sat in silence trying to take in all that had happened in the last few hours.

It was me who broke the silence. "I've got no idea what's gone on here tonight, Ben. Why do you think all this happened?" I asked.

In a flash and without pausing for breath, Ben replied: "From what I was told, some Duke got shot a thousand miles away and the Austrians thought it a good excuse to settle a few scores. The Germans, who were good mates with the Austrians, decided to help them out, but the Russians, French and British were unhappy about this. They were even more unhappy when Jerry thought it a good excuse to obliterate France and Belgium, although I can't really see the connection, because the chap who got shot wasn't French or Belgian and the fellow that shot him wasn't French or Belgian either." He gulped in a deep breath and sat back smiling smugly at his razor-sharp wit.

"He wasn't a Duke, he was an Archduke," I corrected.

"I don't care if he was a bloody Archbishop. It wasn't worth all this," Ben replied.

"Anyway, that's not what I meant," I replied, "I meant... this... us... the pair of us sitting together in this field. Why has it happened?" I asked.

"I have no idea. Probably because you came looking for me," Ben replied.

"But I didn't come looking for you. I was just here to lay a poppy wreath at the cemetery and visit Curlu – the same as on my previous visits," I replied.

"Are you sure about that?" Ben asked.

"Maybe it was you who came looking for me," I responded.

"Yes, you're probably right. After a hundred years I just decided to pop over on the off-chance that a long-lost relative might have dropped by for a chin wag and a fag. You can't believe how disappointing it's been for me to find out you don't even smoke – a right bloody let-down. Mind you, it would have been worse to find you did smoke but hadn't brought your own fags," Ben replied.

And with that the pair of us burst out laughing. I picked up a small lump of soil and threw it at him and as it hit his chest, he rolled backwards and lay on his back, looking up at the sky.

Without sitting up, Ben spoke: "It wasn't a conscious thing... coming here. I've never been here, at this spot before. I've not been waiting to meet you."

"Do you think the hundred-year thing is the reason? That this was always going to happen? A good chin wag after a century of silence?" I asked.

"I don't know. But if the hundred-year thing is the reason, then why just us? Where is everyone else? Surely there should be hundreds of us here. All drawn back for the centenary. I lost dozens of mates that day and so did Jerry, and yet we're here on our own – so I don't think it is the centenary that is important. It must be something else," Ben reasoned.

"Maybe it's because you had a story to tell?" I said.

"But didn't we all have a story to tell? And let's be honest, my story isn't exactly exciting – quite boring and mundane really. My tale is no more important than thousands of others. Maybe that's the real reason... that I am just like all the rest of the lads and my story is their story, too."

"So, the question we should both be thinking about is this; does the story remain with you, or are you going to tell it for me... for all of us?" Ben asked.

I considered his question – but made no reply.

Chapter 11

Daybreak

After a few moments Ben spoke: "It seems odd sitting here with you, talking for so long. I was never much of a talker. I don't mean I was shy or anything, I was quite outgoing – a bit of a joker... "

"No kidding?" I interrupted.

Ben continued, "I just wasn't much of a talker. This is the longest time I have ever talked with anyone other than our Dad when we walked to work together, and those conversations never lasted for more than 10 or 15 minutes.

"Sometimes in the trenches I wouldn't speak for more than 15 minutes in a whole day. I enjoyed reading and thinking about things more than I liked to speak about them. It's been strange to have talked for so long and about so many different things. I'm glad I've told our story," he said.

I replied: "I'm the opposite really, I spend most of my working day speaking and giving out information, maybe just gobbing off. I don't think I have ever listened for so long or been so interested in what someone else has been saying. But this hasn't been a normal conversation... it's one I never imagined having."

Ben asked: "Does anyone remember us? I don't mean me. You are here, so at least you remember. But does anyone else remember us? You know, all of us. The Foresters? The thousands of us from different regiments and different places?"

"Yes Ben, they do. Nearly every village in Britain, France and Belgium has a memorial to those people from the village or town who were lost in the war. There are memorials to the soldiers of every country, especially Commonwealth countries, the big ones, like Canada, Australia, New Zealand and India – the tiny ones like Fiji, the Gurkhas from Nepal – all of you are remembered. None of you who fought are left now. The last few souls died a few years ago," I replied.

I continued: "In London, they built a big memorial called The Cenotaph, and every year there is a service of remembrance. At the

Albert Hall the Queen attends an annual remembrance ceremony."

"We have a Queen now... not a King?" Ben exclaimed.

"Yes, Queen Elizabeth the Second. She has been our queen for over 65 years. She's getting to be quite good at it now," I replied.

Ben nodded his approval.

I continued: "Over here there are two enormous memorials, the Menin Gate, which is at the start of the Menin Road leading out from Ypres..."

Ben chipped in: "I marched along that road in 1917. I remember the terrible weather. The rain never seemed to stop – I often thought that it should have been a naval battle; it was so wet."

I continued; "The Menin Gate has over 50,000 names engraved on it."

"Good God! That many dead. I knew it was a slaughter... but I never realised it would be so many," Ben exclaimed.

"It was far more than that Ben. That number is only the Commonwealth missing – not the dead. There are military cemeteries everywhere – and that isn't taking the Belgian and French dead into account," I replied.

"Or the German dead," Ben added.

"No, not them either," I replied.

"Bloody hell. I knew it was a disaster, but I never realised just how big a disaster," said Ben.

I continued: "There's another memorial a couple of miles from here at Thiepval. Again, that's a memorial to the missing of the Somme, not all the dead, just the missing, just the Commonwealth missing. There are tens of thousands of names on that memorial."

"Is my name on any of them?" Ben asked.

"Not on either of those. You are named and remembered in a church in Little Coates, on the edge of your home town, and on the memorial wall in the British Military Cemetery in Pozieres, just a few miles from here.

"There are hundreds of cemeteries all over this part of France and Belgium. Some are British, some Canadian, South African, Australian, New Zealander and many are mixed – containing many different Commonwealth soldiers. All the headstones are the same size and shape, made of Portland stone. It didn't matter if you were a General or a Tommy, you all got the same headstone. At least there was equality in death.

"It was decided to let families pay for a personal inscription at the foot of the gravestone, should they wish. There were strict rules though. No more than 66 letters and the cost of each letter to the family was three and a half pence," I explained.

"Three and a half pence? What does that mean? Ben asked.

"Er, it means Three pennies and half a penny," I replied.

"Thruppence ha'penny for each letter? Bloody hell. I suppose by not having a headstone, it saved our Mam a few bob," Ben joked, before adding, "I'm glad to be remembered nearby, close to where I fell, where I am."

I continued: "It's good for the family because it gives us somewhere to come where we can be close to you. Even though we never knew exactly where you were lying, we knew you were close. Now we can be even closer.

"My Mam took some earth from the fields around here and took it home to her own garden. She placed a rosary in an unnamed grave at the Pozieres Cemetery.

"We all remember you at home. I have your photograph on the wall and every night when I walk my dogs down to the gate for a last piddle, I stop at my flagpole and touch your poppy and say goodnight to you. I do the same every morning. I walk my dogs down the drive to the gate first thing, you know... 'At the going down of the sun and in the morning, we will remember them.'"

"What do you mean by that last bit? The 'going down of the sun' bit?" Ben asked.

"It's a poem that was written and is recited at every remembrance service. I'm not sure of the exact words or who wrote it, but it goes something like; 'They shall not grow old, as we that are left grow old. Age shall not weary them, nor the years condemn. At the going down of the sun, and in the morning, we will remember them.' I did my best to recite it for him.

"Bloody hell, I never knew all that...I never knew. I'm not even offended that the time you think of me most is when your dogs are doing their ablutions!" Ben quipped, then, laughing, he straightened his legs and fell back to look at the stars.

I looked up too, and for a few minutes we looked up together. Not speaking, just looking up at the stars, poking through the clear, inky-blue sky, just as they did a hundred years earlier.

Ben broke the silence. "What did you mean when you said you touch my poppy?"

"The poppy is the symbol of remembrance at home. In France it's the cornflower, but back home it's the poppy. Anyway, I bought a big poppy, which is yours, and I have attached it to the flagpole on my drive. Every night and every morning I touch it and say good morning, or good night to you. My own daily acts of remembrance," I explained.

"While your dogs are having a pee?" he asked, seeking confirmation.

"Yes, while my dogs are having a piddle," I confirmed.

"It's nice to be remembered... and with such regularity too!" he replied, and he smiled up at the sky. I imagined my Mam would be thinking, 'You daft monkey! Why did you have to mention the piddling bit?'

I went on, "Remembrance in Britain wasn't always so well observed. In fact, in the 1970s up to about 2000 it really seemed to be on the wane amongst the general public. The ex-services community always remembered, but the rest of the country – not so much. Then we became involved in wars in Iraq and Afghanistan, and the sight of fresh casualties stirred people. Suddenly, it wasn't about a relative who died so long ago, and nobody actually knew, but it was about the young lad down the road who'd been killed, or had returned home without his legs. Now it was about the kid everyone in the neighbourhood knew.

"In 2014 they put on a big event in London that was called 'Blood Swept Lands and Seas of Red'. It was staged at the Tower of London, and they had the poppies falling from the ramparts of the tower like a bloodstained waterfall and running into the moat around the tower.

"Every poppy was made of clay and fired and glazed, you know, like a plate or a bowl. They were all made by hand so each one was different. Each poppy a one off, an individual."

"Just like each of us," said Ben.

I continued; "888,246 of them – one individual poppy for every man, woman and, in some cases, child who was lost.

"Of course, that is only the official number, it doesn't include those who came home alive but broken, and who survived a couple of years before dying of something related to their physical or mental wounds.

"When the poppies were removed, parts of the exhibition were sent all over the country, England, Northern Ireland, Scotland, Wales, and set up for people there to see and remember. At the end of the exhibition the poppies were sold. We bought yours and have it at home.

"This year, 2018, there's another idea called 'There, but not there' to mark the centenary of the end of the war. There will be almost a million silhouettes and clear plastic soldiers that will be placed around the country. Some will be in towns and villages where they will sit in places like churches, schools or other buildings where they once were, so that people who live there today can see them and remember that they were real people, who would have once sat in that very place.

"The idea is for people today to remember how and where you all once lived, not just how you died. That you were all part of a community and now you have been brought back there. It's a good way to remember you all."

Ben sat up again into his customary position. "What do you mean, plastic?" Ben enquired.

"It's a sort of material, a bit like glass in this case, but it is less likely to break. It was first made in America and I'm sure it was around before the war," I replied.

"In America maybe, but Grimsby is a long way from New York!" Ben laughed.

I went on, "They have brought out something called 10-inch Tommies, small plastic silhouettes of a standing soldier, which people can buy and keep, to commemorate a soldier, perhaps a family member lost in the Great War. The money raised goes to support military charities that help today's injured servicemen and servicewomen."

"The Great War. That's an odd name for it," Ben said.

"Yes, Ben. It is a bit odd," I replied.

"Did our Charlie ever speak of me?" Ben asked.

"I didn't really know Charlie. Although he was my Grandad, he died when I was just over a year old. I didn't know him, but he certainly knew me. I remember a story that my Mam – that would be your great-niece Alice – used to tell me about my Grandad. The last few years of his life he was quite ill and often confined to his bed. My Mam told me that one of his great pleasures was having me sit on his chest as he bounced me up and down; although after I once piddled all over him he made sure I always had a securely fitted nappy on before he did it again.

"My Mam worshipped him, and I don't think she ever truly got over his death. She would have been 21 years old when he died, but she would talk about him all the time – she was so proud of him. It was my Mam that told me about you. She told me about how Charlie was heartbroken to lose his younger brother and that he was angry and very bitter about the way your mum was treated after your death.

"My Mam would sometimes see her Dad looking at your photograph and she could see the pain in his eyes and feel his loss and sadness. He told my mum that it was bad enough that his Mam had lost you, but the government had been mean in the amount of pension she was awarded in your name. Charlie felt that you and your Mam had been let down by the government.

"It was never about the amount – he just felt that the payment seemed to reflect that you were worth less to your Mam than someone else's son, brother or husband. He believed that everyone should have been treated equally."

Ben stopped looking towards me and instead stared down towards the ground, down at his feet as he sat cross-legged on the ground. He reached forward and with his right hand picked a small blade of grass, just like a kid does when lost in thought and can't think of anything better to do. Nothing was said by either of us for a minute or so, and then he looked up.

He said; "The government betrayed all of us. The money, which I didn't know about until just now, was the least of it really. None of us should have been here. None of this should ever have happened and I don't just mean to me and my mates. I mean the Belgian and the French lads as well... even Jerry. The whole lot of us were betrayed by our governments.

"Maybe it was different for the French and Belgian lads. I mean they had a foreign army on their own soil, in their own towns and villages, living in their homes. I bet soldiers today are treated better than we were by the government."

"Yes, Ben. It's much better now," I lied, whilst thinking about being sent to war on false intelligence, with inadequate equipment and returning home to a lack of medical and psychological care. I thought of those living with the scars of half a dozen wars, conflicts and 'troubles' that have punctuated the last 75 years of 'peace'. I thought it – but said nothing.

I remembered reading that in 2014 suicides amongst former British military personnel attributable to Post Traumatic Stress Disorder had outstripped losses in the actual conflict for the first time. How the hell was I going to explain that one to Ben?

"Yes Ben, it's much better now." After all Ben's honesty, here I was, lying to him.

Then he asked, "How much did our Mam get for me?"

"I don't know what the weekly pension was, but the lump sum payment made on your death was just short of 21 quid. It was made up in two parts. I don't know what the first part was called, but the second part was called a War Gratuity. I thought that was an odd term to use because these days a gratuity is usually used to describe a tip given to a waiter for good service. It's not much of a tip for a life, Ben. Not much for your life," I explained.

"I don't suppose it was," he replied.

I went on, "It's more than some got though. When I checked the national records the poor bloke who was just below you on the list was valued at just under £7 and that included a War Gratuity of £5. I have no idea how they worked that out. I wonder if it was based on pay that was owed, or maybe how good a soldier he was, length of service, or medals awarded. I have no idea in all honesty."

"Did you have to go all the way to London to read through all those records?" Ben asked.

"No, I looked them up on the internet," I replied.

"What's that then?" asked Ben.

"Well, I suppose it's like a massive big library with millions of books inside that you can look at on a screen – like at the cinema," I replied.

I know my description of the internet wasn't exactly a detailed one and Bill Gates would probably have thought it a little short on technical info, but Bill Gates wasn't available at such short notice, and it was the best explanation I could think of. Then I remembered my mobile phone in my pocket. I put my hand in my jeans pocket in order to produce a miracle of 21st century technology. Bollocks! I thought, as I felt the dead satnav, not my phone. There was little point showing Ben a lump of useless black plastic, so I pushed it back into my pocket. I must have had my hand in my pocket for a bit too long.

Nodding towards my hand in my pocket, Ben said, "There's no need for any of that nonsense – if you're bored with the conversation we could always play cards."

Yeah, 'nice one Ben', I thought!

*****

At 5.35am on the 25th of March 2018 the sun began to rise over Picardy and the former killing fields of the Somme. The horizon to the east began to lighten slowly and I knew that soon it would be time to let Ben go. We both looked towards the slowly rising sun and sat in silence.

Ben spoke first: "I suppose our time's almost up. It's been good to talk again after all this time. Thank you for coming to speak with me."

I didn't speak, I just nodded my head. I didn't want to stand up first, it would be like I was in a hurry to get the goodbyes over and done with, when in reality my only thought was how to stretch out my time with Ben for as long as possible – to hold on to every last second in his company.

Ben was still sitting cross-legged and without uncrossing his feet he rocked forward and rose up to the standing position with them still crossed. Once upright he shook his right foot, then his left foot, and raising his arms to chest level drew back his elbows to stretch out his chest and back.

He drew in a deep breath. Filling his lungs with fresh air like a man who hadn't breathed in the fresh air at sunrise in a long time... a hundred years in fact. Then he took out his packet of Black Cats and lit one up, before blowing out the match, dropping it on the ground, then putting his foot on it, just to ensure it was out.

He offered me the packet: "Are you sure you don't want one?" he asked... again.

"Don't be daft, smoking those things will bloody well kill you," I replied.

"That's OK, I'll take my chances," Ben replied with a smile.

I reached up with my right hand and said, "Give us a pull up, my knees are locked solid."

Ben reached forward with his right hand and grabbed my forearm just below the elbow and I grabbed him in the same place. He heaved me to my feet with ease and as I came up I let out a deep groan. As I stood up, the first thing I did was bend forward and with both hands tried to rub some blood into my legs.

"Bloody hell," said Ben, adding: "I wouldn't worry about the fags if I were you... it doesn't sound like you've got that long left anyway. Maybe you shouldn't bother going home."

I wanted to come out with a smart reply, but I was more concerned with keeping my balance and staying on my feet, so I said nothing. After a few seconds I slowly managed to stand upright. I must have looked like the evolution from ape to human compressed into a few seconds.

Ben picked up his greatcoat and slung it over his left shoulder. He stood looking into the sunrise and I stood looking at him. We were about the same height, 5'8". We had the same short hair except Ben's was light brown, almost fair, and mine was brownish-grey – well, greyish-brown.

And there he stood, just like you would expect a 17-year-old soldier to look. Strong, athletic and youthful – a handsome young man of unlimited potential and with everything to live for.

With the benefit of sunlight, even though his face was slightly dirty, I could see the smoothness of his skin and the light downy hair on his face. 'Yep, dab a bit of milk on it and the cat would be able to lick that 'tache off – definitely no need for a razor,' I thought.

He took a couple of deep drags on his Black Cat and then dropped it on the ground at his feet, putting it out with his right boot. He turned towards me and I saw the light in his green-brown eyes. The same colour eyes that my Mam had. The same sparkly eyes that twinkled with humour; the eyes of a young man who should have had another 60 years of life ahead of him.

"It's time," he said, and as he did so, he stepped towards me and reached out with his right hand. I took his hand in mine to shake it. It was as strong as I expected, but I was surprised to feel how warm it was, almost hot, not at all cold like I had expected. I thought back to when I was seventeen years old and my hands were always warm, no matter the weather.

There was a small trail of dark, crusty blood that ran from his wrist and down the length of his thumb. I saw that the inside of his right sleeve was blood-stained, where the blood from his wound had run down the inside of his sleeve. I was surprised at how little blood there was.

"I suppose that this is where you walk off into the gloom and slowly disappear from my sight, like they do in all the cinema films," I said.

"What would be the point of disappearing? I have nowhere to go. The Somme is where I fell, and it's here where I belong, or it has been until now. Now I'm not so sure what will happen. It might be different. Maybe this is the end of something for me, and the start of something else. I don't know. Still, I suppose you could come back in another hundred years and see if I am still here." Ben laughed, and so did I.

There was a difference in our laughter, though. Ben's laugh was genuine and mine was a laugh that was concealing the tears welling up inside. I realised that I was doing a Donald Trump handshake, you know, still holding onto Ben's hand for far longer than I should have – like I never wanted to let go.

Ben was my last connection to the family I had never known: long-gone aunts, uncles and great-grandparents. Keeping that grip on his hand was like holding on to them and letting go would be letting them slip away forever. I was determined to hold on to them all for every precious second.

During 35 years in the RAF I'd said a thousand goodbyes to those I love, but this felt like nothing I'd ever experienced before. I can only compare it to a sort of vacuum in the middle of my chest – like I'd had as a five-year-old kid when I'd been crying hard for a long time – the point at which the 'boo-hoo' crying subsided into sobbing; just before I'd take a deep, snivelling intake of breath. The free-flowing tears that used to drip from my face and the trails of snot that flowed and mingled with the tears might have been missing, but everything else felt just the same.

Slowly I opened my fingers and released Ben's hand, I just nodded towards him, then without speaking I turned and took the first faltering steps back on to the path leading me back towards the village. My legs were like lead and those first steps seemed to take an eternity, as if I was wading through treacle – but I was determined not to look back.

If I looked back and he was gone, that would be it, forever. As things were, Ben was still there, watching me. If I didn't look back perhaps he always would be.

"You never told me what happened in 1940!" Ben shouted.

I wanted to answer, 'I know I didn't, Ben. You lads suffered enough without knowing that you'd all be let down 20-odd years later.' I thought it – but didn't say it.

"Well maybe we should save that for the next time we meet!" I shouted back. There was no reply and I walked on in silence, knowing he was gone.

Then he shouted, "Be careful, Sunshine Boy!"

The words stopped me dead in my tracks, like an invisible hand had grabbed me by the collar. The only person who ever called me that was my Mam, and she had said it to me for the last time on the 24th of November 2015, almost 2½ years earlier.

He shouted again; "Do you remember we talked about whether you came here for me, or I came here for you?"

I didn't turn, but shouted, "Yes, I remember!"

He went on; "It was nothing to do with either of us. She sent you to find me 4 years ago and she brought us together again last night...She's always closer than you'd ever imagine!"

I turned to shout my thanks and goodbyes, but when I turned I was staring at the morning sun rising over an empty field... and suddenly the tears and the trails of snot arrived and ran freely, just as they did when I was five years old.

*****